This is a work of fiction. Names, characters, places, and incidents are products of the author's imagination or are used fictitiously and are not to be construed as real. Any resemblance to actual events, locales, organizations, or persons, living or dead is entire coincidental. The race to set the land speed record in Germany was, however, very real. Both Rudy Caracciola and Bernd Rosemeyer competed in this race. For the purpose of the story, I condensed some of the historical events into two years, while in reality some of the other historical events played out over many years.

FIRST EDITION

Library of Congress Cataloging-in-Publishing Data has been applied for.

ISBN 978-1-66785-712-1

The main characters:

Rudolf Caracciola - Born a poor Belgian farmer, Rudi is a handsome, up-and-coming Grand Prix driver. He's won almost every racing title and is a rising star in the SS. He learns to love Nazism, but in the process loses his morality and the love of his life.

Bernd Rosemeyer - A handsome, bisexual playboy and gifted Grand Prix driver, he's the pride of Germany. He loves his country but secretly hates the Nazis. He's driven to win so he can prove that he's as good as—maybe better than--those who would have him exterminated. He accidentally falls in love with a woman who is betrothed to his rival.

Nicolette von Dries - Beautiful daughter of General von Dries and accomplished aviator in her own right. She's Germany's answer to Amelia Earhart. She hates the brutality of war but sympathies with the German people. She is devastated when she learns that her true love, the man of her dreams, is not her fiancé but her fiancé's rival and a Jew.

Colonel General Schwartz - A gay SS officer in Berlin, Schwartz has his pulse on everything and everyone. When the moment comes, Schwartz is torn between love and duty and must make a life-or-death decision.

General von Dries - A reluctant general who

invades Poland and kills thousands but saves Germany from starvation. As a solider, he struggles with his daughter's beliefs as well as his own.

Hendrick - Friend of the von Dries' and member of the Polish resistance, he is the only man Nicolette trusts.

August Horch - Auto Union (now Audi) CEO and model Nazi. His decisions have horrible implications for those around him when he chooses between winning and allowing a Jew to win.

Margi Wardenberg - Family friend of Bernd's and a Jew. She provides the moral compass which Bernd uses to navigate his choices.

Dominique Dresden - A woman who knows how to play both sides while taking none, Dominique is in it for herself.

Wilhelm Kissel - Mercedes CEO and reluctant Nazi who knows the fate of his company and its workers are tied to Hitler's success.

TABEL OF CONTENTS

5

Rudi Caracciola

Auto Union Streamliner

Mercedes Rekordwagen

Bernd Rosemeyer

1. FLIGHT OF TERROR

It is 3 AM.

With a violent snort, a substantial line of cocaine disappears up Bernd's nose. He stows a small glass tube, etched with edelweiss flowers, gently in his vest pocket, then pulls out a pack of Junos. The cigarette dangles from his mouth as he lights it; smoke twirls from the ashen end, stinging his already dry eyes on its hurried path toward the nearest draft. Looking in the mirror, he straightens his formal bowtie and wipes his raw nose. "Dashing," he says as he prepares to rejoin the party.

In an opulent Berlin mansion on the outskirts of the city, this reception marks the exclamation point on the Duke and Duchess of Windsor's October tour of 1937 Nazi Germany. The couple is mesmerized by Germany's new leader, Adolf Hitler, who is both charming and terrifying, two of the marks, they know, of a genius—and a psychopath.

Berlin's social and political elite have gathered for the event and the champagne helps erase the unease kicked up by Germany's recent bombing of Spain. Bernd Rosemeyer, dressed for the evening in his tux, stands by the fireplace with a gorgeous socialite in a Schiaparelli evening dress.

Bernd sniffs away the last remnants of cocaine lodged in his sinuses, gagging a bit as it slides down his throat, feeling the numbness instantly.

The pair talk closely in each other's ears. They look impeccable even though they've been hitting club after club, dancing, drinking and drugging; they have been partying for days.

Bernd's grandfather and father owned over four-hundred square kilometers of prime real estate outside Berlin, but when they saw what happened during the Kaiser regime, they liquidated and put the profits into beer and alcohol production, which they believed would never go out of style. Their thinking was that when times are good, Germans drink. Evidently, when times are bad, they drink even more, so the family fortune grew quickly. Bernd used the notoriety and fortune to further his car-racing career.

He loves racing. If there's a better way to live, he hasn't found it. His life is a blur of European debauchery—sex, travel, cars, drugs, and competition. When people ask him what he does for a living, he replies with a smirk, "Anything I want." The Reich has required him, along with the rest of Germany's racing drivers, to become officers of the Nazi Party. He doesn't mind this; the honorary position only grants him even more freedom.

The talk of the party turns to Bernd's Grand Prix racing career; he lights a cigarette and describes to his attentive crowd what it's like to race at speed. The discussion culminates with a question from Cindy, Bernd's infatuation for the night.

"Which is faster darling, a car or plane?" she slurs, beaming.

"Would you like to find out for yourself?" he whispers in her ear. She stares up at him, eyes unfocused. "Come with me, darling." He grabs her hand and together they weave through the crowd, making excuses not to stop and talk with anyone. He leads her out a servant's door and they jump in his Alfa Romeo convertible. He floors it and she squeals in delight at the acceleration. After speeding for ten minutes through the winding road that tracks through the Berlin Forest at a pace that threatens the life of the speedometer, Bernd turns to his bubbling companion and says, "Got a bit of a surprise for you darling."

He turns off the road into a small airfield owned by a local company. The sign on the fence reads "Porsche AG". Walking onto the tarmac from the Alpha, surprisingly unspilled champagne glasses and bottle in hand, they see the sun rising.

"There she is darling, my one true love! The German Messerschmidt Bf 109 airplane. She's more dependable than a German train."

Cindy clutches Bernd's arm in excitement. "Oh Bernd darling, she's gorgeous, pure sex with wings!" She stumbles and the force of her body nearly sends the champagne crashing to the ground, but Bernd's strong grip saves the bottle.

"True, true," he says, pouring a glass. "If you know how to stroke her and treat her right, she'll take you to heaven, whatever that may be." The first rays of sunlight illuminate the aircraft. His chemistry has gotten all mixed up from the events of the past few days, and drug-induced emotion swells inside him.

They climb into the two seat trainer aircraft. The plane starts with a grumble and turns into a roar as they take off. Flying at 1500 meters, they greet the morning and see Berlin from the cockpit. The sun shines through broken clouds. It looks like they're flying through God's pasture in the throne room of the Almighty.

Cindy does not sip, but rather gulps champagne in the plane's front seat.

"Shame I'm not back there with you darling," she teases. She leans back in a slight writhe, casting her eyes momentarily on her pilot. "We could do naughty things in the sky." She's enjoying how the flight mixes with her drug-fueled euphoria.

"Time enough for that when we get back to the ground."

"Oh, you're scandalous, Bernd," Cindy purrs.

Cindy produces a snuff box from her bag and snorts cocaine, spilling her champagne in the process. The plane jerks, startling Cindy into momentary sobriety. "What was that?" she asks.

"That's odd, she seems to have stalled," Bernd replies, flipping a switch. "Hold tight my love, might get a bit bumpy."

Cindy doesn't register Bernd's words—she is far too busy looking at the clouds. She's so high she almost looks catatonic.

Bernd attempts to restart the engine but fails. "What the devil?" he says to no one. A gauge on the control panel tells him there is back pressure in the fuel system. He decides to dip the nose of the plane to attempt a glide.

"Seems there's a small issue darling, looks like a bit of trouble. Vapor lock is preventing fuel from getting to the engine."

Cindy rouses slightly from her stupor, just enough to slur mischievously, completely oblivious. "Just get us back on the ground and I'll show you trouble, Herr Rosemeyer."

Bernd looks around with increasing concern, thankful that his companion is unaware of how grave the situation is—nothing but forest below, no place to glide in. He knows the Messerschmidt has the glide range to cover a good two miles or so at his current speed and altitude, but the forest stretches in all directions for three to four miles.

Bernd contemplates what he has to do. His only chance is to regain altitude and find a clearing. He pulls up on the stick and gains 500 meters of altitude, just enough to clear the forest. He then realizes his seat is the only one with a parachute. He wants to eject, but doing so would mean Cindy's certain death. He considers strapping on the parachute and tying himself to his lovely companion. But she's as limp as a doll. There's no way he could hold her.

He checks the controls and sees that the temperature in the fuel line has cooled. He tries again to restart the engine—it cranks to life and Bernd is relieved.

"Sorry for the drama my love, all good now."

Cindy barely registers the drama. She crumples in her seat.

"I'm bored of this Bernd. I can think of at least three things I could be doing to you that don't involve me sitting in this smelly, dreadful bucket of bolts, let's go home, darling." She slumps as she speaks, her eyes half closed, her neck and arms lolling about.

"On the way." He speaks with his eyes fixed on the horizon. He has barely looked at her during the joyride.

Back in control, he flies the plane higher and turns toward Berlin and the break in the tree line. The situation settles for a moment. Bernd knows that getting the plane back to the ground is risky, but feels relieved to be in control again and heading to a clearing below.

As he lines up his landing, the engine cuts out.

The propeller continues windmilling but does not produce power. The control stick is dead in his hands. He can neither turn nor gain altitude. Overheated fuel has once again caused vapor lock.

Cindy squirms in her seat, in truth more bothered by her confinement in such a small cabin than anything else. "Stop it Bernd, I'm tired and I want to go home now, please darling! I'm not feeling well."

Bernd says nothing.

"Goddammit Bernd, I want to go home, please!" she yells, clutching the sides of her seat and thrashing her body about. Her tantrum produces no effect on Bernd, and she shrieks; "I should have never come with you! Get me back on the ground right now you dirty Jew!"

Focused on the impending disaster, he doesn't register her words. If he had, perhaps he would have used the parachute and left her to die. He glances at her, but doesn't care enough to ask her to repeat herself. She is a folly. Nothing more. His course has taken him to enough of a clearing that he believes he can land the plane, but it won't be smooth or safe. His reaction is swift and final. Just as when he's driving in a Grand Prix, there's no time for contemplation. You act, you survive—you hesitate, you die. He reaches back and fastens the safety belt he's never used before. They were introduced to German fighter pilots in World War I. Bernd has always seen them as frivolous and for sissies. But now that the ground is fast approaching, he figures it can't hurt. He leans forward and sees that Cindy is passed out. *Good,* he thinks, *she'll never know what hit her.* He has no time to try to wrangle her into her safety harness and if he's honest, he just doesn't care enough.

Bernd positions the plane as best he can and comes in sideways toward the clearing. The plane brushes the treetops and startles Cindy awake.

"What the hell are you doing, Bernd! What's happening?" she screams.

"I'm sorry love, but this trip seems to be ending in the least acceptable manner. We're about to crash land. I would—" But it's too late. The plane spins sideways, bouncing off the treetops. He corrects its trajectory the best he can, but they go down hard. The nose of this beauty digs into the ground and crumples as the plane's momentum pushes it forward, burrowing into the earth, throwing up chunks of dirt. His body flies forward but is caught by the belt and he feels it dig into his skin. *Dammit,* he thinks. *This is my favorite tuxedo.* He's not sure if it's seconds or minutes, but the plane finally comes to a stop.

"Cindy?" he asks. "Darling?"

When he receives no reply, he unstraps and feels the sting of blood from where the seatbelt cut into his hips. He crawls into the front and sees Cindy crumpled against the windshield, blood smeared on the glass. He glances from the gash on her head to the door and back again. "Cindy? Darling? It's time to go." He waits, but she doesn't respond. Grumbling, he shimmies to the front and puts his fingers to her neck. And finds a pulse. Relieved, he justifies his decision. "You'll be fine," he whispers. "I'll make sure of it."

He takes a look around the cockpit and strokes the controls as if they were a baby or a lover. "It was fun," he says, balancing in the doorway. He tips an imaginary hat, then steps out of the plane and shimmies to the ground.

Bernd heads north, knowing that will lead to a nearby village. "A pity, really," he says as he brushes a few specks of dirt from his pants. "She was a perfectly good airship."

2.   ZEE DOCTOR WILL SEE YOU NOW

Two SS officers, led by Markus Schwartz, Oberst-Gruppenführer and ranking SS officer of Berlin, enter the office of Dr. Ferdinand Porsche.

The doctor heads Porsche AG, which makes engines for the budding German war effort. His dark, paneled office is adorned with various auto racing trophies and photos of past victories.

A few model engines sit on the conference table. The doctor is always trying to squeeze a few more horsepower out of the engines.

Power is a precious resource these days, be it in an airplane, car or factory engine. In fact, Porsche's focus mainly falls on factory engines, leaving the more mundane aero and auto engine design to his younger staff of mechanical engineers.

Potatoes. Their sweet smell wafts over the country. When cooked with plums, knöla, onions, and pork belly they make the collective country's stomach growl. These days, Germans are starving because they can't buy enough nitrogen-based fertilizer to grow crops. So potatoes have become as strategic as bullets and tanks.

To solve the problem, a rather clever German scientist named Fritz Haber has invented a new nitrogen extraction process, but it requires a tremendous amount of power. The key to the process is to create factory engines capable of delivering the necessary power for full scale nitrogen extraction. So Porsche focuses his considerable skills on an engine design that will help solve potato production. Porsche may be an excellent engine designer but he is also hungry. There is no sign of Nazism in his office, only efficiency and engineering.

"Herr Doctor, we wish to discuss an urgent matter with you regarding an aviation accident." Porsche looks up from the contents of his desk to see that a group of three SS officers have appeared in his office. They stand in an arrow-flank formation, fronted by Colonel Schwartz.

"And for what reason would you consult me? Is this not a matter you should be taking up with Obergruppenführer Göring?"

"The accident we wish to discuss involves one of the Luftwaffe planes that was lent to your company for engine research," Schwartz says. "It was found crashed in the village of Lübbenau. It appears that someone you may know may have taken it for an unauthorized flight which resulted in the accident."

"Why would you think this?" asks Porsche, annoyed that his work has been interrupted over some accident. "We have no knowledge of an unauthorized flight. Porsche pilots are SS pilots, so again, perhaps you should be discussing this with the Luftwaffe."

"Sir, our reports indicate Fräulein Cindy Weber was found in the wreckage, alive but it bad shape. She was last seen with your nephew Herr Bernd Rosemeyer. We understand they departed a Berlin party together the morning of the accident."

"Is she a pilot, Colonel Schwartz?"

"No, she isn't, but Herr Rosemeyer is."

"Ah, so you believe that my nephew stole a plane, crashed it and what … left this woman injured?"

Porsche knows well of Bernd's reputation for partying—so does half of Berlin. He does tend to live fast, but Porsche knows how capable the SS is of lying in order to further their interests.

"No, we merely believe that the circumstances and evidence indicate that someone took our plane from your factory, resulting in the crash. Need I remind the good doctor that our planes are a precious resource and we are attempting to build our air force, not destroy it?"

Porsche decides that even if Bernd did send some bimbo crash-landing in the forest, he himself has far more pressing matters to attend to.

"Allow me to remind you Colonel Schwartz that my nephew is a trained pilot, a model Nazi and a Grand Prix driver who was awarded the Führer's cross recently. While he may be young, he's not stupid, and is an experienced aviator.

"Perhaps the young woman has a pilot friend

who survived the crash and escaped? Perhaps she is working for the allies and is a spy? You said the girl is still alive. Has anyone thought to ask her what happened? Or even if my nephew was with her? Perhaps you should look elsewhere and stop interrupting my work with this nonsense. I have more important things to occupy my time than some plane crash that probably has nothing to do with me."

"You are correct that there are many questions still unresolved Herr Porsche," replies Schwartz, "which is why we came to speak to you directly about this matter. The girl, Fräulein Weber, is at the city hospital. She's been in and out of consciousness and appears to remember nothing after getting to the party with Herr Rosemeyer. She cannot confirm or deny that he took her for that plane ride.

"Be assured we will continue to investigate this matter and should our investigation require it, we will contact you and Herr Rosemeyer with further questions. The Lufwaffe will also expect to be compensated for the lost aircraft." And with that, Colonel Schwartz turns on his booted heel and leaves the office, his underlings in tow.

3. MEET SCHWARTZ

Schwartz takes a Juno from the pack and lights it. Smoke slowly circles around the officer's face as he scans the interior of The El Dorado—one of the few remaining gay clubs in Berlin. It's protected from the ever-increasing scrutiny of the Reichszentrale zur Bekämpfung der Homosexualität und Abtreibung, the office of combating homosexuality and abortion. Schwartz himself ensures the club's safety. It stinks of tobacco and stale beer.

Together in a dark corner, he and Colonel Andreas Bibl are reminiscing about the good old days when Berlin had over forty gay clubs. Things were calmer then.

"So when did you know?" Bibl asks.

Schwartz flicks the ash from his cigarette. "Same as you. I discovered my proclivity toward men in university."

"Ja, remember when we would get a copy of the Der Eigene? I knew then that there were others like me."

"Bibl, there's no one like you. You're an ass," Schwartz says. He sips his beer.

Schwartz is a handsome man. He's well-proportioned and, measuring at almost two meters, he cuts an imposing silhouette in his black SS uniform, both authoritative and appealing at the same time. At thirty-three, he's just beginning to show the signs of aging with a few wrinkles by the eyes and a hint of grey in his jet-black hair. He looks like some noir actor as he sits in the red leather booth, his eyes fixed straight ahead on nothing in particular.

Bibl recoils at the reproach and pouts. "You're just angry!"

"*Ja*, I'm angry!" Schwartz snaps. "That fucking Rosemeyer stole that plane, I'm sure of it. And now I'm going to have to clean up his mess . . . again. I can only help that hapless girl who was with him if she wakes up and remembers that he was flying it. I'm sure it was him. I just can't prove it yet."

"I'll help you Marcus!" Bibl isn't the smartest SS officer Marcus has known but he is ungodly handsome, an SS boy-toy if he's ever seen one.

Schwartz looks at Bibl. He knows Bibl loves him and would do anything to help, but right now, he doesn't want his help. What he wants is to talk to Bernd so he can figure out how to sort this problem.

"No Bibl, I can handle this by myself."

"Fine Marcus, whatever you think is best," he says, his eyes cast at the table. "I'm just trying to help. Just . . . be careful. You know there are people in the SS looking for this kind of thing."

It is true. Since the crackdown, even members

of the Nazi SS are being tried for homosexual offenses. The good news is that the outcomes vary widely. If someone is perceived as a "manly" instead of a "soft" homosexual or is married and feigning a heterosexual relationship, they look the other way.

Schwartz keeps his secrets well-hidden but people suspect him. Even so, the SS leadership gladly overlooks him—he knows their secrets too well. It is a game of mutual concession. A game he plays well.

"I'm always careful," Schwartz says in a low voice, grinding out his cigarette in the crystal ashtray. "I just need to talk to Bernd and get our stories straight before I write up the report."

"Why are you always protecting him? If I didn't know better, I'd say you were looking forward to seeing Bernd. Makes me a bit jealous," Bibl admits.

Schwartz looks into his beer and slowly swirls the dregs in the empty glass.

"You should be. He's a real man."

4.   A MESSAGE TO RUDI

It's a dark, snowy night in Ghent, Belgium. Tiny snowflakes cling to the side of Rudi's face, melting as they travel the short distance to the neck of his upturned coat.

Rudi Caracciola, a handsome, mid-sized man with a dark, Mediterranean complexion, is running late. He promised to meet his childhood best friend, Gunther, at the wedding reception of one of the village's young couples.

Love is in the air everywhere tonight—Gunther and his fiancé Louise have just announced their engagement. The celebration is in full swing at a small but beautiful countryside manor. Outside, a group of Nazi officers clad in their black SS uniforms mill about, smoking and talking.

Rudi enters a crowded, smoke-filled room and sees his friend and his fiancée talking at a far table. A lively song by Franz Grothe, "Der Vorhang Falt" or "The Curtain Falls" plays and a few couples are dancing.

As Rudi approaches the table, he spots a group of SS officers eyeing his friend's fianceé. He sits and greets his friends. As they exchange pleasantries, a Nazi officer approaches.

"Guten abend. I thought this beautiful lady might enjoy a dance with an officer," he says, flashing a pompous smile to Louise. "There's so much Belgian and French garbage here tonight. I felt it was my *duty* as a Nazi officer to clear things up for her. My lady, would you do me the honor?"

Gunther, a fair few beers into the night, rises from his seat, his knuckles tensed and white. Rudi knows Gunther better than anyone, and immediately recognizes that this situation could get bloody—and fast. Rudi uses Gunther's arm to pull himself up from his seat, pretending to be a bit drunk.

"The lady is almost certainly enamored with her Belgian friend tonight," he slurs, his eyes half-closed as he grins. "So I think your offer, as good as it sounds, might be misplaced."

The officer looks from Rudi to the table, his eyes narrowing as he wets his lips. "A woman of this caliber should be associating with her kind, not the swill of Belgium."

Rudi calculates his odds of winning a fight against four men—he swiftly chooses discretion.

"Ah yes, you are almost *certainly* correct my friend," he says, garbling his words. "But alas, this is a special night for them. So if you don't object, they'll celebrate on their own terms."

"Well, I in fact *do* object," the officer sneers. "And by the way, who are you? Have you no respect for the German SS?"

"The name's Rudi. And I'm from Ghent." Rudi sympathizes with Germany's desire to right the wrongs of the Versailles sanctions, but he will never accept the German occupation of Belgium, no matter how the Reich plays up their shared cultures.

"Well Rudi," he says, taking a step closer to his victims. "If you don't get out of my way, we'll have to make an example of you. Just like we're about to make an example of the fucking French dogs."

Rudi feels Gunther shaking in anger next to him. He is now sure there's going to be a fight, and at this rate, his only hope is a surprise attack.

"Of course, Captain Schmidt. I'll just move myself on over to the bar," Rudi says, taking a wobbling step closer to the abhorrent man. "May I get you a drink?" He motions toward the bar and makes to shuffle around the officer. A look of smug triumph rises on the German's face. But before he has the chance to spout another trifling comment, Rudi hits the man in the nose with a right hook.

Rudi turns to Gunther. "Gunt, this night is going to be a bit different than originally planned!"

Gunther looks with wide eyes from Rudi to the Nazi officer sitting on the ground, blood spilling from between his fingers as he cups his hands over his now-broken nose. They've got moments at best before this asshole starts yelling and the other officers see what has become of their "disrespected" comrade. Gunther digs in to his pockets, pulls out a wad of cash and keys and hands it to Rudi.

"Get the hell out of here before they catch you, you glorious bastard! Louise and I can take care of ourselves but if this idiot's friends catch you, we'll all be sorry."

Rudi looks around. He watches as one of the other officers' eyes combs the room, his gaze heading in their direction. "I can't take this! It's your wedding money!"

"Rudi, if you don't get out of here quick there won't be a wedding. My NDS is parked outside. Just get out of here!"

Rudi takes the offerings and grasps Gunther's hand, then turns on his heels, leaves the building and finds the NDS motorcycle.

Dressed in casual clothes, he starts the motorcycle. He's already shivering and the thought of driving the thirty-five kilometers to his family's summer home in this temperature makes his hands feel even colder. The NDS starts just in time as the German officers pile outside and start looking for Rudi. In a cloud of steam and mist, Rudi guns the engine and disappears into the night.

5. RUDI'S ESCAPE

Rudi arrives at a small, summer cottage in the Belgian countryside, close to Liege. He already had plans to go to Berlin—after all that's where the real racing is happening—but he had hoped to save a few more marks before his departure. *Tonight is as good as any*, he thinks.

He packs a few meager belongings; his well-worn and torn racing kit, photos of his mom, dad and sister and a few other items are tossed into a beat-up leather bag with a broken zipper. He walks out into the cold starry night, locking the door behind him, and opens the trunk of an aging blue Peugeot.

He starts the car, but sits and stares for a moment at the old cottage. He realizes that this will probably be the last time he sees it. He and his family spent summers here; while just a poor farm family, they loved their time at the cottage, countless nights nestled by the fire, eating carbonade flamande and drinking Belgian beer. The smell of roasting blood sausage always made his stomach growl. God how he missed those sausages. Rudi loved the closeness and security of his family. They didn't have much but they had each other—and that was a lot in those days.

This was where he had first driven an automobile. There was a dirt track in back of the cottage where his father taught him how to counter steer, shift and look through corners. He practiced every day, even when petrol was scarce— sometimes he'd siphon from the neighbor's farm tractor just so he could practice in the old blue Peugeot.

He honed his skills and entered his first race in Köln, Germany when he was thirteen—these last ten years had sped by. He won that day, to the surprise of others as well as himself. Even though it was just a short, meaningless local race, he knew that day he would be a driver.

Rudy shakes his head as he reflects on how he got to this point in his life. Ten years ago his family started sharecropping the land they once owned after it was purchased by Mr. Goldman, a prominent Jew in Liege. The family couldn't keep up with the mortgage during WWI and were forced to sell it at a pittance. Goldman allowed them to live on the wheat farm if they gave him sixty-precent of the profits in exchange for rent. The catch was they had to pay Mr. Goldman at least five-thousand guilders per year or face eviction. The wheat crops suffered during the war and the Carricciola's fell behind in the payments. A few years ago, Rudi's father had cut a deal with Goldman and agreed to make up the difference by working Goldman's other farms for free. Rudi could almost hear his father's bones breaking when he sat in his chair, exhausted from a hard day in Goldman's farms. Rudi wanted to help, and after one especially hard day of working the fields and thinking about his father, eleven-year-old Rudi decided to approach Goldman with a proposition.

Rudi walked the five kilometers to the

farmhouse where Goldman kept an office in an old barn. The sunlight occasionally punched its way through the low-sitting Dutch clouds like a prize fighter.

"Gutten morning Herr Goldman, might you spare a few moments?" Rudi had nervously said to the towering six-foot Goldman who was in the middle of shuffling papers on his dilapidated but well-organized desk.

"Well, if it isn't Rudi. The son of the bastard that owes me money. What do you want?" Goldman barked.

"Sir, I know we owe you money, and my father has been working hard to pay our debt, but I was hoping you might be able to see if we could come to another arrangement? My father is sick all the time and the extra work isn't helping him. Perhaps I could take his place every Monday and Tuesday and work your south farm?"

"And why would I be interested in that? Your father knows my farm, you don't." Goldman had barely looked at Rudi over his half-brim spectacles that sat on his huge nose pocked marked with age spots. One large and lone hair stuck out his nostril making Goldman look simultaneously like an aging banker and demonic ghoul.

"Well, I was just hoping we could swap my labor for his. I'm stronger and can do the tilling much faster than him. I promise I can keep up. "

"Rudi, your father gave me his word he'd pay

off the debt and I've been more than generous with your situation. It's not my damn problem you Caricciola's are weak and worthless farmers." Rudi saw Goldman's temples throb with every word he spoke.

Rudi had glanced down at his dust covered farm boots and darted his eyes back to Goldman. "But sir, I'm just asking to swap my time for his, nothing more. I promise we'll pay you back, please!"

Suddenly standing, Goldman towered over the child, his full six-foot frame darkening the room as if the sun went behind a cloud. "Enough! The answer is no! Now get out of here before you really piss me off!"

"But please sir, can't you find it in your heart to make this small adjustment?" Rudi had taken a small step towards Goldman and made 'prayer hands" in a final gesture, hoping against hope that Goldman might show some compassion.

"My heart! This is about my wallet not my heart you sniveling piece of shit!"

Goldman had violently backhanded Rudi in the face and split his lip. Rudi, who was a foot and a half shorter than Goldman, staggered back a few steps until he was against the wall. The room was spinning, and he leaned against the wall for support. The backhand hurt like hell but Rudi steadied himself. Staring out the window, he was just able to make out the clouds he saw earlier moving across the Dutch sky. The room immediately got darker and colder.

"You people are all the same," Goldman snarled, "always looking for a handout, always looking to take advantage of people who work harder than you. You think I owe you, you worthless twit? You're just like your father, a stupid, lazy idiot farmer who wants to take advantage of me. Get the hell out of here and don't ever come back unless you've got the money to pay your debts!"

Rudi had flung the office door open and run into the road. He was sweating in the cold air and steam rose from his face. He remembered the taste of iron and blood, bitter in his mouth. He also tasted something else. He tasted revenge. On that day Rudi, filled with rage, had sworn that if he ever made it in the world, he would make sure that Jews like Goldman paid for their ruthlessness.

Rudi opens his eyes and puts the Peugeot in gear. He begins his twelve-hour drive to Berlin and hopefully a new life.

6. GIGOLO IN TRAINING

Three months after the fight, Rudi's friend Gunther has moved to Berlin and has landed a job as a mechanic at the largest Mercedes automotive dealership in the city. Gunther has arranged for Rudi to interview with Director Prost for a salesman job.

The morning of the interview, Rudi leaves his new girlfriend's apartment where he currently lives rent free. He walks everywhere—he has had to sell the old blue pig, the Peugeot, because he's unemployed and has no way to pay for his life just yet.

Rudi met Fräulein Gloria Seibel, a gorgeous brunette ten years his senior, through Gunther's fiancée at a beer garden a few Sundays after reaching Berlin. The beer flowed and before long, Rudi and Gloria were a couple.

Rudi isn't in love, but he needs a place to stay and Gloria is more than happy to accommodate. She loves that Rudi is an up-and-coming racecar driver. It makes her feel reckless.

Rudi feels a bit guilty about the relationship, but treads on. Gloria is a secretary at the Mercedes factory, and he thinks it will be useful to have a 'friend' who might help open doors for his racing pursuits. A free apartment isn't bad either; Rudi is aware they are using each other, but it seems to work for both of them.

Given the uncertainty of the German economy and her lack of a wage-earning husband, Gloria is trying to move the relationship to a more permanent status. She fawns over Rudi and cheers devotedly for him at his races. She's his first true fan and Rudi is quickly becoming accustomed to the attention and admiration.

Rudi's long-term plans don't include Gloria. His goals are higher but the first step is to land a job, which is exactly what he intends to do tomorrow. And for now, he has a free place to live and a woman who looks good on his arm.

7.   RUDI'S NEW SHOES

Rudi arrives fifteen minutes early. He *needs* to land this job. He's wearing the only suit he owns and it's showing its age.

Gunther appears, wiping automotive grease off his hands with a shop rag. "My boy! Good to see you. I see you dressed the part. I'm sure Herr Prost will be impressed—you're even wearing shoes," Gunther teases.

Rudi looks down at his worn, dirty farm boots, then jerks his head up again. He can't be embarrassed today. There is too much at stake.

"Well, if the clothes make a man, I guess I'll be looking for farm work next week."

"You'll be fine. All you have to do is sell Mercedes to the elite. As long as you know the specs of the car and babble on about its horsepower and speed, they'll buy almost anything from us—they've got cash to blow. This is the only Mercedes dealer in all of Berlin so they can't go anywhere else. It's shooting fish in a barrel, my friend. It's good, yes, since this interview is for a commissions-only job. You sell, you eat. Understood?"

"Yes, I understand. I just hope I can sell a fancy car to fancy people looking like this."

"Well the first thing you need to do is sell Herr Prost, here he comes." Gunther gives Rudi a nod, another to the approaching Prost and returns to the garage.

Director Prost is a small man with a large aquiline nose, thinning hair and the most expensive looking suit Rudi has ever seen. His shoes are freshly polished and everything about Prost seems to be in the utmost order. They meet in a gleaming showroom filled with Mercedes 170s, one of the most popular cars in Germany. There's the slightest aroma of oil and leather in the showroom, just enough that Rudi knows he's looking at expensive cars.

"Herr Caracciola, please be seated. I've read your CV—it is mildly impressive. Along with racing you're an ordained minister in the Protestant Church?"

Rudi nods. "Yes, sir."

"This will be a perfectly useless qualification unless you plan to sell cars to the Pope." Prost lowers the resume and removes his spectacles, turning his attention to the Belgian. "A few questions, if you please. What is the displacement of the Mercedes 170?"

"It has a 1696 cc six-cylinder side-valve engine. It also features a synchronized four-speed transmission and four-wheel hydraulic brakes."

"Correct." Prost is pleased, but not yet impressed. "The wheelbase?"

"Two hundred eighty-four point five centimeters."

"Correct. The difference between the "V" and "W" models?"

"The V is front engine and the W is in the rear. I personally find the V to handle better than the W."

"You would do well to keep your opinions to yourself, Herr Caracciola. I have over fourteen Ws in stock and only three Vs. If you plan to make money at this job you will sell what I have in inventory."

"Jawohl, Herr Prost. I understand."

Prost looks Rudi up and down.

"Be here tomorrow promptly at 8:30 AM. In Germany, unlike Belgium, we expect people to arrive for work at the designated time, dressed appropriately and ready to work. Buy new shoes before you arrive tomorrow. You will be paid three days after each sale. Are these terms satisfactory to you Herr Caracciola?"

Rudi and Prost stare at each other for an extended moment, each searching for weakness in the other.

"Thank you, Director Prost. I accept your generous offer."

The director gives him a nod, and the deal is made. On spotless heels, Prost turns and leaves the gleaming showroom to return to his daily activities. Rudi now stands by himself; he looks around and grins. He turns to leave, muttering under his breath, "This job is not the only thing I will conquer Herr Prost. Soon I will be driving your cars and winning races. All in good time, all in good time."

Rudi exits the showroom and enters a shoe shop on the same street.

"Sir, I need a new pair of shoes, the finest you have— but I'm a bit short on funds currently. I just accepted a salesman's position next door and will be able to pay you next week. Does this sound fair to you?"

"You're rather confident in yourself I see," the merchant replies. "Selling a car in the first week of a new job?"

"Sir, I think you misunderstand me. I will sell three cars in the first week."

The man looks Rudi up and down. "I see. Well, if you don't, I know where you work and I *will* have no issue reclaiming these shoes. There will also be a slight finance charge for my trouble. These are yours for thirty marks, which is double the cost."

Doubling the price would usually seem egregious to Rudi, but these shoes are part of the terms and conditions of his new position.

"Thank you, sir, I accept your terms. Size 44, if you please."

8. THE FIRST RACE

It's a beautiful day in Dresden. Today is merely a local race, but it also serves as a qualifier. A win today determines the top three drivers who will compete in the more prestigious European Grands Prix, which have become immensely popular over the past few years.

It is also Rudi and Bernd's first race together. Rudi is a young buck with a borrowed car from his employer, Mercedes. Bernd is a cosmopolitan bon vivant with an eight-man team and the best Alfa Romeo money can buy—but he doesn't care about any of that, he just likes the excitement of winning.

They meet in the pits as Rudi examines Bernd's superior car.

"She's beautiful," Rudi says. "I haven't seen an M128 before. Does she drive well?"

"Like a swan on a pond," Bernd says languidly.

"How long have you owned it?"

"I'm not sure to be honest; it was a gift from my company. Is this your first race at circuit de Dresden?"

"Yes, my first here. I moved here four months ago but I've raced at almost all the best circuits in Belgium. My name's Rudi Caracciola, and I'm asalesman at Mercedes Berlin."

"Bernd," he replies. The two shake hands, their driving gloves already on. "Please give my regards to Herr Prost in Berlin. He and I have done some business together in the past. May I offer some guidance since it's your first time at this track? Follow my line. Use the 'M' on the sign in corner one to start your descent from the bank. Once you hit the bottom, accelerate as much as you can so you're lined up for the straight."

"Great, thanks." He looks past the 'M' on the sign to the brewing skies. "I hope the weather stays dry today."

"Yes, indeed." A car passes the pair on a test lap; the driver accelerates prematurely and nearly hits the top guard rail. Bernd sighs in exasperation. "With these imbeciles on the track, we don't need any more challenges. Who's your mechanic?"

"Gunther Legate. He's on loan from my company—and to be honest so is my car. Had to do a bit of begging to be here today." Rudi had moved his handful of possessions into his very own apartment just the day before. As such, poor Gloria couldn't make it to the race today—too busy crying. "My boss only agreed to loan me the car and mechanic since our first team is racing Imola this weekend. They were preoccupied, so I took advantage and asked for the loan."

"I see." Bernd is amused and impressed by this new character's resourcefulness—he seems like a worthy opponent. "Sounds like you like to gamble. Well good luck today, Rudi. I hope to see you again."

"*Danke*—and good luck to you too."

The weather deteriorates just as the cars line up for the start. Gunther stands next to Rudi, dressed in his mechanics-wear, wrenches and oil cans dangling from his vest. Rudi's helmet bears a Mercedes logo signifying their privateer entry's association with the company.

Smoke and the smell of burning Benzene mixes with the heavy scent of ozone as the sky begins to dribble. Raindrops blend with the oil on the tarmac and multi-colored rainbows bead up from the surface. Thirteen cars are entered in the race; most are driven by well-funded private teams.

These days, racing attracts the rich thrill-seekers of Europe. The atmosphere is a mix of carnival and sport; the Dresden elite are sequestered in the grandstands, while the commoners stand at the corners or straights with picnic baskets and children.

The race marshal approaches the start stand with the checkered flag. He gazes over the field to ensure all are ready. As he climbs the stairs, lightning illuminates the field of cars. A loud crack of thunder makes the already nervous drivers jump.

"All right Wolf, remember this is a loaner. If you crash it, we'll be paying for it until we die,"

Gunther tells his friend.

Rudi checks the levels. "I have no intention of crashing or dying anytime soon, Gunther." He looks at his friend. Maybe it's the lightning, but they both feel like something big is coming.

"Just keep the engine running. Be sure to keep checking the temperature. She's not new and frankly she's not in the best shape."

"On the start, I don't intend to follow anyone's line. I've watched the two previous races and for the life of me, I don't understand why anyone would use the banks like they do. It's time for me to show them how to drive."

"Well Wolf, just do your best like always. Hell, with this rain, just try to keep the car on the road. With any luck, we'll place high enough to cover the cost of the oil and petrol we'll use."

Rudi grips the wheel with calloused hands, staring down the track. "My goals are a bit higher than that, my friend. Get ready."

The starter drops the flag, and the sound of the thirteen accelerating cars rivals even that of the thunder. Smoke fills the air and they dash to the first corner. Rudi has been passed by five faster, better cars before he can even make it to turn one. Suddenly, the sun appears and illuminates the race—it's almost as if God has chosen to watch. The track begins to dry, but Rudi falls farther behind the faster cars. He finds himself in last place on lap ten of thirty.

As Rudi flies past the pits, Gunther holds a sign: TEMP.

Rudi hand-pumps air into the crank case as fast as he can—he's left driving one-handed. His arm quickly tires, so he switches hands and pumps even more vigorously.

As if God has become bored, the sun dims and rain clouds emerge once again. The sky opens and rain falls hard. Within minutes, three cars crash on the rain and oil-slicked track. Rudi is still last on lap thirteen. He sees that the three cars ahead of him have slowed due to the rain. He chases them hard.

The rain helps cool the engine—Rudi pushes harder. He presses gently but firmly on the accelerator and finds himself passing three more cars in turn four. He is now in seventh position. The rain falls even harder—lightning bolts appear every minute, ripping apart the sky. The smell of electricity is everywhere and spectators run for cover, leaving the drivers to fight it out by themselves.

Two cars ahead of Rudi are fighting for position. As he approaches, they touch and spin out. Rudi is now in fifth. The rain falls harder. Rudi uses his new line to pass below two more cars as they rise high in the banked turn. Rudi takes third position. Bernd is in the lead, but only slightly.

Gunther screams from the pits, "My god man, you're in third, keep it up!"

"Just keep running!" Rudi says to himself. Suddenly the second-place car pulls off the track, smoke pouring out of the engine compartment.

There are only three laps left. Rudi pushes hard and has Bernd in his sights. Bernd swings up to use the banking and Rudi easily passes him below.

Bernd's re-entry leaves him two cars behind as they come down the final straight. Bernd's more powerful car gobbles up the distance but he's too late. Rudi crosses the finish line and wins by half a car length.

The tabloids dub him "Rudi the Rain Master" that day.

9. CONFLICT OVER POLAND

Germany is starving. There are over seventy-million people in Germany, Austria and the surrounding republic in 1937. Food is scarce. German agriculture, decimated by depleted and over-farmed soil, simply cannot keep up with this many mouths. Demand is outstripping supply throughout Europe and Hitler already knows that his upcoming war will need a well-fed army.

Hitler plans to solve the food shortage by invading Poland. This move will not only provide more 'living space' for the empire's expansion, but also use Poland's rich soil into the Reich's breadbasket. Germany has been relying on Great Britain for the means to fertilize their soils; now, with the Reich's mounting wish to become completely self-sufficient, Germany looks to Poland's fertile soil for the nitrogen they seek. With the help of Haber's nitrogen extraction process, Poland's resource-rich land will become the breeding ground for German agriculture and ammunition.

"We need Poland by October." Hitler stands looking at a map with his back to High General von Dries. "The Russians may only have a small part of the Western border as agreed to in the Molotov-Ribbentrop treaty. Eliminate anyone who interferes."

"Jawohl, mein Führer, it shall be done. The Poles will resist but they will be unsuccessful," the general replies. "They are not prepared for the blitzkrieg we will unleash. Mein Führer, may I?" he asks motioning to the map. Hitler, turning one eye on the general, gives a small nod.

"The Seventh Army will move from the Southern border"—he places one finger on the map—"through Prague and Ostrava and take Krakow. The Ninth Army will move from Berlin to the East and take Warsaw. The Navy shall approach from the North and easily occupy Gdansk and prevent any re-supply or reinforcement offered by their Nordic allies."

Battle planning comes easily to General von Dries. He fought gallantly in World War I and commanded an Eingreif Division. He and his second in command, Hendrick Wagner, both received the Iron Cross for their accomplishments.

He continues. "Once we have established control, the 1st Engineering Army will move into Wroclaw and Krakow and construct the Haber nitrogen extraction factories.

"This plan will allow us to produce fertilizer in time for the 1939 planting season, assuming Porsche delivers the factory engines in time.

"I respectfully suggest we enlist Mercedes and Auto Union to also work on these engines as they are critical to our plan. I know the autobahn is an important showcase of our engineering, but without the necessary factory engines, nitrogen extraction may be delayed."

Hitler immediately slaps his hands on the table.

"Nein General! They are focused on equally important projects. The autobahn is not only a showcase of German engineering, but it also allows our military to travel at high speeds to anywhere within the Rhineland.

"What the Reich needs is speed! Our blitzkrieg depends on it! Mercedes tells me they will have a car capable of breaking the world speed record any day now. Its design is nothing the world has ever seen; it is a rocket! Soon, our cars will travel as fast as a Messerschmitt. Imagine traveling at 250 miles per hour, General. Tell me that is not a military advantage."

"*Jawohl mein Führer*," says the general.

Dries clicks the heels of his boots sharply, salutes, and leaves Hitler to ponder the map on his wall.

In an unusually good mood on his way to breakfast at the family farmhouse the next day, General von Dries whistles and sings a funny German folk song as he walks to meet his daughter, Nicolette.

"Good *morning* mein Führer!" she sings, her back to her father as she places a jam jar on the table.

The general laughs. "Such pleasantries from my aviator this morning!" he says, giving a little salute to his daughter.

"So what is on the general's itinerary for today?" she asks as they take their seats at the table. They occupy two of four chairs, the other two left empty by the passing of Nicolette's mother and brother.

"Ah, the usual duties of a German general. Mostly expanding the Rhineland empire. We'll be annexing Poland shortly so we can build factories to feed our civilians."

Nicolette looks at her father, her eyes wide. "What?" Her butter knife has come to a halt just above her slice of toast.

"Poland? My *god* father, do we really need to annex another country? We've barely digested the Czechs and Austria, and now Poland, too?"

"Schatzki, you know that Germany is starving. Look at this breakfast. Do you know how many in this country would *kill* for this bounty? If I weren't a German general, we'd be eating broth and twigs. We need Poland for resources, for food production and for labor. Without Poland the expansion stops and millions starve. Poland is not optional. We must take it and turn it into the Reich's largest food production area."

"But with an invasion, thousands will die. Not just Poles, but Germans too! How many more must die just to satisfy our own needs? When does it stop, Father?"

"Poland will quickly fall Schatzki, like a straw house in a storm. Some will die, that is a given in war but they have no appetite for a prolonged engagement after seeing our success in Czechoslovakia—and speaking of appetite, I must finish breakfast and leave. I have many meetings in Berlin today. There is much planning to do. We have factories to build after our annexation is complete."

"This is insane father. Is there no end to this madness?"

"What would you have me do?" von Dries asks through a mouthful of toast. "Sacrifice millions of German lives over a few Poles? We need these factories to feed ourselves Nicolette!"

"It's madness! There must be another way!"

"I wish there was, truly!" Dries' frustration with the war and his daughter is showing. "I take no satisfaction in war; it is simply a means to an end. But it is an important end if we are to expand the Rhineland and feed ourselves!"

Nicolette shakes her head. "I'm sick of war, I'm sick of death." A tear falls. "The only peace I have is when I'm flying, far above the earth, untouched by this madness—and I know most don't have that luxury. It makes me sad to think we've come to this. We're disgusting. We're killing others in the name of surviv—"

"Enough! The Führer's plans are bigger than your tiny, sentimental thoughts. I may not like it any more than you, but I have a job to do and I will do my best to help our country survive."

The general, no longer in a good mood, rises, grabs his jacket, hat and gloves and calls out to have his car brought around.

"Schatzki, I know how you feel and if it's any consolation, I mostly agree with you. But this war has momentum, it cannot be denied. I am just a wheel in a large engine. Once the engine starts, it cannot be stopped. And as a general, I obey orders, and orders I have. Good day Schatzki."

10. Meet Hendrick

After an intense month-long battle, the Poles are defeated while awaiting help from France and the UK that never comes. Desperate, the Poles that can escape flee to Romania.

General von Dries reluctantly leaves his family to start mining and factory operations in the newly acquired Poland countryside where the Wehrmacht enlists Polish prisoners to build farms and mine the land for minerals.

Resentment runs deep and hot in Poland and the Polish underground takes form quickly in Romania. They do their best to sabotage the mines and factories, but have little success. Tragically, the Polish resistance must fight an underground war that forces them to kill their enslaved countrymen being forced by the Reich to turn Poland into Germany's new food production center. Ironically, Poles killing Poles is the only way to slow Germany's roll.

Nicolette stands in front of her bedroom window. She sees lightning splinter the night sky in the distance; a thunderstorm is approaching. There will be rain tonight, she can smell it in the air. Hopefully a clear sky will arrive before morning when she flies. She draws the soft, heavy curtains and gets into bed.

The next morning, in a muddy airfield that smells of oil and dirt, Nicolette prepares to fly an unofficial recon mission over Poland. She needs stick time and she's curious about the real effects of the Poland invasion.

Nicolette's mechanic, Hendrick, is a longtime family friend. Despite being a Pole, he served as second-in-command of General von Dries' Eingreif Division. He now runs a thriving airplane rental and training school; there's a high demand for pilots these days. He's been Nicolette's flying instructor for the past four years, and she trusts him with her life.

Hendrick, standing by an older bi-plane used for training, greets Nicolette before her flight.

"Guten morgen Fräulein von Dries, I've checked everything on R28 and she's ready to go. Keep an eye on the engine temperature, cylinder eight seems to be little grumpy today.

Nicolette pats the side of the engine, a far-off look appearing in her eyes. "Cylinder eight feels the same as I do today."

Hendrick walks around the plane, looking for anything amiss. "Ah, so Fräulein von Dries is feeling a bit under the weather?" he shouts from the other side of the aircraft. "Seems the rain has colored your emotions?"

Nicolette climbs into the cockpit and checks her seat.

"Hendrick, I cannot fathom why we are doing what we're doing. It makes no sense, the fighting, the deaths . . . and for what? More food, more war? It seems it will never end."

Hendrick climbs up the nearby ladder to assist Nicolette with her pre-flight check.

"I understand, Fraulein. I feel the same. You already know how I feel though, nothing has changed."

"Didn't we learn from the last war? I know we suffered with the embargo, and Germany was unfairly sanctioned, but the politics are simply insane."

"I agree, Fräulein von Dries—I see the inequity every day. But the German people seem to love their new leader: they are simple people and will follow blindly if they are told the same propaganda day in and day out. We have become sheep, and the herder is misguided."

Nicolette sighs. "What you say is unfortunately true, Hendrick. The people seem enamored with Hitler. Nothing he says, no matter how vile, is questioned."

"Well," Hendrick hesitates for a sliver of a second, "that's not entirely accurate. There are some who feel otherwise and work toward a different path. You know, the ones I mentioned."

Nicolette looks pleadingly at him.

"Hendrick, I *know* but you can't expect the daughter of a German general to join the Polish resistance, can you?" she says, slumping against the seat, frustrated and conflicted.

"I'm not asking you to join," Hendrick says

quietly. "Just provide a little insight on where things are going."

Nicolette's eyes bulge. "You want me to spy on my own father?" she asks breathlessly. She looks at her feet, her boots caked in mud. She knows, has always known, that she wants to help; but she is afraid, not only for her life, but at the thought of betraying her own father, the only family she has left.

"Not on your father, on war planning. You *must* learn to separate a man from his actions. You know I have the upmost respect for the general; we fought together and he saved my life numerous times. I know he is a good man, but the path we're on is wrong."

"Enough, Hendrick. We've had this talk many times, and while I respect your desire to help your people, I *cannot* spy on my father!"

Hendrick glances at the airfield, then back to the young woman. "I understand, Fräulein von Dries. And I appreciate you talking to me about this. Should you ever change your mind, we can talk again." He jumps into the mud. "Should I let the tower know you're ready for takeoff?"

"Yes," she says, looking into the distant sky. Her mind won't stop churning. "Perhaps being closer to God while I'm flying will help me see the world a little clearer today. I'll be back in two hours." She looks at Hendrick and smiles. "As usual, have our beers ready on my return!"

"Your wish is my command, Fräulein von

Dries."

Nicolette takes off and flies east. Over Poland, she looks out of the cockpit and sees the devastation. Dead bodies litter the fields and refugees flee her plane thinking it's a German aircraft about to strafe them.

The carnage of war is everywhere. Disgusted, she turns her plane toward Germany. She thinks about confronting her father once again about the war. What good will it do? She has been taught to respect her elders and her country. But nothing about what's happening in her beloved country feels right. Should she take matters into her own hands? Spy? How could she? She is torn. Navigating home, she ponders what will happen to her country, her family, and herself.

Nicolette and her father are car shopping in celebration of von Dries' successful annexation of Poland which has taken just under four months. Nicolette has remained silent on the matter since seeing the carnage firsthand. She feels foggy as the pair enter the pristine Mercedes showroom.

"Allo Herr Prost," booms the general. "I understand that you are the best purveyor of Mercedes in Berlin, perhaps all of Germany?"

"Herr General, you are too kind," Prost replies as the men clasp hands. "These rumors are just gossip. I am but a simple man, doing simple work. I only hope that it helps the Reich, Germany and the Führer in some small way."

"A modest man indeed. There's no doubt that the German people need cars. I've heard that in America there is one car for every twenty men, yet in Germany we have one for every two-hundred men. If our economy is to become strong, we must solve this problem, eh Herr Prost?"

"Indeed, Herr General. I listened to the Führer's Berlin Auto show speech and was moved by his vision to create the 'people's car'."

"Yes, I too share the excitement of seeing our autobahns full of KdF-Wagens. Imagine a country where any working man can buy a reliable and inexpensive car that can take him anywhere of his choosing."

"Herr General, when you say it aloud, it brings joy to my heart. The day of the KdF cannot come soon enough."

Nicolette imagines a light blue Beetle driving through the war-torn fields of Poland. She lights a cigarette.

"Yes, not soon enough," says von Dries. But I'm also excited about the new program to set the world speed record on the autobahn."

"Ah! I heard about this just last week. The Führer has enlisted both Mercedes and Auto Union in a contest. Whoever builds the fastest car will win the Führer's favor—and the heart of the German people."

"Yes, the cars being prepared are unheard of. They look like they could fly! I understand that Bernd Rosemeyer himself will drive the Auto Union car."

"Rosemeyer is one of the best drivers in the world. It would bring great honor to Germany if he were to set the world record."

"Not 'if' Herr Prost, *when*. But on more mundane matters," von Dries continues, "I have a need for transportation. The staff car the Wehrmacht provides is often on loan to others and I need access to reliable and stable transportation. So here I am in your showroom. I understand you have a few 170s you could part with?"

Prost senses he can sell at least two or three cars to the general, but doesn't outwardly reveal his excitement—Prost is a true salesman.

"Ja, Herr General. As you know the 170s are the best Mercedes built right now. And surprisingly, I do happen to have a few in stock—they *do* sell quickly. With inflation of the Mark," Prost continues, "it seems people are flocking in to buy them before the price rises again. Only this week, the price went up by thirty percent.

"Herr Prost, am I to understand that the price of the 170 is now thirty percent higher than yesterday?" the general asks slowly. "It seems the director might be using inflation as an excuse to line his pockets?"

"Oh no Herr General, I assure you! I'm sure we can accommodate your request and come to very agreeable pricing terms given the general's official transport needs. Did you say you needed four or five cars?

"I didn't say how many I need Herr Prost; but let's assume it's more than one if we can agree on price."

"Excellent, Herr General. Might I suggest I turn you over to our salesman, Rudi Caracciola? He can explain a bit about the car while I work on the pricing arrangements."

Rudi has been observing the group from afar since the pair walked in. He has heard talk of the general, but never of the daughter. But he's seen enough photographs of the two together to know that this is Nicolette von Dries. She's dressed in a chic summer frock; not Berlin-chic, but in an understated and functional style. She's beautiful to Rudi.

She carries herself with confidence and intelligence, unlike many of the Berlin women he's met so far; they all seem more interested in the amount of Marks a man has than anything else.

"You are too kind Herr Prost," says von Dries. "Just be aware I'm due back at HQ in less than one hour, so let's be quick about this."

"Certainly, Herr General." Prost locates Rudi across the showroom and waves him over.

"Rudi! Please meet General von Dries and his daughter, Fräulein Nicolette." Rudi gives a slight bow at each introduction. "Please take very good care of them while I attend to an administrative matter.

"Herr Caracciola is our newest salesman, as well as a professional racecar driver. He just won the circuit du Dresden in one of our older cars as a privateer entry—he has quite a career ahead of him. There's talk of him becoming a Mercedes factory driver in the near future."

"Heil Hitler Herr General and Fräulein von Dries," Rudi says. "A pleasure to make your acquaintance."

"Heil Hitler," responds von Dries. "So you're the young man who beat Rosemeyer last week?

If you keep that up, you may find yourself racing Rosemeyer on the autobahn in a Rekordwagen car.

"Indeed, Herr General. I've heard the rumors about these cars, and all I can say is if they're half as fast as they claim, I will certainly be driving one against Rosemeyer."

"A very confident driver I see. We need more men like you in the Luftwaffe, right Nicolette?"

From what I saw, they don't need any more "confident" men—if that's what you want to call it, she thinks.

"I suppose so, Papa," she says, forcing a small smile.

"Fräulein von Dries, you are familiar with the Luftwaffe?" Rudi asks as the three peruse the showroom models.

She looks at the salesman. "I am a pilot, Herr Rudi. I fly, but not often enough and certainly not for the Luftwaffe," she says. Rudi nods; further impressed.

"It takes over a hundred men to hand-build these cars," Rudi says, showing off the gleaming Mercedes. "The entire car, including the engine, is made in Stuttgart and each takes about seventy hours to complete. You see this windscreen? Bullet proof! The first of its kind; very useful in aviation. It also provides security for German statesmen should the need arise," he says with a nod to the general.

The general's mouth twitches up at one corner. He drifts away to inspect a dark blue 190.

Rudi turns to Nicolette. "A pilot! Then you certainly understand that the power-to-weight ratio is critical to an airplane and an automobile."

"Preferably a one-to-one ratio," she says, her mouth blooming into a slight grin. She hates to admit it, but she is always pleasantly surprised when a man does not underestimate her skill and experience as a pilot. "But my R28 falls significantly below that, Herr Rudi."

"Hahaha, yes I'm sure it does. My 120 Mercedes is also far below that. Well, I see the Fräulein is not just a pretty face. You understand technical engineering better than most."

"I understand many things Herr Rudi. One of which is that you're about to lose a sale if you don't hurry up with my father." She tips her head in the general's direction, who stands, fiddling with his shirt cuffs. Rudi gives her a look of thanks and hastens to von Dries.

Nicolette doesn't meet many new men—she's too busy flying and working on her plane—so the interaction with Rudi is unusually pleasant for her. She likes the way Rudi carries himself.

She finds his confidence and politeness intriguing. She spends most of her time at the airfield, which is populated almost exclusively with gruff pilots and mechanics; despite being the general's daughter, she avoids soldiers and officers at all costs. Yes, she's intrigued by this racecar driver, though she can see his ego is substantial.

Prost returns and requests the general come to his office so they can finalize the paperwork on the purchase of four new 170s. Rudi calculates his commission on such a large sale.

Left alone, Rudi and Nicolette make small talk about horsepower, weight to power ratios and transmissions—all components and functions found in their two vehicles of choice. She loves this opportunity to talk about technical details with someone who seems genuinely interested; she enjoys this interdisciplinary camaraderie. He's never met such an intelligent, humble, well-rounded woman.

"So, Fräulein von Dries. Would it be too forward to ask about your relationship status? I was hoping that you might be interested in attending one of my races as my guest."

"Yes, you may ask."

"Um, so . . . what?"

"You wanted to know my relationship status."

"Yes . . . um—"

"So ask!" She laughs.

"Ah! So, are you seeing anyone Fräulein Nicolette?"

"I see many people every day Herr Rudi," she says with a coy smile. "What about you Herr

Rudi, seeing anyone?"

"No, no, I'm unattached at the moment." It's true. Despite what he has been telling quite a few lofty ladies of Berlin in recent weeks, none of them have captured his attention as Nicolette has. He grins. "Why are you being so coy? Or perhaps you're the type who likes to see a man squirm."

"You have no idea what you're getting yourself into Herr Rudi," she says, smiling, despite her best efforts to remain serious. "Contact me with the details of your next race. I make no promises, but perhaps I'll buzz the race track in my plane—maybe even land if you're winning."

"In that case, Fräulein, I will win every race until you grace me with your presence."

"Over the past four years, and with continual improvements, we have developed the Volkswagen, which we are convinced can be sold not only at the price we want, but also can be manufactured in ways that use a minimum of workers to produce the maximum amount.

"The model that has resulted from years of work by Dr. Porsche will undergo testing this year. It will enable millions of new customers with limited incomes to afford a car. We owe the best cars in the world to our directors, engineers, craftsmen, workers, and salesmen.

"Today, I am convinced that in a short time we will also build the least expensive cars."

13. A NIGHT TO REMEMBER

It's 1 AM. Bernd has been circling the Berlin Airport for forty minutes in his plane waiting for the fog to clear. The short flight from Leipzig, the home of Auto Union's factory, should have taken less than one hour. This is the first time he's flown since his accident with Cindy, and he's relieved to know that she's recovering nicely . . . although the doctor's say her situational amnesia may be permanent.

He had spent the day with the engineers testing the new design known as the Streamliner. When Berndt first saw it, he wasn't sure if he was looking at a car or a plane; its sleekness was beguiling.

The Streamliner sat silently in the factory, its bright aluminum bodywork glistening under the lights.

The car was like nothing that had been seen before. It looked like a shark, its tall dorsal fin sticking up behind the cockpit, its front air intake looking like a mouth ready to eat anything that came close.

Most notably, its wheel arches covered the entire area around the tires, thereby reducing airflow. This amazing feature also presents a significant problem.

Since the wheels were covered, the front tires could only turn six degrees, thus making turns almost impossible. The car was designed for straight-line speed and nothing else. Turning was limited to small corrections, which, when traveling at 250 miles per hour, translated into large corrections very quickly.

The car featured a rear diffuser that created a revolutionary aspect *downforce*. As the air passed rapidly under the car, the diffuser disrupted the airflow and created a vacuum which sucked the vehicle closer to the road. This vacuum created over 1200 pounds of downforce, almost as much as the car weighed.

The cockpit was sparse: just a seat, a wheel, a few gauges, and pedals for operating the massive 12-cylinder engine capable of producing almost 500 horsepower.

The most amazing feature was the bubble canopy that had to be removed so the driver could enter. It looked like it belonged on a fighter plane—and given that the Streamliner looked more like a plane than a car, it looked appropriate.

Once the driver was seated, the canopy was bolted onto the car. Should things go wrong there was no way for the driver to get out without a mechanic and spanner, something which sat heavily in Bernd's mind as he walked around the car.

After the fog finally clears, Bernd lands and taxis to his waiting Auto Union sportscar. The transition from plane to car is always strange, like going from running to crawling. He laughs as he drives down a newly constructed portion of the Autobahn—the plane has made his present 120 kilometers per hour feel so pedestrian.

Bernd parks outside the Kit Kat Cabaret and approaches from the back alley—there are too many stargazers and fans at the front, and he wants to get inside in time to see Dominique Dresden before she performs.

In the shadows of a weak street light, a midget and a leggy showgirl stand by the rear entrance smoking. He nods and enters.

Passing other performers and staff, Bernd makes his way to Dominique's dressing room where he finds her applying her final touches of makeup.

"Where have you *been*?" she asks, her wide eyes meeting his in the mirror.

"Sorry darling, long day, and then there was fog at the airport. But I'm here now! Alles gut?" He kisses her lightly on the top of her head.

"You're such a bore sometimes Bernd. And yes I'm ready to go. Shan't be long tonight—are we still on for Rebecca's fête?"

"Wouldn't dream of missing it," he says.

"There's a big group of Nazi officers in the front row who are beyond drunk. Be a good boy and sit close to the stage so you can lend a hand if things get out of hand?"

"Of course. But isn't that Maurice's job?"

"Haven't seen him tonight, I'm on in five!" she says, kissing his left cheek before scurrying to the stage.

"Break a leg darling!" Bernd calls after her. He meanders out of the dressing room and finds the usual table reserved for him.

"Champagne, Herr Rosemeyer?" the maître d' asks.

"Yes Maurice, the usual if you please."

"*Jawohl*, right away monsieur."

The emcee cajoles the crowd into a hearty applause for the previous act—ten showgirls who left nothing to the imagination. To say the girls were nude would be an understatement, and the crowd claps and yells their approval.

"*Mein Damen und Herren, Mesdames et Messieurs*, Ladies and Gentlemen! *Guten Abend, bon soir, Wie geht's? Comment ca va?* Do you feel good? I bet you do! *Ich bin euer, je suis votre compere*.... I am your host.

"Now, the Kit Kat is excited to present to you a vixen who's twirled her tassels from London to Lisbon, the international "Good Bad Girl", please welcome the stunning and mystifying Dominque of Dresden!"

Standing, slapping each other's backs, the drunken group of Nazi officers wolf whistle and scream their approval as the first notes of a belly dancing song called "Ya Washeshni" plays.

Dominique enters the stage wearing a chiffon Arab robe which she slowly drops to the floor. She performs her usual routine, culminating in an erotic Arabian gyration to the beat of faraway drums. The crowd is mesmerized by her movements and erupts into applause when she saunters off the stage.

Bernd drains his glass and meets Dominique in the dressing room where she gathers her items. They slip out to his waiting car.

They cruise down the back alley; small, oily puddles from the light rain that fell at dusk glisten in the moonlight.

"Should only take a wink to get to Rebecca's darling. Hold tight!

"Mind my hair Bernd!" Dominique whines as he starts to speed down the city streets. "Why must we always drive with the top down?"

"Because it's freeing darling, nothing can stop us tonight!" he says, turning with a smile to his passenger. Dominique wraps a scarf around her head.

Arriving at Rebecca's mansion, Bernd and Dominique quickly make their way to the main salon where the party rages away. Cocaine and champagne are the usual staples of the Berlin party scene, but tonight is special. Tomorrow is a huge Grand Prix in which Bernd is racing. The top teams from Italy, France and Britain are here.

Bernd has big plans; the German cars he's racing have the most powerful engines in the field. Germany was banned from producing any engines that could potentially be used for military purposes under the Treaty of Versailles. With the treaty now ignored, Germany is producing the fastest engines and cars possible. He can easily outrun any of the European teams in a straight line, but will find himself challenged in the corners.

Monsieur Davenport, the lead driver for the French team, is busy snorting a rather large line of cocaine he's carefully prepared when he catches Bernd's eye and walks over. He is dressed impeccably, in a way only the French can achieve. Davenport touches Bernd's arm.

"Bernd, 'ow wondeurful to szee you!"

"Ah David, my friend! You look smashing tonight as always. How are things?"

"Supehrb, supehrb! Looking forwad tu ze race tomorrow. But first I thought I might enjoy myself a bit...."

"I always took you for a man who enjoys life, mon ami. So what are your plans for tonight?"

"Well, frankly, I'm stuck here with my team who are a bit *boh-ring*. Too focused on work as they say?"

"Ah well, to be expected given the race at

hand." Bernd sips his champagne. "Perhaps we can find a way to make your night a bit more, shall we say, enjoyable?"

"You have my attention, mon ami."

"I happen to have come with that lovely creature over there," says Bernd. "Perhaps you know her, Dominique of Dresden?"

"Ah yes, I have seen her performance before—when I was in Berlin last summer. She's magnificent!" the Frenchman says, watching as Dominique laughs and paws at the sleeve of a drunken, uniformed officer. "Perhaps you can introduce us. But I was hoping to spend some time with *you* tonight my friend."

"You are a lucky man, David. I was thinking the same…. Perhaps the three of us could mysteriously disappear for a while."

"You must be part French, mon ami."

Bernd grins. "I'm part something, but I don't think it's French. Let me grab a bottle. Meet us upstairs, third bedroom on the right."

"I shan't be late, nor will I disappoint."

14. CHURCH

Nicolette and her father haven't been to church in months. This is not because they have lost faith, but simply because their favorite church sits in the Mitte district in the heart of Berlin, and getting there takes an hour.

But today is going to be different. As they arrive at the *Berliner Dom*, the Berlin Cathedral, the morning sun greets them with a soft kiss. The green and gold of the building call out, dazzling in the light, as they ascend the steps.

When she was a little girl, her father would bring her here and they would climb the 103 steps to the top of the dome to look at the city. From here, they could see all of Berlin in its glory. Her father would make a game out of identifying the different landmarks. She loved being this high; it was almost as good as flying.

The Protestant pastor here is quick and to the point—something she appreciated both as a little girl and now as an adult. Nicolette agrees with the work ethic promoted in Calvinism. It just seems right; work hard, be disciplined and frugal, and the world will be better. Very German.

But once Bach's Keyboard Concerto No. 1 in D minor erupts from the massive pipe organ, she knows the service is over and the *real* fun is about to start.

It is then that the smartly dressed congregation

spills into the huge courtyard of the church. A sacrament of coffee, tea and sandwiches are lovingly offered, brought by the women of the congregation. Nicolette loves the competitive aspect; every woman proudly displays her offerings and tries to one-up each other over who has the best strudel recipe.

Between exchanging pleasantries with members of the congregation, Nicolette wonders why it has taken her so long to attend a service. An hour isn't very long, and she always finds peace here, just as she does when flying—it's meditative. She loves the grandeur of the building, and the warmth and companionship of her fellow Germans make everything else going on in the world seem slightly more palatable. Most importantly, the gathering provides an opportunity for friends and family to gather, eat, and reminisce. Here, gossip isn't encouraged—it is required.

Nicolette and her father munch on strudel and chat with Fräu Heidelberg about her son's academic successes. As they discuss the benefits of team sports on the development of young people, Rudi Caracciola approaches with a small plate stacked precariously with a tower of sweet confectionaries.

"Fräulein von Dries, General! So good to see you!" the driver says, nodding to Fräu Heidelberg.

"Herr Caracciola, what a surprise! Good to see you as well," the general replies.

"It was a lovely sermon, don't you think? I especially liked the part about work. It made me realize I have much left to do in this world."

Born of Max Weber's book, *The Protestant Ethic and the Spirit of Capitalism,* work is viewed as a noble value, a way for the poor and downtrodden to lift themselves up to God, and is a basic tenant of the Protestant theology.

"I agree, Herr Caracciola. It was almost as enjoyable as all these strudels," Nicolette says, as she flashes a grin to Fräu Heidelberg.

"You should try this one—apples and raisins," Rudi says, offering Nicolette a large strudel covered with confectionary sugar. She takes a bite.

"Oh my, that's delicious!"

"If you liked that, there's some Buchtel you simply must try. Might I borrow you for a moment, Fräulein Nicolette? I told Fräu Simon I'd bring her more customers! That is of course, only if the general can spare you for a moment."

Nicolette nods rapidly, her hand over her mouth as she works to lick the remnants of powdered sugar from her lips.

"Fine by me, Herr Caracciola."

Rudi and Nicolette make their way through the congregation. Everyone is laughing and talking, fueled by the sugar which had been in short supply five years ago. Today it flows like the

Danube River.

"I'll say, I didn't exactly expect to see *you* here, Caracciola," Nicolette says as they peruse tables laden with sweets.

"Well then I'll take it you didn't know that I'm an ordained pastor of the church?" he says warmly.

"I didn't! That's wonderful. How long have you been in God's care?" Nicolette replies, a bit surprised by the revelation. She had assumed Rudi was a run-of-the-mill thrill-seeker—usually not the most religious, nor even moral types of characters. It seems Rudi is more complex than she had originally thought.

"Oh, since a young boy, probably around ten. My family back in Ghent attended church every Sunday and I guess it just rubbed off on me. I found peace through worship and I pursued my religious studies—and the next thing I knew I was a pastor." They both chuckle. "It's funny, I never really thought myself to be a religious man."

Nicolette can't help but smile. "I understand the feeling. I love attending service too. It helps me see things clearer. It restores my faith in the world."

They look at each other for a moment, then Nicolette continues down the tables.

The two fall into step once again, silent for a moment until—

"I've been thinking about you, Nicolette."

Nicolette's eyes continue over the sweets, though her heart seems to be beating a bit faster than usual.

"Really? And what was it you were thinking?" She faces him.

"Well, if I'm being honest, you've been in my thoughts since we met at the dealership. I was hoping to see you at one of my races but . . ."

"Yes," she says, shaking her head, her nose slightly scrunched up. "I've been meaning to attend, but I've been a bit preoccupied."

"School?" he asks. His tone doesn't sound like he was too wounded by her absence—Nicolette is relieved.

"Partly. Studying aerodynamics isn't for the faint of heart, so it's kept me busy. Between studying and flying, my time is a precious commodity these days."

"Hmm, I see. Well, try this, and maybe it will convince you that spending time with me is worth it." Rudi hands her a small buchtel and motions for her to take a bite. As she does, the sweetness mixes with the morning air and the flavors dazzle her tastebuds.

"Oh my—" she says.

"So if I can't get you to come to a race, maybe we could try for something that is shorter—you know, given your schedule. Say something like . . . dinner?"

"Well Herr Caracciola," she says, "are you asking me out on a date?"

"Yes, Fräulein, I believe I am."

"Hmmm. Well you *do* seem to know your way around a dessert table," she says, smiling.

"Sweets for the sweetest woman in all of Berlin!"

She laughs. "Rudi, you'll have to work on your conversation skills if I'm to go to dinner with you. We can't go to dinner and talk about desserts all night!"

He feigns surprise. "You mean to tell me that flowers and sweets aren't the way to every woman's heart? Well then, I accept your challenge. We could talk about many things: aerodynamics, cars, planes, politics, your family...."

"Politics? I'm not sure that's a good idea."

"True, it *has* been too depressing for light conversation these days-- so much talk of war."

"Ah, so you're concerned over Germany's annexation of Austria?"

"Well, let's put it this way. While I believe Germany has a right to peace, so does Austria. We just need to find a solution that works for everyone."

"Hmmm, a pleasantly enlightened view! Perhaps I underestimated you, Herr Caracciola?"

"Most do," he says with a lighthearted shrug. "I may be a poor Belgian farmer but I've got plans and thoughts, Nicolette. Big ones. Things I'd love to share with you."

She is admittedly a bit stunned by the young man's forwardness.

"Well in that case, I accept your dinner invitation. Perhaps we can be friends after all."

"I was hoping to be more than friends, but I'm happy to start there."

"All right, Herr Caracciola. But this isn't a race, is it? Or did I simply miss the checkered flag?"

"Perhaps it is," he says, his steady gaze unfaltering. "If it is, it's a race I intend to win."

"Ah, I see. And this race. What is the prize, Rudi? A trophy?"

He shakes his head. "A trophy is just a piece of metal that symbolizes a victory. No, a tiny tin cup isn't what I'm after. The real prize in *this* race, Nicolette," he leans slightly closer, "is your love and respect. That's what I'm racing for."

15. I'D KILL FOR A KIT KAT

No drug is illegal in pre-war Germany. Presently, Eukodol, a chemical cousin to heroin, is becoming Deutschland's drug of choice; even Hitler has developed an affinity for it. Dr. Gilbert Morell—or 'Dr. Feel Good'—Hitler's personal physician, often prescribes it to the Fürher.

It's a night like any other at Berlin's Kit Kat Club, another night of sex and drugs.

The club is packed at 2 AM and the crowd has just finished being entertained by none other than Dominique Dresden. The crowd is still electrified by her performance.

Seeing friends in the audience, Dominique joins a table after her show. Colonel Schwartz, Colonel Bibl, Bernd, and a few others are having drinks, enjoying the atmosphere that only Berlin's nightclub scene can provide. They greet Dominique enthusiastically and congratulate her on her performance.

Schwartz beams at the performer. "You were absolutely smashing tonight, dear! How was the Croatian tour? The sun looks absolutely marvelous on your skin. Can I offer you something to drink?"

Dominque brushes away a stray strand of hair that has fallen across her forehead and says, "Thank you Herr Colonel, so nice of you to say. Yes, I'd love a Bees Knees please! Oh, plus some

Pervitin and a pack of Junos."

A Bees Knees is a gin-based cocktail, first invented by Frank Meier, an Austrian-born, part Jewish bartender who was the head bartender at the Ritz in Paris in 1921. It's Dominique's favorite cocktail these days.

Schwartz takes a slip of paper, writes out the order, and places it in a small glass tube, screwing a cap on its end. He settles the tube into a hole in the middle of the table and pushes a button. The pneumatic system whisks the order to the main bar for processing.

The pneumatic system is all the rage these days and can be found everywhere: nightclubs, telephone centers, offices and, of course, the German Wehrmact where it's used to efficiently move war planning paperwork.

Bernd lights a cigarette and sucks aggressively at the nicotine. He offers the pack of Junos to Dominique and says, "Did you have a nice time in Croatia dear? How long were you gone?"

She takes a Juno, taps it gently on the table and says, "Fabulous time! So lovely there. And the people. So interesting. I was only there two weeks but would go back in a heartbeat."

Herr Hans Braun, one of Dominique's many admirers approaches the table with a bottle of champagne. Braun owns a small but significant engineering shop in Frankfurt but is visiting Berlin for business. He is a known Jew but is tolerated for his technical expertise.

Braun greets the group enthusiastically. "Wie gehts, wie gehts Fraülien Dresden! Allo everyone! Wasn't Dominique wonderful tonight?"

The party murmurs its agreement.

Braun strikes a match for Dominique, the sudden brilliance momentarily illuminating Dominique's heavily made-up face. She bends slightly to light her cigarette and blows smoke out of the side of her mouth as she disinterestedly drawls, "*Danke* Herr Braun, nice to see you again."

Looking for acceptance which doesn't come, he demurely says, "So, I was hoping for a chance to chat with you Fräulein. I'd love to talk to you about a private show in Frankfurt. Perhaps you could spare me a few moments?"

But the performer is not paying attention. Dominque has spotted a couple in the throes of a long kiss and watches them intently. A few moments pass and she turns unhurriedly back to Braun. "As you can see, Herr Braun, I'm a bit occupied right now," she says.

Braun senses he's being dismissed. "I understand . . . and wouldn't dream of interrupting. Perhaps later then?" he asks.

"Perhaps. Guten nacht Herr Braun," she says as she waves goodbye and shoos him away simultaneously.

He bows and departs abruptly, leaving the

table to settle itself once again.

"That man, I really can't stand him," Dominique says, bored and condescending. "He's always bothering me for a private. Stinking Jew." A waiter places her Bee's Knees and pack of Junos gently in front of her and she smiles sweetly.

"Well you can't fault a man for being attracted to you, Dominique," Bernd says matter-of-factly, though a tinge of alarm can be detected in his tone. Sometimes Dominique can be too heated, even for him.

She guffaws slightly. "If it were just that. But he's a dirty Jew, he smells of garbage. The sooner they're gone, the better." She stabs out her cigarette roughly in the ashtray.

"Seems a bit *harsh*, darling," Bernd says, growing more frustrated. "The man's an admirer trying to pay his compliments. And if one is going to be an entertainer, one doesn't get to pick their fans."

"Yes, well I'm *sick* of his kind!" Dominique huffs, her voice rising with annoyance. "They all think they can do whatever they want, talk to anyone they want! They're a sick and demented lot, all of them. They have no sense of decorum or status; they wander the earth looking for a way to exploit people. They're just disease-ridden, filthy people!"

"Dominique, really? He's just a *fan*!" Bernd says loudly, partly to be heard over the noise, partly because he's angry. Since abandoning Cindy Weber at the site of the plane crash, he finds he has more of a conscience. Although he did tell about the plane crash to a nearby farmer who helped Cindy get to the hospital, he constantly feels guilty about his missteps. Tonight is another example of how his morals are changing, evolving; he can no longer accept the persecution of those who are simply born on the wrong side of a cultural ledger.

Dominique sips her Bee's Knees, still oblivious to Bernd's reproach. She lets out a sigh of exasperation which turns to relief. "The only admirers I need are at this table! Correct, colonels?" she chirps.

"I can only speak for myself," Colonel Bibl says, perking up immediately, "but to say I'm your biggest admirer would be an understatement, Fraülien!"

Dominique shakes her short hair and smiles, well-aware of the admiration she garners from so many. "The only fans I want or need! Come Colonel, shall we dance?"

"I'd be honored," Bibl says, rising from his seat and extending his hand to the performer.

Schwartz watches as they make their way to the dance floor. He glances back at Bernd. *Alone with Bernd—this night may be worth it after all,* he thinks. He fondly remembers the time they spent together in Frankfurt. Just him and Bernd. Bernd had been reluctant at first, but he was thankful for Schwartz after he cleaned up that mess with Cindy Weber. Bernd never asked Schwartz how he did it, but somehow Schwartz convinced the girl it wasn't in her best interest to remember the night of her accident.

"Well, it seems those two are hitting it off—wouldn't you say," Schwartz remarks.

"They are truly a match for each other, Marcus," Bernd says. He and Schwartz watch as Bibl swings Dominique into a playful dip. "Hmm, impressive! I had no idea Bibl could dance."

"Well, Bernd, I must say, you're quite impressive yourself," Schwartz says. "The racing, the women, the wealth, the looks. It's amazing. A true man." Schwartz speaks gingerly. He hopes, has been hoping for weeks, that the night might turn out like the one they shared in Frankfurt.

"Marcus, you're too kind. Can't have my opponents see you making me blush," he jokes. *He's always so ungodly charming, so impossible to read.* Bernd stands, grabs his coat and gives Schwartz a nod.

"Wish I could stay, but I've a big day tomorrow."

Schwartz feels his opportunity slipping through his fingers. "Oh, come Bernd, stick around a little longer...."

Bernd cocks his head to the side. He

recognizes a certain look in the colonel's eye. "What, like in Frankfurt? Perhaps another night Marcus..."

Schwartz may be one of the most influential men in Berlin, but he is powerless when it comes to Bernd. He sighs quietly, shakes his head once.

"A shame, I was . . . looking forward to spending more time with you...." He searches Bernd's face for just a moment too long.

"Marcus, what are you talking about?" Bernd asks, shifting his coat from one arm to another.

"It's just that . . . well . . . I thought there might be...." Schwartz struggles, unable to hold Bernd's gaze.

Bernd sees a deep disappointment creeping over Schwartz's face; he exhales. "I see. Marcus, look at me." Schwartz's eyes dart to Bernd's. "It's a crazy time right now. Let's be happy with what we've had, not dwell on what could be."

Schwartz, seeing that his hopes will remain unrealized, gathers himself and attempts a stoic face. "Of course. You're right, I've no idea what I was thinking."

Bernd smiles. "*Auf Wiedersehen*, my friend," he says, touching Schwartz's shoulder lightly as he takes his leave.

Bernd makes his way to Dominique and Colonel Bibl. They're buying more Pervitin, a methamphetamine, from the bartender.

"I'm leaving darling," Bernd shouts to Dominique over the music, interrupting the transaction. "Just wanted to say goodbye, always lovely to see you. Colonel Bibl, a pleasure meeting you," he says with a nod.

Dominique whips around to face Bernd. "Oh Bernd, don't leave yet," she whines. "I was hoping you, me and the colonel might have some fun tonight!" She bats her lashes, the eyes below quite bloodshot indeed.

"Sorry, love, I've got some other plans, big day tomorrow. Raincheck?"

Dominique pouts. "I hope it wasn't what I said about that nasty Jew, Braun?" she asks, looking at him with her careless eyes. "You seem upset."

"No, love, it wasn't what you said."

"Then stay with us! I promise to make it a wonderful night," she squeals.

Bernd pecks her on the cheek as he pats her bottom. "Sorry *liebling*—have fun without me."

"Fine," she says coldly, upset at the rebuke. She spins away from Bernd and grabs Colonel Bibl by the arm. "Come on Colonel, let's dance!" she   yells.

From the dance floor, she watches Bernd leave. Rage fills her tiny frame, the methamphetamines quickening the pace of her heart, already beating fast with hate.

16. FRIENDS OF FORD

In May of 1920, Henry Ford published "The International Jew: A World Problem" and shocked most of the civilized world. In 1922, its German translation catches Hitler's eye while he's imprisoned for his attempted coup.

Hitler reads it while writing Mein Kampf in 1925 and is moved. His autobiography, which details his political ideology and his antisemitic beliefs, mentions Ford by name. Ford is the only American mentioned in Mein Kampf.

Hitler writes in Mein Kampf, *"Every year makes them [American Jews] more and more the controlling masters of the producers in a nation of one hundred and twenty millions; only a single great man, Ford, to their fury still maintains full independence."*

In another letter written in 1924, Heinrich Himmler described Ford as *"one of our most valuable, important, and witty fighters."*

With this in mind, Hitler decides to write to Henry Ford to request his support.

April 20, 1936.

My dearest friend Mr. Henry Ford.

I write you to express my gratitude and support for your recent views regarding the

Jewish plague the world is experiencing.

It is my sincerest hope that together, we can help eradicate this plague for the betterment of mankind.

As you know the Ford Cologne AG company is an important participant in the German economy which provides employment and transportation to our great Nation.

Again, I congratulate you on your business success both here and in America. Your embrace of modernism is refreshing and more importantly, the means to create a more perfect world.

Unlike FDR, who would seek to cause more chaos associated with the uninhibited frenzy of market speculation, you have chosen a more noble and worthwhile approach.

While I had great hopes when the New Deal was announced, I see that he [FDR] has become beholden to those who would pursue profits and expansion at the expense of their own citizens.

I write to you to establish a friendship of mutual respect and admiration. We depend on Ford AG for many services and resources and look forward to continuing this important work in the near future.

Please write to me when convenient so that we may further our discussion and friendship on these mutual beliefs.

With respect and best regards, your friend,

Adolph Hitler

May 14th, 1937

Ford, an aging, grumpy, and ill-mannered man is in his office reading the letter. The air is filled with American cigarette smoke and the scent of well-oiled machines. He calls Edsel, his son and president of Ford into his office. He still can't quite get used to his newfangled phone system and stabs endlessly at the buttons until his son answers.

Ford barks into the phone, "Get up here, now!"

Before Edsel has a chance to close the office door, Ford asks, "Did you see this letter from Hitler?"

Edsel is tired. It's tough keeping up with the old man. He may be seventy-five years old but Ford Sr. never stops, "Yes, your office sent me a transcription a few days ago. Looks like you've made a new German friend. A friend we don't need right now." He slumps into an office chair directly facing Ford Sr.

Henry Ford is a man of action so he constantly fiddles with something—this time, it's a set of gears from one of the new transmissions his company is building.

"The man may be a bit harsh, but he makes sense. FDR can piss up a rope with his New Deal bullshit. What America needs is more workers and less unions, God dammed communists," he growls.

Lighting a cigarette, Edsel contemplates his father's statement.

"Maybe, but we've received memos from the Cologne office. Seems they've had several visits from the SS and they're worried." Edsel hopes that this new information, casually offered, will help Henry realize he's playing with fire.

"Worried about what?" Henry barks. He exhales smoke. It floats into the still, Dearborn office air and circles around Edsel's head.

"Worried that the Nazis will nationalize the factory. They're beating the war drum pretty loud right now. Their factories aren't anywhere near as sophisticated as ours."

Henry's face turns a deep shade of red as he processes Edsel's words.

"No shit, why would they be? They're assholes and couldn't find an orgy in a whorehouse. We're the only company in the world right now that can make cheap cars quickly."

Edsel knows he's got to be careful with Henry. If he says the right thing, the wrong way, shit could spin out of control. He'd like to see Henry more engaged with the US war effort and not screwing around with the Nazis. The Ford Motor Company was still licking its wounds from the last congressional oversight investigation in which they strongly recommended that Ford get with the US war effort. That's when Henry told the congressman he'd be happy to do so if the US government would pay their bills on time. Needless to say, the meeting ended with some choice words being exchanged. Henry always spoke his mind, which left a lot of cleanup work for Edsel.

"Yes, true. It also helps that we've got raw materials like rubber, steel and aluminum. Seems they're just as interested in these as they are in our factories."

Henry, being the old horse trader that he was, smelled a deal.

"Hmmm, I won't allow them to nationalize our factories, fucking fascist assholes! Maybe we can make a deal? Maybe they won't take our goddamned factories if we ship them some of the materials they're looking for?"

Screwing around with the Germans right now would bring more scrutiny upon the Ford Motor Company, which is exactly what Edsel is trying to avoid. Shit! This deal, *any* deal with Nazi Germany would be like hanging a bullseye on their back.

Edsel jumps out of his chair, accidentally knocking over the standing ash tray and sends ashes and butts flying everywhere.

"FDR and Congress would go apeshit if we did that, Dad! You can't build tanks and jeeps for the U.S. and give Hitler materials he'll use for war! You'll be looked at as nothing but a war profiteer!"

Henry narrows his eyes as he leans back in his large, black office chair. He runs his hand through his grey, thinning hair and smiles slightly.

"Bullshit, son. Just watch me."

Henry Ford didn't get to where he is by inaction. No, he got where he is by seizing opportunities quickly. That's how you win: you act fast while others are still thinking about the problem.

Ford immediately picks up the phone, fumbles with it for a few minutes and gives up, swearing at the new technology.

"Get me the goddamn Cologne office, Cindy!" he bellows to his assistant.

After ten minutes of dialing and talking to international operators, Ford finally speaks to the Cologne office and instructs them to get in contact with the SS and float the idea of an exchange: leave Ford Motors alone and we'll ship raw materials to you secretly. Ford's plan is to leak the materials out of the Cologne factory so there's no trace of any exports coming from U.S. Ford operations.

With orders given, the Ford Cologne office, headed by Michael Green, the president of Ford AG, responds by contacting the SS.

Green, sitting in his austere office, picks up the phone and calls Colonel Schwartz to negotiate the deal.

"This would be very interesting Mr. Green, but I'm unclear how you would ship these materials. Wouldn't U.S. customs take issue with these shipments?" Schwartz asks.

Speaking in his native Texas drawl, Green says, "You just leave that to us Colonel—we know how to make it happen, it'll be slick as a whistle. The manifest will show that the materials are property of Ford USA and are being transferred to our factory in Germany."

"I see. So once the materials arrive in Cologne, we can take possession?"

"Yep, just pull the trucks right on up to the factory. You got trucks, right?"

Schwartz can't help but grin a little.

"Of course."

"Well then, you wait until dark, right, then, we'll get Marty—Marty is so crooked that if he swallowed a nail, he'd spit up a corkscrew. He'll open up the gates, and you and your compadres drive up to the back door and load'er up."

"What?"

"I can explain it to you, but I can't understand it for you Colonel! Jesus son, you just wait until dark, drive in and load up! You understand?"

"Your language is ... strange Herr Green."

"Well yours is as handy as hip pockets on a hog, Colonel. It ain't much better."

"Herr Green, I fail to see the relevance in any of this!"

"Look Colonel, we'll get the materials to you as promised, you just make damn sure you have a check ready. Make it out to Ford USA. Mr. Ford ain't running no charity."

"*Ja, ja,*" Schwartz says, still trying to understand a good half of the words that have come through the receiver. "We'll make sure to have the funds ready."

"Yeah, make sure of it. In good old US greenbacks too, none of that Deutsch mark bullshit, that shit ain't worth wiping your ass with."

"I'm getting very tired of your insults Herr Green!"

Green blows smoke into the phone.

"Ain't my problem, Willy. For someone who needs this stuff, you're all hat and no cattle."

"Hat, Cattle! You imbecile! Do you not realize who you are talking to!"

"Yeah, I do, Colonel. Look, I'm not trying to cause any trouble so don't get your tail up. Just pick up the stuff and bring the check. We'll get 'er done. Okay?"

"You'd best, Herr Green. Call me when the materials arrive."

"Count on it, Willy."

The line clicks.

After six months of supply, Hitler is pleased with the resources and is enamored with his American friend. Hitler decides to award Ford with a new medal, the Grand Cross of the Supreme Order of the German Eagle, and conveys this with a letter to Ford. Henry Ford is the first American recipient of this order; it is the highest honor Nazi Germany can give to any foreigner and represents Adolf Hitler's personal admiration and indebtedness to Henry Ford. Hitler plans to present it to Ford in a pompous ceremony only the Nazis can pull off upon Ford's arrival in Germany.

While Ford may be dumb, he's not stupid. The optics of him going to Germany to accept a medal from Hitler are absolutely horrendous. Ford doesn't need any more "Congressional oversight". Edsel has made that clear.

Ford writes to Hitler and graciously explains that he'd love to visit, but simply can't get away. You know, work and all.

Undeterred, Hitler decides to send the mountain to Mohammed and deploys SS representatives to Dearborn, Michigan.

At a ceremony hastily cobbled together at the Ford headquarters, Henry is presented with the Grand Cross of the Supreme Order of the German Eagle on his seventy-fifth birthday.

Ford stands in his office awkwardly as a Nazi photographer snaps a few pictures of him with his new medal.

"Aw shucks, thanks guys. This is one nice looking medal. Reminds me of a Cracker Jack toy." Ford winks at Cindy. She rolls her eyes.

Captain Markus, a tall officer with an angular face who is leading the SS delegation, smiles and bows, pretending to understand the joke.

"*Jawohl*, with our deepest regards Herr Ford. The Führer sends his best. Heil Hitler!" His comprehension of English isn't very good.

"Fuck that shit," Ford mutters under his breath.

Ford twiddles his thumbs until the congregation has left. He closes the door and looks at the heavy medal in his hands. *It's a pretty darn nice medal* he thinks as he inspects the meticulous detail in the metal work.

"Fucking Nazis better pay their bill," he says as he tosses the medal in the trash bin by his desk.

17. THE EAGLES NEST

The Eagle's nest, or *Kehlsteinhaus,* is at the summit of the Kehlstein, a rocky outcrop that rises above the Obersalzberg near the town of Berchtesgaden. It's used exclusively by members of the Nazi Party for government and social meetings.

Today it is serving a different purpose, one tailored to cars and the autobahn.

The CEOs of Mercedes and Auto Union, along with a few staff members, have reported to this heavily guarded location at the request of none other than the Führer. There's a hint of mystery in the air; the request simply invited them to a weekend of relaxing discussions regarding the future of the German auto industry. One does not deny Hitler an audience and live to tell the tale these days.

The CEOs are flown to a small airfield near Berchtesgaden and picked up by SS officers. The drive from the airfield and up the mountain takes longer than expected. It's a steep climb to get to the Eagles Nest, and the Mercedes truck is laboring at this altitude with the additional weight of five extra men and twenty cases of wine. Wilhelm Kissel of Mercedes and August Horch of Auto Union sit in the back of the truck.

"I should have eaten before getting on the

plane." says Wilhelm, wiping away a feverish sweat with his handkerchief.

"You should have made a better truck," replies Horch, seated across from Wilhelm on the opposite bench seat.

"Screw you August, we're at four kilometers, I've already got a headache." Maybe it's the altitude or maybe it's the diesel fumes spewing from the back of truck.

August rolls his eyes and looks out the rear window. "This truck is a piece of shit, the F122 would have jumped up the mountain and we'd be eating fresh deer and truffles by now," he says with a scowl.

Wilhelm shrugs and looks out the back of the truck, the beautiful mountain scenery sliding away as they ascend.

"Who eats fucking deer?" he asks.

After a long and uncomfortable five hour drive up the mountain, the CEOs and staff are dropped at the opulent main entrance of the Nest. The men pile out of the truck, stretching in the process. The air smells like pine. Luggage is sorted and the men enter the building, contemplating the weekend.

After everyone gets settled, they gather in the large anteroom decorated with priceless art, animal heads, and carpets, all pillaged from exotic and far away locations. The CEOs and their staff are seated in overstuffed leather chairs and sofas surrounding the fireplace. A few staff members are milling about, idly chatting and waiting for the meeting to begin.

The evening is clear, dark and cold. Hitler's staff has started a fire in the gargantuan fireplace which adds an ominous, smokey glow to the dimly lit room.

Hitler, Göring and Schwartz, along with several SS staff officers, enter the room. Everyone stands. "Heil Hitler!" the group says in unison.

Göring, flanking Hitler's right side, takes command and says to the entourage, "Guten Abend, and thank you for coming. We have a lot to discuss, so without further ado we'll get into tonight's agenda.

"As you know, the German economy is dependent on the success of industry— specifically the auto industry. The Führer," he says, motioning to the nation's leader to his left, "in a moment of enlightenment, has seen the path forward for this industry and wants to share his vision for the future. In short, it is through innovation. This is why you are here tonight.

"As you know, the new autobahn will be completed in a few months. But the Führer wants not just the people's car on the autobahn—he wants the fastest cars in the world.

"Beginning tomorrow, your companies will accelerate the development of these autos. They will be the greatest cars the world has seen. We will hold a competition in 1939 between these cars to show the world that German engineering is superior. The winner will receive most, if not all, of the Reich's future military business."

August, sensing an enormous opportunity for Auto Union, immediately stands.

"An excellent idea, General! Might I ask what the speed goal is?"

Göring nods to Horch and once again addresses the congregation. "As you know, the current speed record is 312 miles per hour held by Eyston, an American at the Bonneville Salt Flats. You shall beat this."

Immediately, August realizes that he may have been a bit too eager in his support of the project.

"Ah. General—yes, I'm aware of this record. To beat it, we'd need an engine capable of generating over 700 horsepower—and we have only successfully made engines in the 400-500 horsepower range. Those which are more powerful are used for airplanes. They're too big for cars."

Wilhelm drums his fingers on the leather arm of his chair. He's already doing the calculations in his head, and he's worried. He too is perplexed by the project. Don't they realize the complexity they're asking for? What if they can't deliver? He knows that failure to deliver will result in *consequences*—even though he enjoys watching August squirm, he decides the best course is to ask more questions without directly supporting August's position.

"It's true. Mercedes only recently built a 600-horsepower engine for the Messerschmidt and it weighs over 300 kilograms. Might I ask what the goal in this exercise is?"

August, now wishing he was back at the office, sees an opportunity to humiliate Mercedes and Wilhelm—always a good way to take some of the pressure off himself and Auto Union.

"We've already been told dummkopf," August chides. "It's to show German engineering supremacy! I apologize for my colleague's slowness. His mind is as slow as his cars."

"Screw you August." Wilhelm now wishes he had let August stew in his own eagerness.

Göring ignores the squabble, continuing, "Gentlemen, please focus on the matter at hand. How long will it take to design and build a car capable of beating the speed record?"

Wilhelm stands. He's got to be careful. He can't be seen as weak or unsupportive, but he's got to recalibrate expectations. "That's impossible to calculate, General!" he hears himself saying. He regrets this immediately. He quickly begins again. "We would need several years to study the problem, to test designs and build prototypes."

August chuckles. "Typical Mercedes. I would expect we could do this in less than one year," he says, putting on his best smolder for the Reich.

The veins in Wilhelm's neck bulge as he yells across the room, "Really August? Do you have a secret engine stored in a cave that I don't know about? The power-to-weight requirements for this are unheard of! Why you'd need a power source that hasn't been designed yet. Then there's the special tooling and jigs, the suspension, aerodynamics and—"

August, now happy with his initial goading and Wilhelm's reaction, smirks and interrupts.

"Wilhelm, maybe you should step aside now and let me take this, it's clearly too big a job for you." August waits for a response, knowing that he's made Mercedes look like the fools they are.

Wilhelm is furious he let himself get put in this position, vowing never again to come to Horch's aid.

"Screw you August, we are kicking your ass all over the Grand Prix circuit you little prick and you expect me—"

"Stop!" Göring barks, and the room immediately falls silent. "I think we've heard enough from our guests. Let us adjourn and consider this over dinner and drinks. If you please . . ."

August and Wilhelm exchange a long, cold stare. This is battle, just like on the track — attack and counter attack. August may have won this lap, but Wilhelm knows this race isn't over yet— it's just beginning. Wilhelm collects himself and marches toward the dining room. August smirks and nods to his staff members as his opponent exits.

The group moves to the dining room where they are greeted by the scent of grilled meats and vegetables mingling with pine wafting in from the open windows.

Everyone sits down, Hitler at the head of the table, backlit by the glowing fire.

The Führer stands and raises his glass. "To Germany and the world speed record!"

"Prost!" The group responds in unison, drinks deeply in unison. All is silent for a moment.

Göring, ever the statesman, rises from his chair. He cradles his glass in one hand as he addresses the table.

"Gentlemen, I know the task before us is daunting, but we have faith in your abilities. Germany has already built a state-of-the-art highway system that rivals anything in the world. It took the Romans more than ten years to build the first roads which connected their empire—we did it in less than two years. This is why Germany will succeed."

Schwartz, whose rise in the SS can be directly attributed to grandstanding, senses an opportunity to impress Hitler by echoing the leader's own thoughts, mixed with a few points of his own.

"To further add to the general's comments," he

begins, "I for one believe that this is our true destiny. Never before has the world seen a more powerful race, a pure race, a race touched by divinity. We proved that in the 1936 Olympics, and *we will* become gods!" He pauses. "The world will tremble when they see our might." He smiles slightly and raises his glass.

"To Germany!" Göring booms.

The crowd murmurs in agreement and dinner is brought out.

It is a feast for kings; wines, fresh game, sausage, schnitzel, and breads are passed about and the mood slowly turns from anxious pressure over an assignment into a celebration of the future. The men continue to feast and drink until satiated, their stomachs firmly filled.

The table is cleared and brandy and cigars are offered around. The men break into small groups and chat by the fire. The cigar smoke mixes with the woody smell of the fireplace and contentment descends over the group as night falls.

The group slowly dissipates, some going to bed, some retiring to the garden for smoking and more drinking, some moving upstairs for companionship.

As the guests and staff choose their activities, Hitler stands at the top of the staircase and observes how his soldiers are choosing to spend their time. Everything is catalogued in his mind. Nothing goes unnoticed by Hitler.

18. HITLER'S DREAM

I am swimming beneath an ice-covered lake. It is as cold as the moon. The sun is shining through the ice. I can see bubbles that have formed in the ice. They are trapped.

I have no trouble breathing, even at great depths, as if I am a fish. I can swim like this for days.

I am searching for something in the ice, in the walls, in the water. Searching for life, for power, for the sun, for myself.

I see a bright light below me. It illuminates a path. A path I must follow.

I want this. I want it with all my being. I desire this thing, this thing that is bright. This thing that will give me power, this thing I need to rule the world. It is me.

19. Making plans with August

August Horch is busy. He's signed up to develop the fastest car in the world and he has singlehandedly created the largest automobile company in Germany by combining three struggling German companies with Horch Auto: DKW, Audi, and Wanderer.

The four interconnected circles logo he chooses represents the four companies, now integrated into one company: Auto Union.

Dr. Ferdinand Porsche, who is an independent automotive engineer and designer, is on the Auto Union payroll designing engines—big engines. His engineering skills are the heartbeat of Auto Union and Horch needs help if he's going to compete with a company such as Mercedes.

Porsche knows that placing the engine behind the driver helps with a car's balance. This is critical because his engines Auto Union has adopted are massive and heavy—a 4.4-liter V-16 engine that produces 500 horsepower at 4,500 revs per minute.

With the engine placed mid-ship, the car's center-of-mass is perfectly located and greatly improves handling. The engines are heavy and cramming a massive one in the front where the steering occurs creates huge amounts of understeer.

While Porsche makes significant advancements in Auto Union's designs, the chassis and suspension work is the product of a younger engineer named Fritz Müller.

Designs are progressing on the chassis, but August worries about the engines. He needs large amounts of power if Auto Union is to deliver a car capable of satisfying Hitler's demand for the world speed record. Porsche's massive engines are an adequate start, but he needs more horsepower than the current design provides; 295 horsepower is only about half of what he needs, and his attempts to integrate two of these beasts into the car have been simply unfeasible.

The weight of the two engines would make it ungodly heavy, which would both reduce top end speed and make the car as big as a ship. No, what he needs is more displacement and horsepower from the same size as the current sixteen-cylinder Porsche engine.

So he takes a cue from Mercedes. Some might say he stole it.

Although Mercedes has kept with a front engine design, their engines use a supercharger and the results are impressive. With a lower displacement than Porsche's design, Mercedes produces a whopping 354 horsepower with only eight cylinders.

Yes, supercharging is the way to go. The supercharger is a relatively new and simple innovation. It uses a set of rotors to take air in and compress it, thereby making the air denser. Denser air carries more oxygen which provides more combustion. More combustion makes higher horsepower; a simple, practical, elegant solution to a complex problem. This brings joy to August's tiny heart.

All he needs to do is take Porsche's sixteen-cylinder design, add a supercharger, and the engine should easily produce 600 horses—or so he thinks.

He just needs to manufacture these complex engines, build superchargers, test them, install all of it in an upgraded chassis capable of supporting the additional weight, work out the aerodynamics, and then build five to eight cars.

Easy, if he had three years and unlimited resources.

Oh, and he also has to do this while meeting the Reich's unheard-of demands for more war machines.

The problem is, he has only nine months, and August is feeling the pressure.

In a small office above the factory floor, Horch stands looking out a window. He sees hundreds of men working. Some are moving assemblies to their next position, some are unloading coal, iron and zinc from train cars, some are stoking the forge to keep it at the necessary 1200 degrees to cast the aluminum the factory will use to make engine blocks.

The forge, which looks like a huge, maniacal face belching smoke and dust, sits silently in the corner. A deep, angry fire can be seen inside the forge's gaping mouth. It looks like hell. An eerie glow from the fire casts shadows of long, nightmarish workers against the walls.

It reminds Horch of a Hieronymus Bosch painting he once saw: Christ in Limbo. In the painting, Jesus enters Hell to rescue the souls of the righteous before they are eaten by a fire breathing devil. If the forge isn't Hell, it's close.

Nick Müller, August's right-hand man, enters the office.

"Herr Horch, we need to discuss a few items."

Horch sits at his desk, and without looking up, says, "Let me guess. You need more time for everything."

Müller stands stiffly. "To be precise, Herr Horch, we need to focus on the immediate items. We're behind on the R543 Junker project. We've only produced twelve engines this week and the schedule calls for eighteen."

"So work an extra shift!"

"It's not just a matter of staffing," Muller replies delicately. He knows Horch's temper and how quickly it can explode. "The forge, as you know, produces zinc, magnesium and aluminum oxides which are causing the workers to become ill. We lost thirteen percent of the forge line last week."

Horch stares at Muller with a scowl on his face. "Thirteen percent capacity or thirteen percent of the workers?" he asks. His scowl does not falter.

"Um, thirteen percent of the workers are now dead. So we've lost forty percent capacity." Muller braces for the onslaught he knows is coming.

"Forty percent! That's unacceptable!" Horch bellows.

"Yes sir, but unless we vent the forge, we'll lose more," Muller replies, taking a half step away from the desk.

"You idiot! Venting will cost money *and* time!" Horch rips open a desk drawer and riffles violently through the contents. "Talk to Captain Schmidt. Tell him we need more forge workers if we're to stay on schedule," he says, angrily sucking his tobacco pipe.

Müller thinks that maybe framing the issue as a long-term solution will help Horch see it more clearly.

"Sir, I will speak to him, but if we don't vent there will be more deaths and we'll have to replace more workers. As you know, it takes time to train them. Shouldn't we try venting? It would appear ..."

"Müller, are you not hearing me?" barks Horch, "The Jews the SS sends us are scum and there are thousands of them. I couldn't care less if they die! Keep us on schedule."

"Yes sir. I must warn you, it's not going to be easy getting this many men—"

"So use women, they can be trained easier than the men. And don't stop with women, ask for teenagers, they should be strong enough at, say, thirteen to operate the jigs on the forge."

"Uh, but sir, they will be more susceptible to galvie flu than the men!" Müller knows showing compassion for Jews, immigrants or gypsies is dangerous, but Horch needs to realize that his solution is worse than the cure.

"Am I not making myself clear, Müller? We are not Henry Ford with an assembly line and healthcare. That bastard has figured out how to make cheap autos by the thousands. We do not have the same luxury and concerns as Mr. Ford. We need workers and we need them now!"

"Yes sir, I will contact Captain Schmidt immediately and make the request." Müller sees there is no hope to change Horch's mind.

"Good. And tell Schmidt we're doing him a favor by taking these Jews off his hands. It's one less thing the SS has to deal with. They would have killed them anyway. Better we get some productivity out of these scum."

He points at his employee with the mouthpiece. "I want these Jews here yesterday, Müller. Am I making myself clear?"

"Yes Herr Horch, perfectly." Muller exits the office. *Just another shitty day at Auto Union,* he thinks as he walks slowly back to his office to make the call.

20. A Different Perspective

Across town at the Mercedes factory, things are different. Wilhelm Kissel is sitting at his desk thinking about lunch.

In front of him are piles of reports detailing production schedules and goals, inbound shipments of raw materials from his new source, the Ford Motor Company, and most importantly, his teams' standings in the European Grand Prix.

Kissel is a driver at heart. Ever since he was a young boy growing up in Haßloch, all he wanted to do was race cars. Now instead, he's forty-one and running Mercedes, focusing more on war than racing. He's had a headache for the last three years.

Kissel's love of motorsports started when he was fourteen, during the first World War. He drove a beat up DKW but loved it—it was a pure escape from the death he saw around him.

He and his friends were too young to be recruited for the war, so they would spend endless nights tearing down the DKW only to rebuild it, trying to make it slightly faster for their races around the war-torn countryside.

How he missed those days—the simplicity, the joy, the friendships.

Now, his world is filled with Nazi war planning.

At first, he agreed with Hitler. A case could be made that Germany was unfairly suffering due to the negotiated treaties that sprang from her defeat in the previous war. He saw firsthand the devastation that surrender had brought about. It had permeated the fabric of Germany; shortages, unemployment and civil unrest were everywhere. A corrupt and inept government only made matters worse.

When Hitler entered the political stage, his speeches brought hope to many in the country. A hope that the German people could regain their pride and become integrated with the rest of the world, but with more fairness this time. Yes, as a country they needed to atone for their past sins, but the severity and disdain shown to Germany over the past two decades was devastating and humiliating.

Kissel is snapped back to reality by a quick knock on his office door. His vice president, Hans Fischer, pokes his head through the doorframe.

"Guten morgen, Herr Kissel. Do you have time to discuss today's item?" Fischer asks politely.

"Herr Fischer, of course, come in!" Wilhelm says, waving Fischer to take a seat. "Always have time for you, my friend." He straightens a stack of papers on his desk.

"Just a quick note on the status of new venting we've installed," Fischer begins. "The supplier finished the last bit of work a week ago and we've performed all of the tests. Ventilation has increased forty-eight percent on the factory floor and we've been unable to detect any toxic fumes. I believe we're ready to re-start the forge and of course, production." He's relieved the retrofit has gone smoothly and that Mercedes has chosen to make the workplace safer.

"That's excellent news," says Wilhelm. "I've been worried since the last report. Without workers our factory can't produce, and if we can't produce, the SS will pay us a visit, which I prefer to avoid." He winks to acknowledge Fischer's work.

Fischer nods. "Very good," he says. "We will re-start the forge which should only take a day. We'll be ready to resume forge operations the day after."

"And the new block design? Has it been reviewed and deemed ready for casting?"

"Yes sir, the V12 plans are ready, and the mold too."

"So assuming the casting goes as planned, we should have the first V12 block by Friday?" Wilhelm is immensely excited by the prospect of putting this absolute beast of an engine in the new Rekordwagon.

"Correct, Herr Kissel," replies Fischer. "At that point it will move to engineering for the build out, and then to testing. It should be ready by mid-March, which puts us slightly ahead of schedule. But keep in mind that anything can happen during build out and testing, so our cushion can easily evaporate."

Wilhelm has spent more than twenty years building cars. He knows all too well that things can and will go wrong during testing.

"Well, if the unforeseen happens, can we steal testing time from the Messerschmidt team?"

"We could, but it would mean that the Messerschmidt schedule would slip," Fischer replies as he thumbs through a report. "The Luftwaffe has already called many times. It seems we're the critical link in the development of their new airplane. Missing a schedule with them will have repercussions."

"Anything associated with the Wehrmacht has repercussions," Kissel says. "I'm damned if I miss their schedule and damned if I miss Hitler's demand for the world speed record." The scream of the lunch whistle sends workers scurrying to the cafeteria. There may be an impending war, but workers are still well fed and appreciate the little perks of working for Mercedes. "I miss the old days, Hans."

"Wilhelm, I wish I could help. But the die has been cast. I will do my best to juggle both of these projects, but we can only do so much."

Kissel nods, his eyes closed. "Just do your best Hans, I'll try to buy us more time with the SS in case things take an unexpected turn for the worse."

The business at hand addressed, Fischer turns the subject of their conversation. "By the way, congratulations on last week's victory at the Nürburgring. It was a great race—and not just because Mercedes won. I like that boy Rudi."

Kissel beams. "Thanks Hans, it was a good race. Rudi's been with us for nine months now and has become quite a driver." His smile falters. "He's also grown into a full Nazi, which makes the Führer very happy and me a little sad. Actually, I'm more than a little sad. Germany seems to be a raging cesspool of hate and antisemitism these days. And I've heard rumors about Rudi's attitude towards Jews," Kissel says as his voice loses pace and tone like a misfiring engine. "We're so different than the Germany I know and love."

"Yes, well, his new girlfriend is very interesting don't you think? I understand she's quite the pilot. If we get ourselves into a pickle, maybe she can talk to the Luftwaffe for us," Fischer replies with a small smile.

"Not a bad idea Hans," Kissel grins, but his eyes squint with apprehensiveness, "but I think the Fräulein has a soft spot for the SS considering her father is General von Dries."

Fischer shakes his head. "That's not the rumor I've heard. I understand her to be good friends with Hendrick Wagner. You remember Hendrick?"

"The Polish officer?"

"Yes, the same. I believe you served with him in the eighteenth division?"

"Yes I did. He was a good leader and knew his way around airplanes. He's an excellent man," Kissel says in a tone of awe. "But I did hear he's not the best Nazi these days given the Polish invasion. Seems he might be harboring some ill will." Kissel lowers his voice slightly. "I've also heard he's still connected to, shall we say, his old friends in Poland?"

Fischer takes a moment to think about this. Softly, he begins, "Friendships are strong between Poles and they have long memories. It wouldn't surprise me to find he's working for the resistance."

"Then that *would* be odd, a general's daughter associating with a known sympathizer? Maybe you're right Hans, a friendship with the Fräulein couldn't hurt ..." Wilhelm trails off, the gears in his head working to calculate whether Hendrick and von Dries' daughter are working together. "We may need some new friends if we miss the Luftwaffe's deadline."

"I'll try to make some discrete inquiries."

Wilhelm shakes his head in admiration of his vice president. "I'm not sure what I'd do without you, Hans."

"Probably get in a lot of trouble," Fischer replies, laughing heartily.

21. FRANCE IS CALLING

France's reputation as the cradle of motorsports is well deserved. Le Mans, Circuit du Sud-Ouest, and of course Paris–Rouen—the first motoring contest ever recorded— were just a few races that cemented its place in automotive history. So when the French Grand Prix returned to the Reims-Gueux circuit in 1938, the country was electrified with anticipation.

The Reims-Gueux circuit had its straights widened and facilities updated for the race, making it a perfect place for spectators, which is convenient given the crowd size. After the Nuremberg law stripped German Jews of their German citizenship in 1938, some 900,000 German Jews fled to France. It is no wonder then that the stands are filled with over 20,000 German Jews.

The sky over the track is mottled with white puffy clouds traveling low and slow over the French countryside.

As the sun struggles to burn off the morning haze, it glistens off the aluminum skin of the Mercedes Silver Arrows, poised for another win. They sit silently in the chilly morning air, waiting to be unleashed.

The sounds of hammers and engines revving create an orchestra of noise that makes it difficult, but not impossible, for Rudi and Wilhelm to talk.

"What?" Wilhelm yells.

"I *said* this place stinks of Jews!" Rudi says.

Wilhelm ignores Rudi's comments. "Let's concentrate on the race strategy," he yells. "It's going to be a tough race. You and Manfred need to work together."

Rudi spits at the ground; he's getting over a small head cold. "Don't worry about me, just keep Manfred where he needs to be—behind me defending our position."

Wilhelm knows about prima donna drivers. He's worked with them all his life. They're always overconfident before a race, a coping mechanism they use to psych themselves up. But he's not so sure about Rudi. Caracciola has become increasingly difficult and shows an utter lack of team respect.

"There will be no team orders," Wilhelm says flatly. "It's every man for himself out there."

Rudi looks up from the glistening spot of spit he's deposited on the oily tarmac and shakes his head. "And what would Göring have to say about that?"

"I run this team Rudi, not Göring."

Rudi spits again. "Well, then run it properly and keep Manfred in his place," he says as he grabs his helmet and well-worn gloves from the pit bench.

"Just focus. Auto Union has their Type D here and we know it's fast in the corners," Kissel says, gazing up at Rudi from his seat on the bench. "And watch out for Bernd."

"I'll worry about Bernd," Rudi barks as he slips on his gloves. "You worry about getting me the best car. And do something about the Jews, they're practically standing in the middle of turn four!"

"I'll speak to the track officials, but it's a sellout. More people than expected." Wilhelm's face is scrunched up in a grimace against the hazy light of the sky.

Rudi does not look up as he adjusts the fit of his glove. "Well it won't be my fault if someone spins and they get killed." As the words slip from his lips, Rudi recalls his encounter with Mr. Goldsmith, the Jew who bullied his father and split his lip. Rudi's tense over the race and his flashback to Mr. Goldman only compounds his hatred of Jews.

Wilhelm sighs. "Just keep the car on the track, Rudi."

"Don't I always?"

The race is long.

Two hours in, Rudi is trailing behind Manfred but sits ahead of the two Auto Unions led by Bernd. The Auto Unions are nipping at him but he's keeping them in check.

Every time he goes through turn four he sees the 'ghetto stands'—full of Jews cheering the Auto Unions. God how he hates them.

With only four laps left, René Carrière, a French driver, spins in turn four. His Talbot Darracq clips a gutter and launches over the barrier, straight into the Ghetto stands.

In the middle of the crowd is a family of four who just arrived in France after escaping from Germany. Two small children are standing with their parents, watching the Talbot silently approach, its driver already separated from the car, flying through the air as if he was a trapeze artist.

The Talbot lands and bursts into flames, immediately killing the family. Several other spectators are caught up in the flames. The crowd runs from the flying debris and more spectators are hurt from the rush of the mob.

They thought they had escaped from the horrors of Germany. They were wrong. Somehow German engineering is still finding a way to kill them.

Rudi passes the scene and sees the carnage. Unaffected, he continues the pursuit of Manfred.

The flag drops and Manfred takes the win. Rudi passes a few seconds later, taking second.

After the trophy presentation, Rudi, Manfred and the rest of the team return to the pits to pack up the gear. Rudi is sullen and bitter. He should have won this race! Manfred must have had a faster car. He makes a note to talk to Wilhelm—this *cannot* happen again.

"Congrats old boy," Manfred says to Rudi as he unzips his race suit, "looks like you just didn't have it today!"

Rudi throws his gloves at the pit bench with force, as he shouts, "Screw you Manfred, I know what you did!"

Manfred knows Rudi all too well. He's been expecting a tantrum and Rudi's delivering—so he decides to egg him on. Manfred knows driving is ninety percent mental and ten percent physical, so he relishes the opportunity to get under Rudi's skin.

"Drive better?" he asks, smiling.

Manfred can see Rudi's face turning bright red through the grease marks covering his face.

"No, you had the faster car!" Rudi shouts, pointing to Manfred's Silver Arrow.

Manfred laughs loudly. "Well you're right, I did have the faster car. Because I *drove* it faster than you!"

"Screw you!" Rudi screams, spittle flying. "You were lucky today, that's all, Manfred!"

"Well, look at the bright side: you got second place. A nice one-two finish for Mercedes," Manfred says. He has quickly become bored with Rudi's diatribe—he's too tired for these theatrics.

"No." Rudi grabs his jacket and points to the stands. "The bright side is that there are a few less Jews in the world." He storms away.

22. A Picnic & Proposal

In the Champagne region, close to the track, lies Reims, a beautiful French city built by the Romans. The city is easy on the eyes, its gothic architecture breathtaking.

The Musée Saint-Remi, formerly the Abbey of Saint-Remi, has a quaint park off the eastern vestibule. Autumn sunlight streams through the trees where Nicolette and Rudi are sharing a picnic lunch of bread, cheese and wine, the abbey's columns soaring above them.

Rudi pours a glass of wine for Nicolette, shaking his head. The Sancerre perfectly captures all the flavors of the sun and flowers of the Loire Valley; slightly sweet and dry with a hint of lemon.

"I can't *believe* Manfred," Rudi says. "I should have won that race."

Nicolette sips from her glass. The fruitfulness of the wine suits the dappled sunlight perfectly.

"Well, as you like to say, the better man won."

"What? Manfred is not a better driver than me!"

Nicolette senses she may have been a bit too direct with her response. She tries to recover. "Well, Rudi, he was yesterday."

Rudi shakes his head vigorously. "He was lucky. The Jews distracted me. They were practically standing on the track!"

Nicolette is annoyed. She knows Rudi will fight like hell to run from reason, and she doesn't want to spoil this beautiful day. She sips again from her glass.

"You'll get over it, Rudi," she says gently. "There's always another race."

"Yes ... well, I *will* win at Monza."

"Of course you will."

Rudi is tense, but his anxiety is diminishing with the help of the wine. His mind shifts to the real matter at hand. He feels a fresh kaleidoscope of butterflies flutter in his stomach. "Do you like the park?" he asks.

"Gorgeous," Nicolette replies, smiling placidly. "The abbey is divine."

He's nervous. It's not every day you propose to a woman, but it's not anything he can't handle; after all, he's faced more danger in his life than most men. How could a marriage proposal be more frightening than risking your life in a Grand Prix race?

He licks his dry lips.

"Yes, it's beautiful," he says as he puts his hand over hers on the picnic blanket. "It would make a wonderful place for a wedding, don't you think?"

Nicolette smiles at Rudi quizzically. "Rudi, this park is beautiful, but you already knew I thought that didn't you? You sir, know how to impress a lady."

She's a bit taken aback; he may be an ordained minister, but Rudi's never preached to her about matrimony before.

She looks at the towering abbey windows and thinks about a wedding, her wedding. She can't deny her feelings for Rudi have grown over the last few months— something that she wasn't expecting. She's fallen in love with him. She thinks about Rudi often; his smile and ease bring her joy and a sense of stability in this crazy world.

Sometimes she catches herself smiling for no reason when she's with him, and then she realizes that it is Rudi's passion and drive that she admires, qualities that she herself pursues and possesses. She sees a mirror in Rudi, a mirror that reflects some of her own beliefs.

Images of her own wedding swirling in her head, she murmurs, "Hmm, I suppose. Seems rather large. . . I always thought I'd have a small wedding."

Rudi resumes breathing, relieved. The mention of a wedding didn't fall flat with Nicolette. "Small?" A beaming smile has stretched across his face. "But why? You're a general's daughter. You'll have many to invite."

The excitement has now arced to Nicolette, it has jumped like electricity between two poles in a Tesla coil. She senses that Rudi is on the verge of asking a very important question. Could this really be happening, right here, right now?

"Perhaps," she says, smiling. "I hadn't thought that far ahead."

"Well. . . perhaps it's time to think about it?"

"Think about what?"

Rudi pauses for a moment; he is emboldened with confidence and wine. He looks into her eyes.

"Nicolette, I know we've only been together a short time, but I know I love you . . . you must know that by now? I think it's time we make plans for the future."

Nicolette now sees why Rudi planned such a marvelous picnic; but she's going to have some fun and play it out as long as she can.

"Oh really? Love me, do you? And what might those plans be, Herr Caracciola?" she coos as she looks deeply into his eyes.

A slight breeze carries the scent of freshly cut grass through the air as Rudi, one knee on the slightly damp lawn, pulls a box from his pocket.

"I want us to marry, Nicolette."

"Oh my dear!"

Everything is perfect. The sun caresses the

couple; Nicolette looks radiant in front of the abbey. This is the moment, the moment Rudi has practiced in his head a thousand times.

"Ever since I first met you, I've been in love. You're the most amazing woman I've ever met, Nicolette. You are, without any doubt, what my heart desires. You are what I need.

"I need you in my life Nicolette, and I promise to be the man you need. I promise to be everything you want, now and in the future, if you'll take my hand in marriage."

Nicolette's heart races and her face feels like it's on fire; she's dizzy, the ground feels like its falling away from her.

As she looks at Rudi, she tries to take everything in, to capture the moment. Time stops for Nicolette. This must have been just like when her father proposed to her mother. Her mother, God how she misses her. She wishes she was still alive, to see this, to be able to share this with her mother.

"Oh Rudi. This is amazing!" she whispers. "I don't know what to say."

"Say yes!"

Nicolette shakes off the fog of bliss and tries to focus on what Rudi has just asked. "Have you spoken to my father already?'

"Of course—and he has given me his blessing."

"Oh Rudi, it's so *sudden*!" she says breathlessly.

"Say yes my love, please!"

Her head clear, her heart full, she touches Rudi's cheek. "Well then . . . yes! I will marry you!"

They stand in the lawn hugging and kissing as the clouds pass over them and the French countryside.

23. BERND'S SECRET

Bernd's childhood friend, Michael Wardenberg, was in real estate in 1930. He speculated heavily in commercial buildings—everything from little shops to large apartments. His career flourished, and he owned more than thirteen properties in the Berlin area. Life was very good, until it wasn't.

In 1933, he went bankrupt; ironic since Jews are supposed to be brilliant businessmen. When the sanctions hit, he was overextended and faced financial ruin. No longer able to make payments, he jumped from the window of his eight-story building he had bought in 1931, leaving behind his wife and two children.

Margi, Michael's wife, picked up a job in a factory, but, as a Jew, she doesn't make much and she is faced with living on the streets with her kids. She is trying to save enough to get out of Germany—which can't happen soon enough. She can see the changes taking place and it troubles her; she fears for her children.

Her cousin in Bratislava will put them up on their farm if they can just get out; but getting out of Germany is almost impossible. Every time she tries to leave, the Nazis refuse her request for travel papers to Slovakia, claiming there are too many security risks in the area. She is trapped and she feels the noose tightening.

When Bernd finds out about her predicament, he secretly rents her a small apartment in Berlin. Located in Berlin's Scheunenviertel or the "Barn Quarter", it is modest but has plenty of room for her and the kids. He gives her a monthly stipend so they have more than enough food and the children can go to school.

Bernd goes through the motions of being an SS officer—he knows the SS is watching him closely. They suspect him of sympathizing; his comments at parties are often relayed back to Hitler and the SS, who have eyes and ears everywhere.

The Jew Star is becoming more common now. In a 1938 meeting, Colonels Göring and Goebbels decided to implement a new system that would help stigmatize and identify the Jewish people. They decreed that all Jews over the age of ten were to be marked with a "Jewish star": a white band affixed with a blue star of David, worn on the upper right arm. Those who don't comply face heavy penalties.

Bernd has seen the spread of this mania firsthand. Every race now has a section for Jews—at the most dangerous areas on the track. Most of the drivers are complicit with this. Bernd has heard quips from Rudi and the other drivers, "If you crash, just aim for the Jews."

With the Jews in the Rhineland now easily identified, it's just a matter of time before Margi and her children will be forced to move from their apartment to the Jewish Ghetto. Margi tries to keep a low profile. She knows that from the Judenhäuser, it's just a matter of time before they are sent to a camp. Margi quits her job so she will be less visible to the SS, knowing and dreading that she is becoming even more dependent on Bernd.

Bernd knows there would be hell to pay if Germany's Formula One hero—not to mention an SS officer—was found sympathizing with a Jew, but he doesn't care; his predicament comes secondary to Margi and her family.

Margi loves and appreciates Bernd, both as a dear friend and for what he is risking for the benefit of her and the kids, but she is a proud woman. It kills her to have to live like this. The suicide, the harassment and the mounting threats are taking a toll on her and the children. All she can do is wait for a chance to escape, but time is running thin.

Bernd can only visit with them about once a month, when his busy schedule allows. Today, like all days, he takes heavy precaution, sneaking up the alley to enter the apartment. He knocks lightly on the door in the predetermined, coded pattern.

Margi catches the noise from the kitchen and rushes to the door. She opens the door and he silently steps inside, shutting the door after him.

"Hello, Margi. How are the kids?" he asks as

she gives him a warm, grateful hug and a kiss on the cheek.

"They're good Bernd, good given what's going on."

The two walk farther into the apartment, Bernd removing his coat and hanging it on the rack in the living room.

"Have they been keeping up with school?" he asks.

Margi chuckles, rolls her eyes with a loving smile.

"Yes, yes, we have our nightly fights about homework but they know they can't win a fight with me!"

Bernd takes a seat at the small dining table.

"Indeed!" he says, assuming a deep, booming voice. "You are the most fearsome schoolmaster I've ever known!"

Margi mockingly wags her finger at Bernd and says in a severe, stuffy voice, "Zee shall do the assignments or face my wrath!" as she takes a seat across from the driver. They both laugh. The mood lifts.

Bernd sighs, looking at Margi with admiration, with awe.

"I don't know how you do it Margi. Really, you're amazing."

Margi smiles, shaking her head slightly.

"What choice do we have? All we have are each other now, and we look after each other. Not so hard to understand." Margi sees concern in Bernd's eyes.

"I'm just surprised that you can keep it all together, really. I doubt I could do the same if I were in your shoes."

Margi feels a pang of pain and fear in her chest, but pushes it away as best she can.

"That's quite the compliment coming from the famous Rosemeyer, the bravest man in all of Germany!" she says with a smile.

"Brave? *You* are the brave one, Margi. You and the children." He glances toward their bedroom. "I'm working on the papers. Maybe next week according to the Exit Office?"

The subject of the Exit office causes Margi's blood pressure to rise.

"*Bah*, I hate those swine! Last week I was so close to getting the exit papers but that pig Meyer refused it, all because I didn't have the stamp from immigration!"

"I know, I know," Bernd says, shaking his head in agreement. "I spoke to immigration, who said they can't give you the stamp until the Exit Office approves the request. Some days I want to shoot the lot."

"Welcome to the club."

The children run into the kitchen shouting about who is to set the table for dinner. They exclaim happily when they see Bernd and immediately cling to his arms. After they get their sought-after hellos, the two children follow their mother around the kitchen as she gathers utensils and settings. They are as close knit as a family can be. The respect and love they show each other touches Bernd's heart. He thinks of his own family— loveless, entitled, wealthy, and indifferent. The differences are as wide as the Rhein River is long.

After dinner, Margi pours two shots of schnapps into tiny glasses.

"I'm worried, Bernd," she says. "You are taking so many risks by helping us."

Bernd, looking at his glass, picks it up and drinks.

"Margi, don't worry about me, everything is under control. I've still got a few friends who are willing to help. It seems there are others like us who don't like the way things are going."

"I know Bernd, but your kindness has consequences—consequences that will cause problems for you. I can't risk that, I just can't deal with another . . . " Her throat catches. She takes a sip of her schnapps.

"It's okay Margi," Bernd says softly. "We'll get through this. Just another week and you and the kids will finally be out."

"And what then?" she asks, her eyes darting between Bernd's, searching for answers. "Even if we can get out, what about you? You know they'll find out and they'll come for you!"

Bernd laughs a little.

"Me? The famous Rosemeyer?" he jests gently. "I'm Germany's fastest man alive! An SS officer! The bravest man in Germany, according to the adoring public!"

Margi looks at him, takes the rest of her shot, and twitches her mouth into a tiny smile. As she places her glass on the table, she looks down—then into Bernd's eyes. He tries to look back at her, to hold her gaze steady, but eventually he looks down to avoid her eyes.

"I'll be fine Margi," he says, doing his best to sound dismissive. Deep down, Bernd knows that he won't, and he's okay with that.

By the time Bernd leaves the apartment, it's dark out. The streets are empty; people are avoiding the piercing rain that's coming down. Restaurants and cafes are crammed with people taking shelter.

A woman across the street watches Bernd leave from the steamed-up front window of a small cafe. She writes something in a small notebook. If she was in a different part of town,

138

people would recognize Dominque Dresden. But on this side of the Spree, she's just another made-up face.

24. RUDI MAKES A TURN

Things are going Rudi's way.

He's won almost every race lately and people are noticing him. Recently drafted into the SS, he's being provided with access to powerful people and more money than he's ever had.

His relationship with Nicolette is blossoming. They've found a certain rhythm; she attends the races, celebrates with him and they spend evenings and weekends together talking about cars and airplanes and fervently discussing the war. They are in love.

As is often the case, people who become wealthy and powerful get lost and look for direction from others. Rudi's new friends are leaders in the Nazi party, and they're guiding Rudi toward darkness and hate.

At first he struggled to find resonance within the fanaticism, but he now sees that Jews are scum and that Hitler's solution is the only way forward.

Rudi is a new man, not a better man. This becomes evident on an October day when he coincidentally crosses paths with his old friend Gunther as Rudi and Nicolette walk through the Königsplatz.

They greet each other by the fountain, then take a step back to avoid the spray being picked up by a mild northern breeze; the water droplets create a small rainbow over the group as they speak.

"You old dog! How are you Gunther!" Rudi booms.

"I'm well, so great to see you! Congratulations on the win!" says Gunther.

"Thank you! It was an easy race, honestly," Rudi replies.

"And who is this?" Gunther asks as he nods politely to the beautiful woman on Rudi's arm. Her style of dress is subdued, but the quality of her garments speaks volumes.

"Ah, please meet Fräulein von Dries," Rudi says. He thinks Gunther, of all people, should remember her—he saw her in the Mercedes showroom no more than six months ago.

"A pleasure, Fräulein!" Gunther bows and shakes her hand gently.

"Nice to meet you Herr Gunther," Nicolette says enthusiastically. "I've heard many stories of you and Rudi terrorizing the countryside."

Gunther gives a jolly laugh.

"The pleasure is all mine! So Rudi, last I saw you, you were selling cars, and now look at you!"

"Yes, that was a long time ago. After winning so much, Mercedes noticed my excellent driving and, well, the rest is history, as they say," Rudi says cockily.

Gunther is a bit taken aback by Rudi's ego. "Ah I see, lucky for you!"

"No, no luck Gunther, pure skill. Right, Nicolette?"

Nicolette feels uncomfortable with Rudi's crowing. "I think luck had some part, Rudi," she says in monotone.

Rudi, now on a roll, continues.

"Ahhh, but that's nonsense, every time I go on the track I'm ready to win. Why? Because I've spent years preparing and training. I'm simply the better driver. If others did what I did, they'd have a chance, but they just don't want it as bad as I do. Don't you agree, Gunther?"

Gunther, looking to salvage the encounter, tries to help Rudi explain his luck.

"Well you did train a lot back in Ghent!"

"Exactly, Gunther. If you had trained like me back then, instead of wasting your time as a mechanic, maybe you'd be racing against me, eh?"

Nicolette's mouth has fallen slightly agape in shock at Rudi's careless words. "Rudi, that is *enough*! I'm sure Gunther loves what he does!"

Gunther eagerly accepts the cover Nicolette provides.

"You're right Fräulein, I like being a mechanic. I like fixing things. I'm still at Prost's dealership. Still love it." For a moment, Gunther feels ashamed of his lack of shiny accomplishments, but just as quickly he realizes that it's not him who should feel shame, but Rudi. His old friend is a prick.

"How quaint. And what about the girl, did you ever marry?" Rudi says, looking over Gunther's shoulder toward something shiny in the distance.

"Last October," Gunther says dryly. "Pity you couldn't make the wedding."

"Yes, that was a most unfortunate conflict. I had to attend the SS's opening of the Opera House. Big ceremony . . ." The faraway look disappears. "And they needed the Famous Caracciola there. So much going on now . . . there just wasn't any time."

"Congratulations on your wedding Herr Gunther!" Nicolette says. Gunther sees pity in her eyes, pity not because Gunther is any lesser than Rudi, but because he is being made to endure such an awkward conversation.

"Yes, Gunther married the only woman in Ghent that would take him, right Gunther!" Rudi jokes.

Gunther wrings his hands behind his back sheepishly. "Um . . . well we're very happy. We're expecting a child in about five months."

Nicolette flashes Rudi a look and congratulates Gunther on the upcoming birth.

"Yes, marvelous, we need more mechanics!" says Rudi. "Maybe your son can work on my car someday."

"Rudi," says Nicolette, the anger becoming palpable in her stern speech, "you should send a gift."

"Yes, yes, I'll have Mercedes take care of it, my love."

Gunther tries to turn the conversation around. He can't believe his old friend has turned into such a conceited jerk; he hopes that Rudi is just having an off day.

"So where's the next race Rudi?" he asks politely. "The wife and I would love to come cheer you on sometime, but tickets are expensive."

"Monza is next month."

Gunther knows the track well, it's a beast of legend—one of the biggest races of the season.

"Such a great track! Any chance you have a spare ticket?"

Rudi thinks for a second about Gunther, a poor mechanic from Ghent in the VIP standing next to the others.

"Um, sorry no," he blurts. "Mercedes only provides a few VIP tickets each race and I'm afraid they're all taken."

"Oh, I see," says Gunther, visibly disappointed

but barely surprised by Rudi's flimsy answer. "No worries."

Nicolette can hardly bear any more of this ridiculous encounter.

"You could take mine, Herr Gunther!" Rudi immediately grows angry.

"No! that's not allowed, Nicolette. The tickets are for VIPs and Gunther would need a general ticket." Rudi can't believe that Nicolette has offered him her ticket, doesn't she understand the social order? She's a general's daughter for Christ's sake!

Nicolette resorts to sweet talk.

"Oh surely the great Caracciola can make an exception," she coos, hugging his arm.

"No, I'm sorry," he says. Everyone knows he isn't. "Maybe some other time."

Gunther senses the battle is lost.

"It's okay Rudi, I understand. And thank you for the offer, Fräulein von Dries." Gunther bows his head slightly to her, and her eyes give a silent apology.

"Yes, well, we've got to be going now Gunther. Another meeting awaits." Rudi shakes the mechanic's hand, all force, no feeling. "A pleasure to see you again, and say hello to Marie for me."

"Louise. *Louise* will be pleased to hear you're

145

well," Gunther says. Nicolette closes her eyes.

"Oh, right. Well, give our best to Louise."

As they separate, Nicolette can't believe how badly Rudi treated his old friend. As they stroll down the Königsplatz on their way to dinner, Nicolette stares into the distance and thinks about Rudi. He's changed. His ego has become a huge weight in the relationship, and she can feel the heaviness of it. It's a tightly wound ball of narcissism and selfishness. Their encounter with his old friend Gunther was an embarrassment and his constant berating of the Jews is repulsive. Nicolette wonders if Rudi really is the man she can marry.

25. Saving Rudi

It's the tenth race of the season and Bernd and Rudi are fighting it out for the championship. It's a beautiful November morning with clear skies and a brisk temperature, a temperature that favors the big, hot engines of Mercedes.

This race is important; only eight points separate the two and a victory for either will place one of them in the lead. Sporting the highest banked turns on any circuit, Monza, a 7.2-kilometer beast, is built for speed—for all fifty laps.

Initially built in 1922, it has undergone many changes over the years. It consists of two different courses, often combined into what drivers call the "Monza Monster."

It's especially challenging in that two, long, high speed straights are connected with two highly banked turns. The thirty-five-degree banked turns stretch twenty meters toward the sky. There are no guardrails on the turn; if you carry too much speed into a corner, the track will throw you off into the huge pine trees below.

This section is then connected to a parabolic and an oval, forming one of the highest speed circuits—and also one of the most dangerous.

In the 1933 Italian Grand Prix, teammates Giuseppe Campari and Baconin Borzacchini met their ends on the track. In the same race a Polish driver named Sanislaw Czaykowski also perished at the hands of the Monza Monster's banked turns.

Given the danger, Monza is one of the most popular circuits for fans and drivers. The fans love to see the drivers try to tame the beast— sometimes successfully, sometimes not. The drivers crow loudly about defeating the monster; in reality they pray they survive and thank God when they do. Monza has the habit of turning atheists into religious men.

The weekend has been productive for Rudi and Bernd. Practice and qualifying have gone well and Rudi has the pole position, with Bernd starting in third.

Rudi's teammate Hermman Lang is in P2 and Bernd's teammate, Hermman Paul Müller is P5. It will be a battle royale between the Mercedes and Auto Union teams once again. The wild card is Richard Seaman, a Brit who secures P4 in a private entry Mercedes W125.

Rudi and Lang are also driving Mercedes W125s while Bernd and Müller have the new Auto Union D model. Both cars are incredibly powerful, but their handlings are no match for the lighter, though less powerful Alfa Romeos and Maseratis which round out the field.

Rudi and Bernd idle in the pits outside the Mercedes garage before the race.

"Herr Rosemeyer!" Rudi shouts over the preparatory din. "Good to see you again. Quite a race in Monaco; I missed you at the party."

"Ah, I was only there for a bit, my friend," Rosemeyer replies. "I met some new friends by the pool that evening and left a bit early. My friend Dominique was performing at the Opium Club and my other friends were eager to see her show."

"Ah, well at least you showed up today. I was concerned we were going to have to race without the famous Rosemeyer—it would make my victory hollow!" says Rudi, laughing at his own joke.

"I see you're feeling very confident, Caracciola, considering what happened here in the last race."

"They were good drivers but amateurs. We will have no problems today," Rudi says in his now ever-present boasting voice. Bernd is unamused by Rudi's lack of respect for those brave drivers whose lives were lost.

"Yes, well, I hope you're right, Rudi. I have some plans for tonight and I'd hate to miss them. How's the new car?"

"The D is better," replies Rudi. "More horsepower and nimbler. The new independent strut suspension Auto Union has developed is promising."

Bernd contemplates this information; it could be useful in the race, he thinks.

"This track is all about horsepower, my friend," Bernd says.

"But the banks require suspension or all the horsepower won't mean anything," Rudi says in a matter-of-fact tone. His desire to show off has him thoughtlessly revealing information that a competitor could exploit. "I'm actually more worried about the new Ferrari. Have you seen it? Enzo outdid himself. It's just a matter of time before Ferrari makes an Alpha meaningless."

"Yes, agreed," Bernd says, tucking away even more information about the competition in his mind. He makes a mental note to always chat with Rudi before a race; his talkativeness is a gold mine. "I like the shape of it as well—reminds me of Monique from Rome, has the same figure."

"Monique you say?" Rudi says with a sly smile to Bernd. "Seems you have a girl in every town." Rudi's voice bears a faint note of jealousy.

"Should I not?" Bernd asks rhetorically as he raises his hands to the abundance of the world. "I'm living the life, my friend. I just need to win today and the championship will be all but mine!" he says, hoping to plant a seed of doubt in Rudi's head.

Rudi is oblivious to Bernd's challenge.

"Funny, Bernd; I was thinking the same thing."

Rosemeyer and Caracciola hold each other's gaze for a moment; both feel today's competitive flame begin to stoke within them.

"Well, good luck today and give my regards to Nicolette—I assume she's here?"

"In the stands as we speak," Rudi replies. "Good luck!" he says. They separate and make their ways back to their respective pits.

The crowd is enormous at Monza. Not only is the circuit a legendary attraction with its banked turns, but the fans have come to see their three favorite automobile icons—Alfa Romeo, Maserati and the new Ferrari—duke it out against the German-made Mercedes and Auto Union.

For the spectators, it's about national pride. Anything wearing an Italian badge crossing the finish line in first place will be a win over Germany, their neighborly Fascists to the North. There's no love lost between Mussolini and Hitler these days, and there's no lack of competition either.

The race marshal ascends to his perch; it provides a perfect view of the long straightaway so he can easily see who crosses the finish line. The new tarmac is as black as night; it smells of petrol and fear. Shining heat leaks from the racetrack in evil waves, distorting the cars and fans.

He cautiously pulls the checkered flag from the quiver holding the remaining flags—blue for passing, red for race stop, black for disqualifying cars, yellow for caution and white for last lap. His eyes turn to the huge clock over the bridge and he waits for the hands to strike 3 PM.

At 2:50 he yells through the PA system, "Drivers, start your engines!" A cacophony of noise erupts and a flurry of activity descends on the grid: mechanics making last-minute adjustments to the engines, pit crews gathering up equipment, drivers placing their ineffectual helmets on their heads, race officials shooing away pesky fans.

At 2:59, Rudi lowers his goggles and adjusts their fit. Bernd does the same and looks around. He knows the long dash to the first turn will be a challenge; the Mercedes has a few more horsepower than him, so Bernd needs a good start. Bernd targets Lang as his first victim; get past him by turn one and then he can concentrate on hunting down Rudi.

The engines in every car are now revving at 3000 RPM; they sound like a swarm of angry wasps. The sound is deafening, the crowds are going wild. It's Rudi's favorite time of a race—the anticipation of a fight is so thick he can taste it in the back of his throat.

The starter drops the flag and twenty cars scream down the straightaway in a cloud of blue smoke to the first turn. Rudi has a fantastic start and is three cars in front of his teammate Lang. Bernd is a quarter car back from Lang, enjoying an excellent start as well.

Cars are already hitting 120 miles per hour as they enter the first turn, swinging up to the top of the banked pavement. Each engine is wide open and tearing at itself as it moves the pistons faster. Drivers are tense on the first lap; the stress almost unbearable. You can't win a race in the first lap, but you can easily lose it.

Exiting the first turn, it's Rudi, Lang and Bernd all separated by about a car length. They enter the second banked turn.

Behind them, Vittorio Belmondo, a privateer driving an Alfa Romeo, miscalculates the exit of turn two and strays wide, making contact with another privateer driver, Hans Stück, in an Auto Union C. The cars touch and sparks fly. Stück loses a front wheel which causes him to veer suddenly to the left, taking out Christian Kautz in an MB W125. The crash is spectacular; the crowd cheers madly. Belmondo, unfazed by the accident he has caused, looks back and waves at the disarray. He's a gladiator. This is racing.

After fifteen laps, Rudi is opening his lead and is five cars ahead of Bernd and Lang who are exchanging positions almost constantly. Bernd, with his upgraded suspension, takes Lang in the corners; Lang powers back on the straights.

Eventually on lap twenty-five, Bernd makes a pass stick and Lang falls back by two cars. Bernd has his sights set on the leading Mercedes— driven by Rudi. He can see the number on Rudi's car: #2. *How appropriate,* Bernd thinks.

Tazio Nuvolari, driving a brand-new Ferrari, is so spooked by the banked turns he stops and gives his car to Giuseppe Farina who succumbs to a mechanical failure on lap twenty-six. The new Ferraris are fast, but have reliability issues.

On lap thirty-eight, Bernd gets a good exit out of the chicane in turn ten and catches Rudi. As Bernd attempts a pass, Rudi moves suddenly to block him. He comes within centimeters of colliding and Bernd has to lift the gas pedal slightly to avoid a crash. All is fair in war and racing, as they say.

On lap thirty-nine, Bernd, Rudi and Lang are mixing it up with the slower cars. They carefully pick their way past them, which is always challenging. Bernd gets another good exit, this time out of turn fourteen, and is neck and neck with Rudi as they enter the next turn, a slightly banked turn that leads into the finish straightaway. Bernd floors it, passes Rudi and holds it. Bernd is now leading the race of Monsters.

It's lap forty-three. Rudi has learned that Bernd is vulnerable on the chicane; he brakes too hard and too long, his speed dropping too low to parry a counter offensive. Rudi waits until just the right time and floors it while Bernd is exiting the chicane. Rudi regains the lead.

With seven laps to go, Rudi is two cars ahead of Bernd and driving like he's possessed. They're confronted again with slower traffic and Rudi, Bernd and Lang pick their way through, careful

154

to give the slower cars plenty of room.

In the VIP stands, Nicolette is screaming her support for her boyfriend—her fiancé?

"Go Rudi, go!"

On lap forty-eight, Seaman spins just before turn one. Rudi must take an unexpected line into the first bank; he holds on, but barely. Bernd and Lang pass the struggling Rudi and take over the lead.

Rudi recovers and catches a draft behind Lang, slingshots himself into turn two. Lang and Bernd touch wheels, causing Bernd to spin. Bernd veers off the track and into the infield, where he sits in his car in a cloud of smoke, dust and humiliation.

He watches Rudi enter the turn with too much speed. Rudi loses control and flies off turn two at over 100 miles per hour. His car is a missile, Rudi a mere passenger. His car gains altitude as it reaches its apogee, the height of the arc.

Bernd watches from his car; he can see flames coming off the back of the Mercedes. For a moment Bernd thinks, *this is what a comet looks like.*

Rudi's car loses momentum and gravity takes over. Bernd hears the impact over the din of the race when Rudi's car hits the pine tree with a sickening thud.

Rudi's car now begins an anguishing, leaden tumble through the trees, each limb wreaking more havoc on the car. Bernd watches the slow-motion tragedy unfold. The car hits the ground and amazingly lands on its bent but intact wheels.

Nicolette screams but she can't be heard over the cheers of the crowd. This is what they came to see.

Bernd jumps from his car and sprints up the track to a path that cuts under the banked turn. He runs down a long hallway that connects the infield to the park that sits directly behind turn two. He smells burning benzine, oil and rubber, along with something else. The thought makes him sick.

As Bernd runs to the Auto Union, he sees Rudi hanging halfway out of the car, surrounded by tiny flames. Marshalls and other staff stream out of the tunnel, running toward the burning wreck, but Bernd calculates that it will take too long for them to arrive and provide help.

Bernd grabs a nearby water bucket and runs toward the car. He throws the small bucket of water at the flames, but barely any hits the car.

Bernd struggles to free Rudi. The heat is becoming more intense and Bernd knows he needs to move quickly

The smell of petrol is intense and getting stronger—it's just a matter of time before the car explodes.

With all his might, Bernd lifts the unconscious Rudi from the car and drags him five meters away. The car suddenly explodes, knocking them both to the ground. The pine tree catches fire as if to say *we're not done here yet.*

A huge overhead limb cracks loudly, breaking off from the tree. Bernd looks up and sees a giant branch covered in benzine falling quickly, directly toward him and Rudi. Bernd grabs a moaning Rudi, can only move him two meters— but that's all that is needed. The limb lands a half a meter away from where the pair just sat.

A small grass fire now ignites where the resting limb is still burning.

Bernd looks at the fire, then begins to stomp it out with his feet. The marshal, just arriving, sprays it with an extinguisher.

"Sorry about the tree," Bernd says.

After the ambulance arrives and loads Rudi for transport, Nicolette appears with her father and his entourage.

"Oh my God! Bernd, are you okay?" cries Nicolette.   "Where's   Rudi!"

"He's okay, my dear. Maybe a broken bone or two. And I'm fine too," Bernd says, sitting on a tire wall. Bernd is amazed that Rudi was so lucky today. If the car had landed upside down or if the fire was more intense, Rudi would have been dead.

Nicolette's silhouette is backlit by the still-burning wreckage of Rudi's car.

"I was so worried when I saw him fly off the track, I thought—I thought he was dead!"

"He's stronger than that, Fräulein von Dries."

"I can't thank you enough Herr Rosemeyer," Nicolette says. "I'm truly grateful. I don't want to think about what would have happened if you hadn't been there."

"Well, we can't have a respectable young woman like you marrying a ghost, can we?" He grins.

"No, no." She smiles, but her eyes brim with tears. "I'm sorry, I'm still a bit shaken up."

Bernd feels a pang—compassion, guilt for joking at such a time?

"Please don't worry about Rudi, he's tough," he says, rising from the tire wall.

"I know, I know." She shakes her head quickly, trying to come back to her senses. "But thank you again. I'm going to the hospital with him. Is there anything I can do for you?" she asks, looking over her shoulder at the departing ambulance.

"Yes, just one thing. Tell me who won."

Rudi is flying in a spaceship through the stars. He looks out the window and sees a Nazi submarine. The sailors on the deck wave to him. He waves back.

He looks around and sees that his ship is landing in a beautiful meadow. Clouds float by. He sees the Alps, the sun shining brightly on its snow-covered peaks.

He descends from the craft; he's barefoot and his feet sink into the warm, moist turf as he touches Earth. He wiggles his toes and they sink farther into the warm soil. He's startled by a large group of jet-black crows flying overhead—there are hundreds, then thousands. The sound of their cawing and flapping wings is growing louder and louder.

They fly into a large shape, familiar but indistinguishable. Then with a sudden flurry of activity, the shape morphs into a German eagle. It's huge, as big as ten airplanes.

He's now flying a huge German eagle, sitting in the pilot's seat. He looks out the window and sees a large city; it's smoking and bombs are falling everywhere. Out of the window he sees a Junkers 87, a German dive bomber, releasing hundreds of bombs. They fall to the city below.

Flames are everywhere; they rise and touch the German eagle's wings. The city is destroyed, bodies in the rubble. He has destroyed a city with his eagle.

Nicolette stands over Rudi. His eyes are closed, his head bandaged. Hospital machines whir and beep as they deliver life.

Nicolette sees his eyes darting under his eyelids. They are moving rapidly, talking to her, sending her a signal. Suddenly, he quietly whispers, "Adler."

Nicolette takes Rudi's hand gently in her own. She's thinking about the race, the crash. She thinks this sport is madness. What good is it? Risking your life to beat another man across a finish line? For what? Who benefits?

In these few days since the accident, her feelings toward Rudi are mixed and jumbled in a way that makes her nervous and confused.

His recent actions and words seem to be at odds with her own beliefs—beliefs she thought they shared. He's on a path filled with hate, yet he claims his love for her is complete. How can one hold so much love and so much hate in one's heart simultaneously? It makes no sense to her.

She's seeing him more clearly—a driven and egotistical child more than a gracious, warm and loving man.

She remembers Bernd's brave actions and wonders why. Why would Bernd do what he did? Why would he risk his own life to save Rudi? Who is Bernd?

She doesn't like what she has been seeing in Rudi—she's beginning to better understand Bernd, and she likes what she sees.

26. The Encounter

Margi sits on a bench under a leafless Aspen tree in the weak winter light. She spent the morning window shopping in the hopes of finding a few meager Hanukkah presents for the children, toys she might afford, but came up empty.

Now, under a brittle sky filled with dark clouds, Tim and Ann are playing at the local Monbijoupark. The day feels choppy to Margi; sounds of the city echo off the buildings and mix with children's laughter as they walk home from school. It leaves her unsettled.

The *Sturmabteilung,* or brown shirts, are out in force today, adding to her anxiety. With over three million members, they are hard to avoid. A small group of three young men are patrolling the park, looking for trouble. Their primary duty is to protect Nazi rallies, but they often look for gypsies, Communists, Unionists or Jews to harass.

On the other side of the park, Nicolette has just left her favorite butcher shop. She holds a large package of Rudi's favorite schnitzel. She promised to cook tonight to celebrate his recovery and the impending announcement of their wedding.

Her feelings are muddled; she's excited about her wedding and her prospective life with Rudi, but Rudi has changed since the crash. He's become more distant and fanatical; he only talks about two things, Hitler and racing, and never about their future or wedding. Maybe he just needs some time.

The crash. Thank God Bernd was there to pull Rudi from the flames. Bernd. Why does she think of him every time she thinks of Rudi?

The brown shirts are questioning a young man when Tim and Ann run by playing tag. Tim is chasing Ann and is about to catch her. She shrieks and dodges his hand; her Blue Star falls off her jacket, unbeknownst to her.

A brown shirt picks up the star and looks around.

"Hey Jew, you've lost your star! Get over here!" he yells.

Caught up in the chase, Tim and Ann continue their game, headed away from the brown shirts.

"*Halt*! You two children!" the brownshirt shouts. The other Sturmabteilung look on as he steps toward the children.

Tim and Ann stop. They know how easy it is easy to get in trouble these days, especially when the brown shirts are around. They walk toward the young men, their heads hung low in fear.

"Yes, you two, get over here!"

"What is the meaning of this?" the brown shirt asks aggressively. "Jews must wear their stars at all times!"

"I'm sorry, sir," Ann says, looking at the man. Her heart is beating like a rabbit's and tears of fear well in her eyes. "It must have fallen off when we were playing."

"What is your name?"

"Ann, sir."

"Ann what?"

"Ann Wardenberg."

"You are a Jew?"

"Yes, sir."

"You know the penalties for not wearing your Star?" the brown shirt says coldly.

"No sir, I—" She tries to gulp down the lump in her throat. "My mother says I have to wear it all the time. I'm sorry, sir," she stammers.

Ann lowers her head. Tim, standing next to his sister, is scared for her, but anger boils inside him. He hates the Nazis and how they treat his family.

"The fine is fifty Marks and suspension of food coupons for one month. Do you have fifty Marks, Jew?" the brown shirt barks.

Margi, who has been lost in reverie on the bench, now senses something is wrong. She hears her daughter's voice, barely audible. The children stand before the brown shirts and she jumps up from the bench as if it had burned her.

"Excuse me sir, what's the trouble?" she asks politely, nervously, as she rushes over, clutching her thick sweater to her body.

"This Jew is not wearing her star. It is of no concern to you," he says flatly.

"These are my children, sir," she explains, hoping for the best but expecting the worst. "She was wearing her star, it must have fallen off, I tell them they must alwa—"

"You know the penalties! Do you have fifty Marks?" he snaps.

"No, um, what? Surely you don't mean that? This was a simple mistake, they were playing," she pleads.

"The fine is fifty Marks, Frau Wardenberg. Go get it from your husband if you don't have it," he says in a bored, unamused tone.

People are gathering around the scene now, some sympathizing with a mother trying to protect her children, others seeing yet another Jew causing trouble.

"I have no husband. I don't have . . ." She hangs her head.

"Why am I not surprised? Bastard Jew children running around and a whore mother with no money. The penalty is fifty Marks, and if you can't pay it I will take these children to the Neustrelitz."

Nicolette rounds a corner of the park and sees the crowd. She walks over to get a better look at what's unfolding but the crowd is making it difficult to see.

"No, please!" Margi pleads frantically. "I don't have the money right now but I can—I can pay you soon. And we'll put the star on right away!"

"Nein!" the brown shirt barks, spittle flying from his small mouth. "No exceptions, you must pay now or I will take both children to the Neustrelitz!"

Nicolette pushes her way through the crowd.

"No! But even Tim has his star!" she cries.

"Shut up you Jew rat! You must pay—"

"Excuse me Herr . . ." Nicolette says loudly.

The brown shirt is startled by the interjection. He turns to meet Nicolette's fierce gaze. "Who are you?" he barks.

"My name is Nicolette von Dries. I'm the daughter of General von Dries," she says firmly yet politely, hoping to calm the chaotic situation.

He recognizes the name immediately. The brown shirt straightens his posture.

"Ah, your papers please Fräulein von Dries?"

Nicolette hands the papers to the brown shirt. As he reviews them, she looks Margi in the eyes, trying to convey wordlessly to her and the children that it will be all right.

The crowd has become bigger. The sympathizers now outnumber the brown shirt supporters, but the crowd is silent.

The brown shirt tenses as he looks at Nicolette's papers. He knows she is powerful and could make things ugly for him. Assuming a newfound air of respect and politeness, he hands the papers back to Nicolette.

"Yes Fräulein, what can I do for you?"

"I'd like to know what is going on. What have these children done that has attracted such a large crowd?"

"They have not worn their stars as required and are refusing to pay the fine, Fräulein."

"Ah, I see. This is a serious offense, Herr—?"

"Herr Martin," the brown shirt clicks his heels and salutes.

"A pleasure, Herr Martin," she forces herself to say. "I'm sure my father will be impressed with you when I tell him of this incident."

"Danke, Fräulein. Now please excuse me while I complete this arrest."

"Herr Martin, perhaps *we* can solve this problem so you're not bothered with a trip to the

Neustrelitz. We need you patrolling, not filling out forms," she says, hoping to make the brown shirt feel important.

"It is my duty to take these children to the Neustrelitz," he says robotically.

"Yes well, perhaps if the fine was paid we could avoid all of this?"

Nicolette produces a fifty Mark note and gives it to the brown shirt, knowing he'll pocket the money.

"Ah, well then, yes. Since the fine has been paid I suppose we can release these two."

"Your reasoning is sound, Herr Martin, and I will let my father know you are taking your duties seriously." She's lying. If anything, she'll tell her father these brown shirts should be shot for harassing two small children and their mother.

"Jawhol, Fräulein. Good day to you." He motions to his companion that they are done here.

"Good day, Herr Martin," she says as the men turn and walk away from the crowd.

Nicolette turns to Margi and the children, who are huddled together, shaking. They know they nearly lost each other—the thought is terrifying.

"Come. Let's get you home," Nicolette says softly.

"Thank you Fräulein, thank you," says Margi.

"Where do you live? I'm sorry, what's your name?"

"My name is Margi Wardenberg, and—I'm sorry. I can't repay you but maybe I can work for you, I'm an excellent seamstress and can do laundry or—"

"Margi. Don't worry about the money," Nicolette says, smoothing Margi's hair where her children's crying faces have pressed it up. "Now, where do you live?"

"We live at 122 Munich in the Barn Quarter."

"Okay, off we go then!" Nicolette ushers the family out of the park, each member within her wingspan.

The group walks the short distance to the apartment and enters the building. Everyone is feeling better, but Ann's sniffles return in waves. As they walk up the stairs to the third floor, Margi lets the children take the lead and falls behind to speak to Nicolette.

"I can't thank you enough, Fräulein, and really, I will do anything to pay you back. I just don't have any money at the moment but I will—"

Nicolette once more cuts her off at the mention of money. "Margi, it's fine. You don't need to repay me. I'm just glad I was there to help. Mothers and children need to stay together, don't you think?"

"Oh yes, Fräulein, yes," she says. "It's been so hard since the passing of my husband. I'm all the children have now."

"All the more reason to make sure you stay together."

Entering the apartment, Nicolette looks around and sees a well-made home, nicer than she anticipated, nicer than a mother of two with no husband and no job would have. A small menorah sits on the mantle above the fireplace and holds two candles that have burned and died.

"May I offer you some tea, Fräulein?"

"That would be lovely, Margi—and please, call me Nicolette."

"Right away Fräulein, shan't take but a minute or two. Please take a seat at the table." Margi pads across the floor to the small but efficient kitchen to put the kettle on. As she does, the children gather around Nicolette, showing off their beat-up toys and asking her why she's so pretty. Nicolette laughs and makes small talk asking them the names of their toys. She loves the children's banter and their little laughs fill the room. They gradually make their way to Tim's room where they continue to play.

Nicolette sits at the table and looks around.

Bric-a-brac adorns the room, bearing memories of better times. There are wedding photos of a young couple on the wall: a handsome man and woman in a synagogue. Photos of children and family are on a small table next to a lamp. She spots an interesting photo of a large family gathering and takes it in her hands to look closer.

There are two men in the photo surrounded by children and friends. Both are smiling and laughing. It looks recent.

She doesn't recognize the man on the left, but assumes he must be Margi's husband. The other man looks familiar. She holds her breath as the realization comes over her.

"Margi," Nicolette calls to the kitchen, "is this a photo of Bernd Rosemeyer? Do you know him? Was he friends with your husband?"

Margi arrives at the table with a tray full of rugelach, tea and cups. As she pours the tea, Margi glances quickly at the photo Nicolette is holding.

"I, um. Herr Rosemeyer is a famous racecar driver."

"Yes, my dear, he is. How do you know him?"

"I, um, I don't know him. Maybe my husband knew him? I'm not sure really," she says as she finishes pouring the tea and takes a seat at the table. She holds the cup in front of her face and blows away the steam, trying to protect her eyes from Nicolette's quizzical gaze.

"How odd that you have a photo of a man that your husband knows well, but you don't?"

Margi takes a sip of tea, then says softly, "My husband knew many people. He was a very successful real estate businessman. Perhaps I'm mistaken as to who this man is." She gazes blankly at the picture as she speaks.

"Oh, you're not mistaken. I saw Bernd two weeks ago when he saved my fiancé's life. That is Bernd."

"Bernd saved your fiancé?" she asks in amazement.

"Yes, Rudi Caracciola is my fiancé. He and Bernd race together. Bernd saved Rudi at Monza a few weeks ago. I owe this man my fiancé's life!"

"I see," Margi says softly.

"Sorry, what do you see?"

Margi sets her cup gently on the table and tilts her head down slightly. "Herr Rosemeyer is a very generous and kind man, Fräulein. That is all I can say."

Puzzled, Nicolette replies, "I see. And I also agree with you, Margi."

Margi looks up at Nicolette, sees a beautiful, kind woman in front of her. She can't tell her the truth about Bernd—it's too dangerous even though she trusts Nicolette implicitly after her rescue. Instead, she reaches into her pocket, pulls out a Star of David necklace, and places it on the table between them.

"Take this, I want you to have it."

Nicolette picks up the necklace and holds it in her hand, examining it delicately.

"It's beautiful, I can't take this!" she exclaims.

"Please, it's the least I can do, you saved us," Margi says with pleading eyes. "It was my husband's."

"You're very kind Margi, but no, I can't."

"Please, please! It would mean so much to me for you take it. Perhaps you can give it to someone who needs to believe there are still kind people in the world."

Nicolette looks at Margi and sees a beautiful, caring mother struggling through a crazy world. She doesn't want to think about what she must be going through.

She stands up and hugs Margi. "I think I know someone who could use this."

27. Berlin Dinner

It's cozily packed at Zur Letzten Instanz, one of Berlin's most exclusive restaurants. A small Christmas tree, adorned with tiny Santa Clauses, stands in the foyer, greeting its patrons with holiday cheer. Rudi and Nicolette shuffle in from the cold, removing their heavy coats, and are greeted by the maître d'.

"Guten nacht Herr Caracciola, Fräulein von Dries. Good to see you both! Are you ready?"

"Danke, Klaus, the usual table if you please," Rudi says as he hands their coats to a young woman.

"Of course, of course, nothing but the best for Germany's fastest man and the beautiful aviator!"

Seated at the table with menus in hand, Rudi and Nicolette are the focus of whispers and stolen glances from nearby admirers.

"You seem to be drawing much attention tonight, Rudi," Nicolette says as she surveys the buzzing room.

"Ah, you know how it is my dear. Everyone wants to meet me these days."

"Yes, I guess I do see it. Funny, but I'm not sure I like being under such a powerful microscope."

"You'll get used to it my dear," he says, dismissing her discomfort with the flash of a cocky smile. "And it does have its perks."

A complimentary bottle of champagne is placed in an elegant stand beside their table. "See? It's not so bad," Rudi crows. "Champagne, darling? It's a 1922 Bisquit Dubouché, from the northern region of France I believe. A bit complex, but traditional."

"Just a splash," Nicolette says politely as the server suspends the bottle over her glass. "So how was your day, dear?"

"Fantastic! I met with the Mercedes team and development is on schedule. The new car is going to be absolutely beautiful. Der Spiegel also wants to do a photo shoot of me that will appear with the article. They tell me I'll be the very first driver to grace their cover!"

"That's great news, dear. Perhaps you can become a male model if this racing career doesn't pan out," she says playfully.

Rudi does not recognize the humor, and says conceitedly, "You're funny. But yes, I would make a great model, wouldn't I?"

"Only if you wear a helmet and cover that face," she quips.

"Funny and rude, how did I get such a catch," Rudi says, who is slightly annoyed at her jab.

"I had an interesting day, thank you for

asking," says Nicolette, eager to change the tone of the conversation.

Rudi spots a table of well-known admirers out of the corner of his eye. "Hold on dear, let me just say hi to Herr Folcker, I know he's a big fan."

Rudi saunters over to Volcker's table. It's filled with festively dressed couples celebrating the holidays —drinking, eating and smoking. Rudi works the table like a politician. He's got everyone laughing and smiling. After fifteen minutes of glad-handing, he returns to his solitary fiancée.

"Sorry dear, but Herr Volcker was telling me about an amazing trip to the Alps that he took last month," Rudi enthuses as he takes his seat. "Apparently he used llamas for the ascent! I didn't even know what a llama was until he explained it. They're these strange creatures that apparently can go for days without food and are well suited to the altitude—from Peru, I think he said."

"Yes well, about my day . . ." Nicolette says unamused.

"Oh, right, sorry, please continue, it was about flying?"

"No, no I didn't fly today. What I did was—"

"No flying?" he says, motioning for a waiter. "Oh, you should try to fly every day, my dear. Keeps your skills sharp."

"Would you like to hear about my day or not?" she asks sternly.

"Sorry, yes, please."

Nicolette places her menu on the table with a thud. "I helped a woman find her lost child. She was distraught, the poor thing. Happened at Monbijoupark. She was so grateful, she offered me tea."

"Oh that *is* nice" he says, after only paying half-attention to Nicolette's story. "Thank God you were there to help. How in the world did she lose her own child? A woman like that shouldn't be allowed to have children!" he says with disdain.

Frowning, she responds, "It happens, Rudi. Sometimes we get distracted. You're familiar with that feeling, correct?"

"Can't say I am," he says, his eyes momentarily catching on a shining beer being carried behind Nicolette.

Nicolette ignores his small-brained comment.

"Well, she was very grateful, so we went to her house for tea and you'll never imagine what was in her home."

"A llama?" Rudi jokes, laughing at his own wit.

"No, but close. A picture of Bernd Rosemeyer!" she says with awe.

"Bernd? Is she a racing fan? Why didn't she have a picture of me?" he asks, his brow furrowing. "Ever since the crash, Bernd is getting more credit and exposure than me even though I still hold the record for the most Grand Prix victories. Did you tell her I'm going to be on the cover of Der Spiegel? Maybe we should send her an autographed copy when it comes out?"

Ridiculous, Nicolette thinks, rolling her eyes. Rudi does not notice. "She's not a racing fan, Rudi. So sorry to tell you that not everyone is a fan. The picture was of her husband and Bernd. Looked fairly recent."

"Interesting," he says, resigned. "So she knows Bernd?"

"It wasn't entirely clear. She seemed to know of him but not know him personally, which I found odd." She thinks more about her strange encounter with Margi.

"That is odd, but so is Bernd. He knows a lot of women, if you know what I mean."

Nicolette nods slightly. "Yes, I've heard those rumors but this was strange. She seemed to not want to admit she knew him."

Rudi, now certain he knows why this woman wouldn't acknowledge her photo of Bernd says, "That's obvious! It's because she knows who the best driver is and didn't want to embarrass you that she had a picture of Bernd and not me. Perfectly understandable.

"Ready to order my dear? I'm starving!" he says and calls out to the waiter.

"Yes, yes. I can tell it's going to be a long night. Perhaps I will have another glass of champagne," she says, her head swimming with thoughts of Rudi and Bernd. It *is* going to be a long night.

28. A RAINY DAY

It is snowing and raining in Berlin, a typical winter day that has turned nasty. Sleet pours from the sky as Nicolette leaves the Mitte shopping area, bags in hand.

She has no umbrella and scurries beneath a nearby doorway, seeking shelter until the shower has passed.

Bernd, peering out beneath his bobbing umbrella as he passes down the street, catches sight of her figure in the doorway.

"Nicolette! What are you doing? Drowning out here?"

"Bernd!" she says, thoroughly surprised. "My gracious, how good to see you! Yes, I'm just waiting until this passes, shouldn't be too long." She stamps her feet, trying to shake off the snow that has accumulated on her coat.

"Nonsense! Come with me, let's get out of this rain! Give me those."

Bernd grabs the bags and holds his umbrella over the both of them. Their shoulders touch as they walk. Bernd gently guides her around the quickly accumulating puddles with his free arm. They arrive at a nearby cafe and take a seat in the front window.

As they remove their gloves and wet jackets and shake themselves dry, steam emerges from

Nicolette's drenched blouse where water has seeped in. Bernd glances down.

"There's mist in the highlands today," he says, amused, nodding to her collar.

Nicolette lets out a burst of laughter, and they fan themselves to acclimate to the temperature as the waiter approaches.

"Two coffees please," Bernd says.

"Excuse me, aren't you Bernd Rosemeyer?" the waiter says excitedly.

"Sorry no, you have me mistaken."

"Oh— sorry, you look a bit like him. Two coffees, right away."

As the waiter departs, Nicolette chuckles. "Do you do that often?"

"Constantly," he says as he looks down, almost bashful. "I love the fans, but sometimes it's nice to be a shadow."

"How interesting!" she says. "I wish Rudi would do that sometimes. He seems to crave the attention," she trails off. "So, what are you doing out in this storm?"

"I was visiting a friend who lives close by and was walking to my car when I spotted you. You know, you're not hard to find."

"Whatever do you mean?" she asks, puzzled.

"Well, when it's rainy and suddenly the heavens open and the bright, beautiful sun shines through, you take notice."

Nicolette blushes and scrunches her nose. "Such a playboy, even in the rain."

"Apologies, my dear, I'm a cad," he says with a cheeky grin.

The waiter sets down the two coffees in front of the pair and departs.

"Perhaps, but a heroic cad. I still can't thank you enough for helping Rudi," she says, exuding pure gratitude from her hazel eyes.

"How is the old boy? On the mend, I hope?" He means it, she can tell.

"Oh, he's doing much better now. I believe he's in town as we speak, meeting with a dealer. They want to use his face to sell more Mercedes."

"They should use yours instead, sell more cars," Bernd quips.

"Oh Bernd, do you ever stop?" she asks, incredulous but amused.

"Only at the end of a race. Even then, sometimes I forget." He laughs.

"So is this a race?"

Bernd pauses for a moment, flashes Nicolette an inquisitive eye. He sets his coffee down and contemplates what he'll say; he looks from the slowly rotating ceiling fan to Nicolette—she's absolutely stunning.

"No. A race has no meaning, just a bunch of gents driving around trying to be the fastest. *This,*" he says, motioning with his arms to the space in front of him, the space between him and Nicolette, "this is a nice coffee with a beautiful and kind friend," he says, warmth in his eyes. "It's far more enjoyable than a race, don't you think?"

She feels a sudden attachment to Bernd; not just a pang of attraction, but a feeling of calm contentment. It confuses her. "Very much so." She glances down at her coffee, then out the window to avoid his gaze.

A passing car splashes watery sleet onto the sidewalk, snapping her out of her reverie.

"So where are you off to next? There's another race in Britain soon, isn't there?"

"Yes, assuming the race promoter gets the permits. The Brits aren't too happy with us right now."

"I heard. Seems the Czechoslovakian annexation has turned some heads our way," she says.

"Guns too. Sometimes I just don't . . . Never mind," he stammers.

"No, what?" Nicolette asks. "You don't what, Bernd?"

"I don't understand . . . why we must always beat the war drum. I know as an SS officer I should never doubt our orders, but still." He looks deeply in Nicolette's eyes—looking for what? Sympathy? Understanding? Compassion?

She nods slightly in agreement. "Funny, I feel the same way. I said as much to my father before we—oh, never mind. Look at us. We should be drinking our coffees and talking about gay and fun things like Fräulein Brock's upcoming ball. Will you be attending?

"Now how could I miss it, knowing that you'll be there?"

"*You* are a scoundrel, Bernd," she says, narrowing her eyes to keep from smiling as she blows steam from the rim of her cup.

"Guilty as charged," he says, nestling deeper into his chair.

Across the street in another cafe, Rudi is watching his fiancée chat with his competitor.

He watched as they entered the cafe and took off their jackets. He couldn't see much after that because the window where they were seated steamed up.

Now the steam had cleared and he could see just fine, could see her laughing, him smiling. Her touching his hand as they joked about something.

He can feel the heat rising in himself, and soon his window clouds over with a steam of his own making.

29. A FAN SAYS HEIL

Walking down Oranienburger Street, Rudi is busy thinking about the new Auto Union car. He imagines what it will feel like when he drives it down the autobahn, hitting speeds of over 250 miles an hour. He tries to imagine how fast his reaction speed should be.

His thoughts are drifting down to more mundane matters when a brown shirt approaches.

"Herr Caracciola?" the brown shirt asks nervously.

"Yes, how can I help you?" Rudi says distractedly.

"Oh sir, I can't believe it's you! I'm one of your biggest fans!"

Rudi immediately puffs up from the admiration.

"Ah well, thank you for your kind words."

"I see you've recovered well, Herr Caracciola?" the brown shirt asks, his eyes wide as he shuffles his feet nervously. He can't believe his luck!

"Of course, of course," Rudi says with a wave of the hand. "It was just a few scratches really. Nothing can stop Germany's fastest driver."

"That is wonderful to hear Herr Caracciola! I

was concerned for you after Monza. I was hoping to see you at Nürburgring this coming Sunday."

"Oh well, you should, it will be a good race. We've got a few teams coming that will make it interesting, but I assure you, I will win. If you're a betting man, put a few Marks on your favorite driver," Rudi says with a wink, then attempts to leave.

"While I wish I could afford to bet, I wish more that I could afford a ticket," the brown shirt says, looking at Rudi intently. "They're expensive these days and I don't make much."

"Ah," says Rudi. "Yes well, I've got be going now."

"By the way, aren't you dating Fräulein von Dries?" the brown shirt asks, following Rudi the few steps he's taken.

Rudi looks at the name tag on the man's chest.

"That's rather personal, Herr Martin, but yes. Why?"

"I met her recently—in this very park just a few days ago," he exclaims.

"Is that so?" Rudi replies, annoyance in his voice. He's really got to be going. "And how did you happen to meet Fräulein von Dries, may I ask?"

"I was about to arrest some dirty Jew children who couldn't pay their fine. The Fräulein paid it for them and took them away, along with their mother."

Rudi dimly recalls the story that Nicolette told him the other night.

"Ah yes, she told me about how a mother had lost her children in the park and she helped locate them."

The brown shirt looks confused.

"No sir, they weren't lost. One of the rats wasn't wearing her Star and I tried to arrest them. But your fiancée helped them. She paid the fine and then they all went in that direction," he says, pointing toward the Barn Quarter. "I thought it was odd, but she *is* the general's daughter so I didn't think too much of it. She seemed nice."

Rudi lowers his voice.

"Who was this woman my fiancée helped?" he asks.

"Let me check my notes." He pulls a small notepad from his pants pocket and flips through it. "Ah, here it is—Wardenberg. Margi Wardenberg. Children Ann, age ten and Tim, age thirteen."

"Thank you for the information, Herr Martin. And the fine? I assume you gave it to the authorities?" Rudi asks, a slight suspicion glimmering in his eye.

"Of course, sir. This is why I have no money

for a grand prix ticket," the officer says piously.

"I see. Herr Martin, please accept a ticket on my behalf. It will be waiting for you at the gate on Sunday."

The brown shirt is surprised at his own good fortune.

"Thank you, sir! That is too kind. You're just like Fräulein Nicolette!"

"I should think not, Herr Martin. Good day."

With that, Rudi resumes his walk, now confused and angered. Why did Nicolette lie? She specifically said she helped locate a lost child. This child was not lost, this child was a Jew. Giving money to a Jew is against the law, she knows better! This would look bad for Rudi should the truth get out, especially so close to the publication of the Der Spiegel article.

And why did the Jew woman have a picture of Bernd? Didn't Nicolette say the picture was of the husband and Bernd? Who was this family that seems to have close ties to Bernd Rosemeyer?

And why was she so cozy with Bernd yesterday in the rain?

Rudi is not a suspicious man, but rather a calculating one—that is what makes him a great driver. And right now, he is calculating a plan to find out what exactly is going on between Bernd, Nicolette, and these Jews.

30. BETRAYAL

In order to join the SS, Bernd had to prove that all direct ancestors born since 1750 were not Jewish. Bernd couldn't do that. His grandfather and great grandfather had both been confirmed Jews with strong ties to the community.

His father and his immediate family had foresworn Judaism. Over the last twenty years they had succeeded in scrubbing any tell-tale evidence of their past.

His father went so far as to pay some local hoodlums to destroy the ancestry records in the synagogue that his family worshiped at. With that mess cleaned up, he had converted the family to Christianity, thereby becoming a good Nazi family. He didn't want to. He had to if they were going to survive in Nazi Germany.

Even through all these mastications, Bernd still needed a loophole. So he provided a German Blood Certificate when applying to become an SS officer. Since the war preparations were making it difficult for the SS to verify Jewish ancestry for many candidates, the certificate was an easy method to welcome those who wished to pledge allegiance to the Reich.

Purity of Aryan heritage was critical to those applying to become an SS officer. They had to swear their allegiance to the Reich and uphold its values and rules, the most important being that they would not support or sympathize with known Jews.

An SS candidate also had to prove to be in good physical shape, unmarried and without a criminal record. These were the easiest parts of Bernd's application, and to top it off, Bernd was Germany's fastest, if not the most famous, racecar driver.

Bernd had become a Nazi officer in 1937, but Rudi knows now that it was a sham.

After learning Nicolette deceived him about the Jewish woman and seeing her closeness with Bernd, Rudi decides to take action.

As he unsheathes his fountain pen to write the letter to Colonel Schwartz, he struggles for a moment. Was accusing Bernd of being a traitor any different from dispatching a competitor on the track? But didn't he also owe it to Germany to help weed out dissenters and sympathizers?

Even though he doesn't have all the facts, he knows something isn't right. What he needs is someone to look into this in a way that will keep him out of the mess, should it unfold.

Yes, Bernd had saved his life, but Rudi can tell Bernd is involved with something. He is stealing something, something precious to him. He is stealing Nicolette—maybe not intentionally, but the results will be the same.

Since the crash and Bernd's heroic rescue, Nicolette's attitude toward him has been different. She still seems to love Rudi and talks endlessly about the wedding, but there is something that Rudi couldn't name—until he saw her with Bernd.

He saw her eyes light up when she touched his arm in the café. He heard it in her voice, heard admiration and respect for Bernd when she spoke of him.

He may owe his life to Bernd but Bernd, as an SS officer, owed his life to the Reich. And he was no more going to let Bernd steal his fiancée than allow him to win a race.

It wasn't that he is a better driver. It wasn't that he is a better Nazi. It wasn't that he is a Mischling, someone who had at least three Jewish grandparents. No, Rudi is doing it because he is jealous of Bernd.

Pen in hand, he sits and writes:

Colonel Schwartz,

I hope this letter finds you in good health.

I am writing to you to inform you about a potential problem that you may wish to address. It has recently come to my attention that a known and high-profile SS officer may have been derelict in his duties.

The officer in question is suspected of not only supporting a Jewish family, but he intends to help them escape to Britain in the near future.

This officer is well known and respected in the Reich. Should this matter not be handled delicately, significant embarrassment would be borne by the SS leadership.

Please contact me to arrange a private meeting so we may discuss this matter further.

Yours truly,

Rudolph Caracciola

And with this letter, full of speculation and lies, this unknown officer has become a person of interest for Colonel Schwartz.

"Guten morgen, Herr Caracciola," says Colonel Schwartz from behind his desk, flanked by Nazi and German flags, in his well-appointed office.

"Guten morgen, Colonel Schwartz," Rudi says stiffly.

Schwartz surveys Rudi Caracciola, the famous driver, as he approaches the desk. He sees a mid-size man with no distinguishing features. Frankly, he's boring compared to Bernd, pedestrian.

"Thank you for the letter," he says after a moment. "I found it most intriguing."

Rudi exhales shortly.

"Yes, well, I wrote it because I know you'll do the right thing, Colonel. This man could cause a lot of embarrassment for us. He's in a very unique position, very visible within certain social circles, as well as the SS."

"I gathered that. So who is this mystery man and what evidence do you have?"

Rudi pauses for a moment, then blurts: "The officer is Herr Bernd, Colonel."

Schwartz is stunned by the mention of Bernd's name. "W- what did you just say?" he stammers.

"Bernd Rosemeyer, sir. My sources tell me that Rosemeyer is linked to a Jewish family living in the Barn Quarter. He intends to help them escape."

Anger begins to boil fervently inside the colonel.

"That's impossible!" he says. "I know Rosemeyer well, and while Bernd may not be as committed as some, he's no sympathizer. What proof do you have?"

"The Wardenberg woman is a known Jew. She is planning to escape and take her children with her. She's probably a spy, too," he adds.

Schwartz sees Rudi in a new light—a jealous little man who would gladly incite rumors if he thought it would help him beat his competitor. Schwartz pauses.

"Bullshit speculation on your part. There's no evidence of collaboration between Herr Rosemeyer and this woman. And a spy? Come now Rudi, I think I know what's going on here."

"I cannot reveal my source, but I assure you that it is reliable!" he says unconvincingly. Rudi is caught off guard by Schwartz's reception of the information.

"Have you confronted Herr Rosemeyer?"

"I have not. As you know, Rosemeyer and I are competitors. For me to question him would lead to allegations that would be difficult to explain. He and I represent the best drivers in the world right now and my accusations would look like nothing more than two jealous drivers fighting."

Well, at least this little shit recognizes the obvious, Schwartz thinks.

"Yes, it would, which is what I believe, too," he says dryly.

"It's not that, you idiot!" Rudi blurts, his eyes wide, his face beginning to flush.

Schwartz stands quickly, fists clenched, and glares at Rudi.

"Sorry, Colonel," Rudi says sheepishly. "I'm just upset. I'm sure if you looked, you'd find evidence that clears or convicts," he says attempting to steady his rage.

"You'd do well to keep your tongue in check, Herr Caracciola," Schwartz hisses. "You are skating on thin ice."

"Sorry again, Colonel. But I'm simply looking after our mutual interests," Rudi pleads. "The Reich does not need a famous driver and officer to be ousted as a Jew sympathizer! It would be embarrassing. For everyone."

Schwartz sits down gruffly, runs his hands through his hair and yanks on his jacket's collar, his breath slowly coming under control.

"Maybe. Tell me about your source." *Could any of this be true?*

"I'd prefer not to reveal my source; they have provided this information in confidence," Rudi says flatly.

"If we pursue this, *I will* find the source," Schwartz says, pointing a finger at Rudi. "And if your claims are unproven, there will be *significant* repercussions."

"Yes, I understand," Rudi says. He's a bit pale.

Schwartz's gaze, fixed menacingly on Rudi's eyes, does not falter.

"Make no mistake Rudi, you are gambling with your life."

Rudi holds Schwartz's gaze steadily.

"I do it every day on the track, Herr Colonel."

31. Timo time

Bernd is at the specially prepared Auto Union garage located directly on Bundesautobahn 5 near Frankfurt. It's been recently built, along with other garages and facilities, for the speed attempt.

The site of the attempt is a ten kilometer stretch of road that connects Frankfurt and Darmstadt. It's a civilian route on the autobahn and traffic is streaming by.

The Rekordwagen sits silently in the garage, its sleek aluminum skin removed so the mechanics can work on the massive 6.3 liter, V16 engine.

Although Porsche's contract with Auto Union has expired, Auto Union is still using the Porsche engine which sits in the middle of the car. It has fuel injection and not one, but two superchargers. It burns a potent witch's brew made up mostly of benzene, and it now produces over 500 horsepower.

Bernd is talking to Timo Glock, a young Jewish mechanic who is getting ready to test the car's engine.

"How are you doing Timo? Alles gut?" Bernd asks benevolently.

"Ja, the super charger was installed yesterday," Timo says, beaming. "We're going to run a few static tests this afternoon on the dynamometer. Hope to get to 700 brake horsepower!"

"Güt, we're getting closer to getting this thing on the road!"

"Yes—I'm still working on the exhaust. Every time she's runs at over 6,000 RPM, I smell something foul. I've tried isolating it, but no luck yet."

"I thought I smelt benzo when I walked in," Bernd says as he peeks into the engine bay and sees the massive engine gleaming in the klieg light. "Powerful smell . . . almost took my breath away."

"I'll get it sorted, Herr Rosemeyer. Even if it kills me," says Timo as he tightens a bolt on the supercharger's return valve.

"Well, let's hope not Timo," Bernd says, looking at the eager young mechanic. Bernd can see he means what he said; he is moved by the passion abounding in this young man.

"I wish they'd let me test drive it for you, Herr Rosemeyer," Timo says, cleaning his soiled hands on an oily rag.

"Hmmm. Have you talked to Nick? He's making the test schedule. I know he's looking for test drivers."

"Yes, I did, but you know," Timo picks up a spanner from the work bench, "I'm not what they're looking for."

"A competent test driver? That should be the *only* thing they're looking for," says Bernd emphatically.

"I wish that was true. Seems they only want drivers vetted by the SS. That's what August's man told me."

"Look, we need test drivers if we're going to make this work. I don't care if they're wearing a star or not," Bernd says sternly.

Timo looks up from the engine. "Thank you, Herr Rosemeyer, I appreciate you saying that." He resumes tightening a component on the engine. "I know this car like the back of my hand and I *want* to drive. But sometimes we don't get what we want, right?" he says, waving the spanner in the air as if he was a majorette leading a marching band.

"This is true, Timo." He pauses. "Are you sure you want to do this?" Bernd asks seriously. "This engine is a beast—it's quite dangerous."

Timo straightens up, standing tall over the Rekordwagon. He looks at Bernd directly and pauses. He respects Bernd immensely; there is a bond between them, both drivers—and both Jews.

He speaks softly. "There are not many things these days that make me happy, Herr Rosemeyer. Driving is the only thing I have left. When I'm behind the wheel, I'm focused. I'm free. It's just me, the car and the track. If forces me to face my own limitations. It's pure. It's the only thing in the world right now that is honest. If a man can't chase what brings him joy or gives him purpose, what does he have left?"

Bernd nods in silence.

"A life without joy is not worth living, don't you think, Herr Rosemeyer?"

Bernd holds Timo's gaze for another moment.

"Let me see what I can do."

A few meters away, a mechanic named Robin Frijns stands by the workbench listening to the conversation. He makes a mental note.

August Horch has told Frijns to keep his eyes on these two and report any suspicious conversations or activities. What August doesn't know is that his superior officer, Colonel Schwartz, made the same request two weeks earlier.

32. STARSTRUCK

After a fire claimed the original Reichstag building, the Nazis relocated next door into Berlin's Kroll Opera House, often referred to as the Krolloper.

It was in this very building Hitler had said:

> *"If international finance Jewry in and outside Europe should again succeed in plunging the nations into a world war, then the result will not be the Bolshevization of the earth, and thus the victory of Jewry, but the annihilation of the Jewish race in Europe."*

It is the new seat of the Reichstag, and it is gleaming this evening.

Rudi looks handsome, proudly sporting his grey SS officer's dress uniform. On his arm is Nicolette, dressed in an elegant black gown. They are there together as a couple and the crowd recognizes their celebrity.

Tonight's assembly is to honor Rudi with a Knights Cross of the Iron Cross, the highest award for an SS officer. The crowd is buzzing with excitement.

Since the NSKK, the National Socialist Motor Corps, is under the auspices of the SS, Bernd has been invited to the ceremony. It is fitting that both the best drivers in Germany, if not all of Europe, are SS officers—living proof of Aryan superiority.

After the brief ceremony, the crowd spills into the nearby Königsplatz square, smoking, talking and making plans for the remainder of the evening.

Rudi is receiving admiration and congratulations from the attendees with glee. A small crowd has gathered around him as he gushes to them about his achievements.

Nicolette has distanced herself from Rudi's court and stands by the fountain, smoking. Bernd approaches her as she exhales.

"You look beautiful tonight, Fräulein von Dries." Nicolette looks alluring, but natural—not too much make up, just enough to set off her hazel eyes. Her gown is elegant and tasteful and her hair is perfectly coiffed.

"Oh, Bernd!" she says, surprised, as she faces him. "Thank you. How are you?"

"Good. Nice evening tonight."

Nicolette takes a final drag from her cigarette and flicks it into the standing ashtray.

"Yes, a bit crowded for me, but an important night for Rudi," she says as she takes her beaded purse from under her arm.

"Yes, very. But he's deserving of the recognition don't you think?" Bernd asks wearily.

"Yes, I suppose so." She glances at her fiancé across the grand hall. "You're alone?" she asks Bernd.

"Yes."

"Unusual for you," she says with a playful smirk as she corrals a section of hair that's fallen lazily to her forehead.

Bernd glances down. "Not really. Sometimes it's nice to stand back and take it all in. Get a perspective on things . . ."

"Indeed," Nicolette says gently. "That's what I like most about flying, actually. You get a different perspective. Helps you see clearly." She looks up to the stars and breathes in the clean scent that comes with a recent rain.

"I can see that. A little distance makes the bigger pictures grow much clearer, somehow."

She smiles. "So, what are your plans Herr Rosemeyer? Big night out?"

"No, not tonight. Big day tomorrow. Everyone is working hard on the Rekordwagon and more testing is scheduled. Never stops these days," he says.

"You sound tired. Or bored perhaps?" There is a note of concern in her voice.

"A bit tired. Not from working but from . . . other things," Bernd replies. A far-off look momentarily clouds his eyes. Nicolette remains silent, waiting for Bernd to reveal what's on his mind.

He looks at Nicolette, backlit by the bright Krolloper lights. "I had a friend— a good friend actually" he says melancholically. "He got tired too. Didn't end well for him."

"What happened?" she asks softly.

"Oh, he got in over his head. Real estate. It got too much and he had no one to turn to for help."

She moves toward him, not on purpose, but in empathy.

"Oh dear, I hope he's okay now?"

"Afraid not," he says, smiling sadly. "Took his own life. Left behind a wonderful wife and two children."

She reaches out, gently touches Bernd's arm. She feels the electricity immediately. She feels the need to gather herself. "Oh my, that's awful," she says.

"Yes. Devastating . . . He was my nephew."

Nicolette looks in his eyes, her soul on fire, unclear if it burns with sadness or with love. She shakes her head and says nothing.

"A sad story. My biggest regret actually," Bernd says, looking off in the distance.

She touches his arm again with more force.

"I'm so sorry Bernd." She feels hot tears forming, but they do not fall.

Bernd gently places his hand over Nicolette's and says unhurriedly, "Thank you my dear. Your kindness is noted."

He removes his hand, unwillingly, from hers, her touch bringing him peace and solace. The release of her hand burns—just letting go, even for the tiniest amount, pains him. He knows he must go. He turns to walk away, then turns back.

"I realize now that you cannot offer kindness too soon. You never know how soon it will be too late." He gives another melancholy smile.

Buttoning his jacket against the cold night air, Bernd walks away alone.

Close to the fountain, but hidden in the shadows of the Opera House, a cigarette glows as a man blinks away the cold. He drops his cigarette and crushes it with his boot. Colonel Schwartz watches carefully as the couple separates. He wonders why Bernd and Nicolette seem so close as he puts his hands in his pockets and walks into the night.

33. TO TELL THE TRUTH

Margi enters her apartment with today's mail. As she stands in the kitchen thumbing through the papers, she notices an official envelope used by the Kommissar. The address shows it's from the Berlin immigration office. She opens it tentatively.

The letter says that her departure papers have been approved and are waiting at the local office. Is it really possible?

All she needs is the stamp and she can escape with the children! After all this time, her efforts are paying off.

Margi hurriedly grabs her coat and makes her way to the office. It's only a ten-minute walk to possible freedom. She feels lightheaded. Could it actually be happening?

Upon arrival, she approaches the small office. She's been there before. It's always been a disaster. Another stamp or another approval needed. Captain Meyer dismissing her pleas for help.

She enters the office expecting to see Captain Meyer. He isn't there. A new officer is—Colonel Marcus Schwartz. She feels her stomach drop like an elevator.

"Güten Tag, Fräulein Wardenberg," he says with feigned glee in his voice.

"Güten Tag," she says hesitantly, confused by the new officer's presence.

"My name is Colonel Schwartz. I'm the Oberst in Berlin. Thank you for coming by the office, your promptness is appreciated," he says happily. "I'm in charge of many things, but mostly special cases that require—shall we say—further investigation." He places his pen on a stack of papers and adjusts the cuffs of his jacket.

Margi is silent.

He plows ahead as if this were just another matter to address in a long list of items. "I understand you and your children wish to emigrate to Bratislava?" he says matter-of-factly.

"Correct, Colonel," she replies with caution.

"I see. And you are a Jew?" he says as he reads from her file.

"Yes, Colonel."

"Mmm, I see. And why do you wish to leave?"

"My husband passed away last year and we have family there. We'd like to make a clean start," she confesses softly.

With deep concern in his voice he says, "I'm so sorry to hear of your loss! It must be difficult to raise a family with no father or husband? No income?"

"Yes Herr Colonel, it has been . . . difficult," she says quietly.

He reads again from the file, finds the ages of her children. "Your children go to the Böhlen Zu Grimma school, I see."

"Yes, Colonel."

Schwartz picks up his pen and absentmindedly twirls it between his fingers, saying, "Tim seems to be a fine child—good grades, likes football, has an affinity for motorsports. And Ann has just started piano lessons. Is she doing well?"

"Yes, Colonel," she says tentatively. "Ann seems to really like cats-cradle."

How does he know these things? Margi sits in silence.

"So the interesting question in your case—and I have your case right here, just requires one stamp for approval—so the interesting question that I hope you can help me answer is how have you managed to provide for your family for almost one year without an income, without a husband?" he asks in a polite, inquisitive way.

She sits silently. She can feel sweat beading on her scalp.

"Yes, I too was stumped when I read your case!" he exclaims as if he and Margi are both detectives working on a case. He shakes his head vigorously and says, "It's odd isn't it? You have a lovely apartment, food, clothing, nothing too fancy, nothing that would be noticed, yet plenty for a family your size."

Her heart races, fearing that this meeting is a setup. Margi tries to extract herself with a plausible alibi, anything. "I sew and do some cleaning. I make enough . . ."

Schwartz shrugs and says, "Yes, I suppose you do. With the sewing and cleaning . . . very interesting." He waves his arms around dramatically to make himself look like he's cleaning and sewing.

Margi says nothing; a bead of sweat travels down her spine.

Schwartz smiles. "Maybe with some help from friends too?" he says softly.

Margi's feet are dancing beneath her chair.

Schwartz can sense her discomfort; he banked on it. He loves this part of his job—he's good at it so he pauses to relish the moment.

Softly and with mocked fondness, he continues. "Yes, friends are important, aren't they Fräulein? Friends can help in many different ways. Why, some can help with money, some with stamps, some with information. It's good to have friends that can help, isn't it?"

He pauses to let his sharp words sink in; Margi squirms in her chair.

The back of her neck feels feverish. How can she get out of here, back to her children! She must warn Bernd. She dreads what's coming next.

"Speaking of friends, I have a friend that you may know? Herr Rosemeyer?" The name smacks her in the face; she stares straight ahead, afraid to move even the tiniest muscle. "I'm sure you've heard of him, fastest man in Germany! Bernd is a good friend, as well as an SS officer," he says sweetly. "Do you know him?" he asks innocently.

Margi blinks away a tear and says nothing.

"Come now Margi, you must have heard of him?" he scoffs.

"Yes, I've heard of him," she says softly.

With great satisfaction and glee, he roars, "Of course you have! He's very famous! He's also very generous isn't he? Maybe almost as generous as me? Me with the stamp. Me who can help you get to Bratislava." He waves the stamp that she desperately needs to escape in the air.

"All I need to know is that you know him and you and your children could be on a train this afternoon. Not too much to ask, is it?" he purrs.

She opens her mouth, closes it again.

"Ah, I see you are reluctant. Perfectly understandable given the situation," he says in his business-like voice.

Beads of sweat have pricked up on her forehead, gleaming visibly under the harsh light of the office.

Schwartz places both hands on the desk.

"Margi, let me put it a different way. Those that work against me and the Reich are not my friends. Often, my enemies do not fare well. Even their immediate families may suffer because of this.

"Those that work with me will be rewarded," he says with a darkness in his voice as he waves her papers.

"So, let me ask again, do you know Bernd Rosemeyer?"

Her eyes dart around, looking to the door, looking for any possibility of escape. Her body quivers with fear.

Becoming perturbed, he sighs. "I see," he says. "Very well. I guess you don't know Herr Rosemeyer, my mistake. Pity."

"What about the stamp?" she asks softly.

"Yes, the stamp!", he remarks with glee, "It would be nice to have, don't you think?"

"Yes."

"But you don't know my friend Bernd?" he asks again. "My friend Bernd would want you to have this stamp. He would want to see you and the children on today's train," he says, giving her a wink and a sickly saccharine smile.

She can't take much more of this, she's going crazy. She feels lightheaded. Her thoughts turn to Ann and Tim. "What do you want?" she blurts.

Schwartz pauses. He sits back in his chair and glares at her. He knows she's finished, but she doesn't know it yet. That son-of-a-bitch Rudi was right after all. Amazing.

"Just confirm that you know Herr Rosemeyer my dear, nothing nefarious. I just need to know that you know him. Then the stamp is yours."

Broken and scared, thinking of her children, Margi confesses, "Yes, I know him."

He jumps up from his seat, clasping his hands together. "Excellent! See that wasn't so hard was it?" he says joyfully, triumphantly.

"What will happen now?" she asks worriedly—she has betrayed Bernd. She didn't have a choice, thanks to the bastard in front of her!

Back in his chair, Schwartz grins like a Cheshire cat. He says sweetly, "Not a thing, my dear. Here, here is the stamp and your papers and you're free to leave with the children. I have a car waiting to take you all to the station."

"My children are in the car?"

"Yes, I took the liberty of picking them up. And don't worry about your things, we will send them to you on the next train to . . . let me see . . . a Herr Oscar in Stupava, near Bratislava, correct?"

"Yes, that's correct," she says, disoriented.

"See, it helps when you work with me, Margi. I take care of my friends," he says as he stands. He's done here, but he has another mess to clean up—and that mess involves Bernd.

"And Bernd?"

He gathers the papers and says, "Bernd will be fine! As I said, we are close friends and I take care of my friends. Don't you think?" he asks as he hands her papers over to her. His eye glints.

"Yes, Colonel," she replies. Shame presses in on her throat.

Margi and her children are on a train. The destination is the detention camp in Sachsenhausen, Germany, not the farm in Bratislava.

34. MARCUS CONFLICTED

Marcus Schwartz sits at his desk and shakes his head. He is reading a report on Bernd—an SS officer, a Hauptsturmführer for Christ's sake.

How in the hell is Bernd in this mess? The Wardenberg woman's records showed Bernd has been giving her money for over a year.

Bernd's antics on the podium aren't helping. Bernd has recognized that the SS is using the Grands Prix as unofficial Nazi rallies, so he's been hamming it up during the closing ceremonies—duckwalking the podium, Hitler impersonations.

"What is the son of a bitch thinking?" Schwartz says aloud to no one.

But no matter what, Bernd is the face of German superiority. It will be a huge embarrassment for certain people if this story comes out.

A knock on the door alerts him to Lieutenant Marco Wittman's entry.

"Is this everything we have on Rosemeyer?" Schwartz asks.

"Here is his full SS file, Colonel," says Wittman, dropping a heavy file on the desk.

Paging through the file, Schwartz reads, "Race CV, commendations, financials, SS application, blood test, physical, ancestry . . ."

"Ja, Colonel. All appears normal, but I decided to review his German blood certificate."

"And?" Schwartz says intently, his head snapping up from the file.

"Looks official. Conducted at Fliedner Clinic. But I reviewed his application and well, I found a few errors. So I looked at his ancestry records."

"Get to the point, Lieutenant."

"Sir, it appears he has direct Jewish ancestry dating back to 1878. At least three grandparents were Jews."

"Shit!" Schwartz shouts. "Are you telling me he's a Mischlinge?!"

"It appears so."

"Then how did he get a blood certificate?" he yells.

Wittman has experienced Schwartz's outbursts many times. "The system is backed up sir," he replies coolly. "We don't have enough people to run all the background checks."

"Shit. This is bad," Schwartz says, his eyes wide, searching for his next move. "How the hell did the SS allow a Mischlinge to become an officer? Did he lie about all of his history?" he asks wildly.

"You will have to ask him that directly, sir.

214

Should I bring him in?"

Shaking his head, Schwartz says, "No, I'll take care of it. But don't speak about this to anyone until I think this through, Lieutenant."

"Jawhol, Colonel. Anything else?"

"No, that's enough for today" Schwartz sighs.

The lieutenant leaves; Schwartz walks to his window overlooking the Oranienplatz.

Oh, dear Bernd, is this true? How fucking stupid are you? That suspicious prick Rudi hit the nail on the head. First with the Jew woman and now this?

How can such a beautiful, talented man be a Mischlinge? Unbelievable. Göring and Hitler are going to go crazy if this leaks. And it will leak.

How many others have you helped and protected? Too many, I suspect. You've burned not one bridge, you've set fire to the entire Spree River and all the bridges over it. I may have fond memories with you my friend, but even friendship has limitations.

35. HENDRICK ON THE ROCKS

Nicolette is at 3000 meters and she's soaring over the Germany countryside. The reflection of the sun off the surface of a thousand small lakes makes the countryside glitter like diamonds.

Nothing can touch her when she's in the sky. It's just her and the plane working together. The plane is running well today; nimble, steady and perfectly coordinated with her actions.

She pulls on the controls and gains another 500 meters; she can see the snow-covered Alps in the distance. It's cold, beautiful, peaceful up here.

She knows that back on the ground things aren't as bucolic and serene. War is imminent. She hasn't seen her father in weeks—which means there's war planning occurring.

After landing, she taxis to her hanger and sees Hendrick approaching. He's wearing his usual grease-stained overalls, a load of aircraft parts under his arm.

"How was it?" he yells over the noise of the decelerating engine.

"Beautiful as usual," she says. "I needed that. It really clears the head."

"Wunderbar! You were gone longer than I expected."

"You're lucky I came back," she jokes.

"Yes, well, do you have a moment Fräulein? I'd like to discuss something with you."

"Sure," she says, sensing something serious may be afoot. "Give me ten, just need to go through my post-flight checklist."

When she approaches Hendrick, there are two beers sitting at a small table in the hangar.

"Cheers, my friend," she says.

They say Prost in unison as they clink their bottles.

"What's on your mind, Hendrick? What can I do for you?" she asks.

He sets his bottle on the table slowly.

"There's something you need to know, Nicolette."

"More bad news? *Not* sure I need any."

"Yes, well, it's about Rudi, I'm afraid."

Images of Rudi's mangled body lying in a car rush through her mind. "What about him? Did he crash??"

"No, he's fine," Hendrick replies flatly. He takes a cigarette from his pack and lights it. He offers Nicolette one but she declines.

"What then?" she asks impatiently.

"Well, it's a bit complicated, so hear me out."

He exhales a large cloud of blue smoke from deep in his lungs. "I have friends, as you know, and they have given me some information that I think you need to know since it involves your fiancé."

"Yes?" she says setting her bottle on the table and leaning forward, waiting impatiently for Hendrick to get to the point.

"There's a Jewish family. The Wardenbergs. They were trying—"

Nicolette jolts at the name Wardenberg.

"Wait, what?" she interrupts. "I met Margi and her kids recently."

"Yes, that's what I'm getting to."

"Okay, okay, sorry, please continue. But hurry up."

He puts his cigarette out in the ashtray. "A week ago they were taken into SS custody and sent to Sachsenhausen."

Her eyes bulge and heat floods her head. "No. Oh that's horrible! But why? And wait—what does this have to do with Rudi?"

"It seems the SS thinks they were receiving help from someone you know."

"What? Rudi was helping them?" she asks, confused. "That's impossible! He doesn't know them!"

"No, not Rudi," he says, shaking his head.

"Bernd Rosemeyer."

"Wha—Bernd is helping them? I don't understand . . ." She gasps quietly. "I did see a picture of Bernd and Margi's husband at their apartment. She claimed she didn't really know Bernd. This is crazy! Are you sure about this? About Bernd helping them?"

"Fairly sure. Besides, it doesn't matter what I think, it only matters what the SS thinks."

"Oh my God, that poor woman! And her children!" she cries.

"Yes, it is sad, but unfortunately not that unusual anymore. There are many facing similar fates these days."

"Amazing. I'm having a very hard time believing that Bernd would help them.... I don't understand. Was Bernd seeing this woman?"

"Not that we know of. It seems that Bernd and Herr Wardenberg were friends—they were related, but that's not important."

"Okay, then what *is* important? I'm still trying to get this in my head."

A breeze rustles the grass in the nearby field.

"It was Rudi," he says.

"What was Rudi?"

Hedrick pauses.

"Rudi provided the information to the SS about Bernd. About how he was helping Margi."

"That's—that's impossible," she stammers. "Why would he do that? He's never even met Margi!"

"Perhaps. But we know he wrote a letter to Colonel Schwartz accusing Bernd of sympathizing. Shortly after, Schwartz met with Margi and well ... she was deported thereafter."

"Oh my God," she whispers. "This can't be true Hendrick!"

"I wish it wasn't," he says soberly.

Nicolette buries her head in her hands.

"I—I don't know what to say. Are you sure about this?" She looks at Hendrick, he looks back, unblinking.

"Yes. We're sure he wrote the letter. What I can't be sure of is why. Did Bernd and Rudi have an issue that you know about? Maybe a falling out?" he asks softly.

"No, no, Bernd saved Rudi at Monza. He owes his life to Bernd!"

"Yes, I've heard that story."

"Why would Rudi turn Bernd in?" Nicolette cries angrily. "This doesn't make any sense, Hendrick!"

"Nothing makes sense anymore my dear. The

world has lost its mind. And I'm afraid I don't know any more than this. But I thought you should know."

The shock and confusion have overwhelmed her; tears are streaming down her face. She beats back her sobs long enough to say, "All I can think about right now is those children!"

Hendrick watches her with pity. He says nothing.

"What am I supposed to do?" she sobs.

He places his hand gently on hers. "I'm not sure, but it seems like you don't know Rudi as well as you think you do. Nor Bernd."

The sun is beginning to set, casting long shadows on the hanger's wall. Crickets are beginning to chirp as they welcome the approaching night.

Nicolette's world, so peaceful just an hour ago, has turned dark quickly.

36. Confession

The Ravensbrück concentration camp is located in northern Germany, about 90 kilometers north of Berlin and roughly the same from what used to be the Polish border.

The camp, directed by Dr. Mengele and housing over 20,000 mostly female prisoners, is the primary medical facility for the SS's ghastly experiments.

General von Dries is reading a report detailing the camp's operations, his aide-de-camp, Colonel Kaufman sitting beside him.

"This is unbelievable," scoffs von Dries, deep disdain in his voice.

Kaufman shakes his head in disgust. "I have no words, General."

"Who would cut open another human's bones and muscles like this? Just so we can test sulfonamide?"

"It's a promising new anti-bacteria drug, Herr General."

"I know what it is, but *Mein Gott*! This report says they are putting things like pieces of wood or glass into tissues, and fracturing bones of the prisoners! They are deliberately infecting them to see if the drug works! It's madness!"

"They call them *Króliki*—rabbits," Kaufman

offers.

"I'd rather be a rabbit than these poor bastards," von Dries mutters. "This is—this is insane . . . simulating a soldier's war wounds just so they can see if a drug works."

"I'm assuming you've read about the women who have been moved to Argentina?" Kaufman asks.

"Yes," von Dries replies; his stomach does a somersault.

"Apparently, they are working on genetics. Some type of Eugenics program . . . clean up the gene pool, or something to that effect."

"Well, at least those are German volunteers and not prisoners."

"Yes, that's true. But I've also heard there are similar experiments on the babies that are born down there. The cruelty is . . . well, it's unthinkable."

Dries drops the heavy report down on his desk. He stares at the cover page, sadness painting his face.

"What have we become, Kaufman? How can we do this to our own? This has to stop!"

"Well, I'm not sure how we can stop it, General. The only option we have is Warsaw," Kaufman replies, lowering his voice slightly.

"We need to make this happen Kaufman. And

we need to do it now."

"Sir," Kaufman says seriously, "Hitler is scheduled for the parade in Warsaw on the 29th. Everything is ready. Hendrick has confirmed the Polish underground has the TNT. The plan is to plant the TNT in a ditch along the parade route and explode it as Hitler's motorcade drives by. Everything is prepared, but we have to wait until the parade."

"Scheisse! I never thought I'd be so happy for a parade," he says, shaking his head, "but the sooner this happens, the better."

Kaufman gives a nod.

"Sir, keep in mind that there are no guarantees the motorcade will take the roads we think they'll use. Anything can happen. We really need to discuss a backup plan."

"What has Hendrick suggested?"

"That we place a sniper in the tower at St. Alexander's. He's been in touch with the priest, who is willing to hide the shooter. The church will provide the widest vantage point of Warsaw square. We're almost 100 percent sure the motorcade will enter the square after the parade."

"I trust Hendrick," von Dries grunts, his eyes still staring blankly at the report. "I trust that man with my life, so if he thinks this is the best back up plan, let's do it, Kaufman."

"*Jawhol*, General."

That evening, von Dries and Nicolette sit in the study of their home, their conversation illuminated by the softly glowing fireplace.

"So how are things, *Schatzki?*" von Dries asks softly.

"I don't know, Father. I feel like everything is falling apart," she replies, tucking her legs under her. She used to do the same thing when she was a little girl and her mother scolded her for snitching the strudel. God how she misses her.

"I'm so sorry, princess," von Dries says heavy-heartedly.

"I'm still thinking about what Hendrick said— I still can't believe Rudi would turn Bernd in as a sympathizer!" she whispers, her voice breaking.

"I know, my dear. But Hendrick has his sources and he's an honorable man."

"I know," she says, tilting her head back slightly as she blinks away a tear.

"Will you still go through with the wedding?"

"I don't know. It's so confusing. I just . . ."

Dries pads across the room in his thick socks, pats her shoulder.

She looks up at her father.

"Do you believe Bernd is guilty?" she asks.

He holds her gaze for a moment, says nothing.

"The only thing he's guilty of is being a good man," von Dries says with conviction.

"Yes, I *know* but do you think he's been helping that Jewish woman?" she asks. Her eyes search in his for the truth, though she knows her father has little more information than she does.

He shakes his head. "I don't know my dear, but you seem to think so."

"When I was at her apartment and saw that photo and how she reacted. It just seems they knew each other, like they were close friends but she wouldn't say."

"Maybe she was trying to protect a friend?" he says, sitting down next to Nicolette on the plush loveseat.

"But why?" Nicolette asks quietly, staring into the fire. "I meant her no harm. I like Bernd too. I'm sure I said as much."

"One can't be too careful these days," von Dries says, watching the glow of the fire dancing on her melancholy profile. "I'm sure she was just trying to protect her children, just as I would. And you are the daughter of a General—a woman like that wouldn't trust you, despite what you did."

Nicolette sighs with knitted eyebrows. "Yes, I suppose you're right."

The pair fall silent for a moment, the crackle

of the fire filling the room.

"Dear," von Dries starts gingerly, "there's something I need to tell you. And I'm afraid you won't like it."

"Not another annexation Father!" she says, facing her father.

"Nothing like that," he quickly offers with a dismissive wave of the hand.

"I can't take any more of this war, it's too much!" she exclaims weakly as she leans back against the seat.

"I know dear, but that's not want I want to discuss with you."

"Well, what is it then?"

He looks at his daughter's face and takes in a breath.

"There are certain things going on, big things. I probably shouldn't tell you this, but you have a right to know. They will have large implications for me—and possibly for you as well.

"What?" she asks, puzzled by his formality. "You can tell me anything. You know that, Father."

He pushes up from the loveseat. "Yes, I do know, which is why I'm telling you." He crosses the room to stand in front of fire, hoping to warm his old bones.

"I don't like the sound of this," Nicolette says flatly.

"Neither do I, but it's something I have to do. Something we as a people have to do. This madness must stop and I'm one of the few people who can end it."

"What are you saying?" she asks, her body frozen still as she watches his back.

He turns from the fire, looks directly at his daughter. God, how she reminds him of his wife.

"Hitler will be in Warsaw for a parade. A parade that he shan't return from."

Her face drops. "What? Someone is going to assassinate Hitler?!"

"This is all I can tell you for now. You need to be prepared to leave Germany immediately on the 28th."

"I won't leave without you!" she cries and runs to hug her father.

He embraces her, stroking her hair. "You won't have to," he says, his cheek against the top of her head. "The parade is in Poland where I will be. It's to take place three weeks from now, on September 28th."

"W-what? What are you saying?" she whispers into her father's chest.

"You will receive word from me on that day. You are to fly your plane to Warsaw and meet me there. If you don't hear from me, then nothing happened and it will be business as usual."

She looks up at her father, tears streaming down her face. "Oh Father, this is insane! What if you're caught? What will happen to you, to me, to us?" She once again searches for answers in his eyes.

"Dear, if I'm caught, Hendrick knows what to do," he says. His years of military service have trained him well to maintain composure during any circumstance, but his daughter's shining, pleading eyes tempt tears to well in his own. "He will make sure you can leave Germany, get somewhere safe."

"I hate this, I don't want you to do this!" she says, attempting to break out of her father's arms; he holds her steady. "Please! You're all I have in this miserable world!" she cries, softly pounding her fists against his barrel-sized chest.

He smiles at her with melancholy eyes.

"And that is why you'll do exactly as I say. This miserable world can't be left to fester. I have to stop this madman before it's too late." He strokes her hair. "Surely you see this?" he asks soothingly, trying to calm the one precious thing he has left in this world.

"Oh Papa, this is horrible," she sobs softly. "I don't know what to say! I know he has to be stopped but I can't lose you too! There's got to be another way!"

He takes her by the shoulders, holds her away from him so she can see his face.

"I'm a soldier princess. I'm supposed to be fighting for our people, our country. Somehow, I've lost my way. We've all lost our way. This is my chance to redeem myself and keep my promise to the German people. It's the only way I know to stop this war."

She looks into his eyes. Breaking free from his grip, she buries her face back into his chest; "Oh Papa, please, no, don't do this!"

"I have to Schatzki," he says, hugging her tightly. "For you and for our people. For our people's spirit. This war has its own gravity, its own mass. We must find a way to break from its orbit or the world will surely perish.

"And remember, trust only Hendrick. He will know what to do."

The fire dies, the wood screeching quietly as it gives its final breath.

37. TIMO DRIVES

The car is like the cold. Cold air is denser and contains more oxygen; with more oxygen comes more combustion. More combustion means more horsepower, and more horsepower is why they're here this morning. To test.

Cold air also helps with engine temperature control, which is giving the mechanics a fit. Timo and Rene, the head mechanic, stand next to the Streamliner, frustrated.

"First it runs hot, and now cold!" he yells. "I wish it would make up its mind!"

Timo pats him on the shoulder, his lips pursed in consideration. "Try covering part of the radiators with something . . . like a piece of aluminum?" he posits.

"Maybe we should disconnect the radiators? That should bring engine temps up," Rene says.

"No, too risky. I don't want to be half way through the test and then run hot."

Bernd joins the troubleshooters at the car. "Timo! You excited about today?"

"Herr Rosemeyer!" Timo says, straightening up. "Thanks for coming today! I sure am! I can't thank you enough for getting them to let me drive!" he says, shaking his head in excitement.

"My pleasure, Timo," Bernd says. "I wouldn't

miss this for the world. It wasn't hard. I think you and I are the only ones that can control this beast," he says, playfully rustling Timo's hair.

"Ja, she's something!" Timo says; he can't stop smiling. "A bit temperamental right now, but we'll have it sorted shortly."

"Okay. Let me know if I can help," Bernd says, moving away from the car to leave the mechanics to their work.

"Will do!"

Across the pits at the Mercedes garage, over twenty mechanics are busy preparing Rudi's car for its first test.

The new W125 Rekordwagen is really not that new. An existing W125 had its horsepower boosted to 765 and its skin replaced with sculpted body work. Instead of radiators for cooling, it uses a chest filled with dry ice. It's an interesting solution to the vexing problem of controlling the engine temperature. Even with super-cooled air, the engine can only run for around ninety seconds before overheating.

The supercharged V12 is massive. It runs on a special mixture of methyl alcohol, benzene, ethanol, acetone, nitrobenzene and avgas. Its massive superchargers gobble up this elixir quickly; the tank can hold only twenty gallons and runs dry after five miles at full throttle.

In contrast, the Auto Union Stromlinien wagen has a massive 6.5 liter, 45-degree angle

V16 engine developed by Porsche. The camshaft, with its thirty-two valves, is enormous. A single camshaft left the vehicle with vibration problems, so Porsche redesigned the camshaft as three separate, geared units which are then screwed together to make a long, durable camshaft.

Its horsepower maxed out, the only thing left to address was weight.

All racing components like on-board air jacks, mirrors and front brakes were either modified or removed. In the rear, the limited slip differential—necessary for a road course—just added unnecessary weight. The transmission was replaced with a simple five-speed gear box and an open differential.

The front end of the car sustained even more changes. Since these cars were built to go in a straight line, steering and suspension needs are minimal. The front suspension is based on the semi-trailing arm design used on existing race cars; this allows the mechanics to easily align the camber, tow, and caster of the wheels and tires.

Steering was severely limited as the car's bodywork covered the front tires. Engineers determined that the lengths of the steering rods could be reduced since the car only needed to turn by six degrees, thereby saving another few pounds. The steering rods were connected via pins and bolts to the steering shaft, and the steering shaft to the steering wheel, thus completing the loop.

Equal but different, the W125 and Stromlinien wagen both raged war on the speed record in their own ways.

Rudi and Hans Fischer are reviewing the work in the Mercedes garage.

"What do you mean?" Rudi says angrily.

"Well, we couldn't afford to close the entire autobahn, so you're going to have to test in traffic."

"Are you insane!"

"Look, we talked to Auto Union. We've agreed to share the cost of closing the road for the record run, but for this test, all we need is a long straightaway. There will be some traffic on one side of the road, but the straights will be clear on the closed side. You'll be fine."

"Unbelievable," Rudi grunts. "We're going to go out there and run at over 250 miles an hour while there's traffic on the other side of the road?" he asks, throwing a hand in the Autobahn's direction.

"It's just a test, Rudi."

"At over 250!" Rudi yells.

"It is what it is!" Fischer responds firmly. "Do you want a test driver? Bernd has one."

"No! No I don't want a test driver! I'll do it, but only once. You better get this sorted by Rekord week, you idiot!"

"I will," Fischer says flatly. "I'll worry about the course, you worry about driving." He walks off, leaving Rudi stewing in the garage.

Timo prepares for his first run in the Auto Union garage. He dons his suit, gloves and helmet and checks the cockpit for any stray spanners or tools. The VIPs have all arrived and sit watching the preparations.

General von Dries and Nicolette chat, sitting next to Colonel Schwartz, Hans Fischer, and August Horch. Bernd is in the Auto Union garage talking to the mechanics.

Schwartz, dressed in his usual black SS uniform, munches on a pretzel. "So General, the time has come!" he says casually to von Dries.

Dries, who is a rank above Schwartz, nods. "The test? Yes, it has, Colonel."

Schwartz feels the carnival-like atmosphere. He sits with a goofy grin and a small smear of mustard on his face. "Who will you bet on today?" he jeers to Nicolette.

General von Dries, watching Timo administering his final checks, says, "Well, I think Nicolette would prefer I bet on Rudi. Though August might have a different opinion."

August grunts. "Sit back and watch. Auto Union will be the fastest today."

Schwartz takes a large bite of pretzel. Speaking through the dough, he says,"*Ja*? Bernd and Auto Union? They have a good chance too, don't you think Fräulein?"

Nicolette's stomach jolts—she's never trusted Schwartz—but she maintains her placid look. "If I've learned anything Colonel, I've learned that in this sport, anything can happen," she says coolly.

"Yes, yes, so true!" Schwartz squeals. "Anything can happen and often does! That's why I love this so much!"

At the start line, Rene leans into the cockpit.

"Ready Timo?" he asks.

"Ja!" Timo replies, flexing his gloved fingers as he grips the steering wheel.

In a cloud of smoke and noise he starts the W125. He waits patiently for the mechanics to re-check everything and for the engine temperature to rise.

Mechanics from both teams stop their work and gather around the start line to watch the event unfold.

Just to the right of the track, officers of the NSKK are manning an electrical recording device that will be used to measure speed. Five miles down the track, another group stands by their device, ready to record the attempt.

The timekeeper checks to see if everyone is ready, then tells the recording crew to begin the session. There is no flag drop on this race, as the cars will be automatically recorded after they trip the start wire on the device.

Timo guns the engine one last time and puts the car in first gear, starting his run. The sound is deafening.

The car triggers the initial recording device; the teams signal that everything is working and the timekeeper gives a final thumbs up.

Timo tears up the autobahn and shifts into second gear. The noise has eased from the distance, but is still too loud for any observer's voice to be heard.

Hitting third and 140, Timo is now just a speck to those watching. He shifts into fourth gear and waits for the acceleration that should come, should punch him right in the back. It never does.

Now approaching the ten-mile mark and turnaround point, Timo realizes he's got a problem. He puts the car in neutral and coasts to the turnaround point as mechanics swarm the car.

The official speed is recorded at 142.3 miles an hour, hardly a record.

The mechanics instruct Timo to drive back slowly to the main garage so they can try to figure out what went wrong.

August gets word from the team. "Shit!" he yells as the walkie talkie clicks off.

Schwartz, who has moved on to a bratwurst, says, "What happened?" as he wipes his mouth.

"How the hell do I know?" Horch barks. "Once he's back we'll fix it and run again." He starts off for the garage.

Schwartz turns to the von Dries family.

"Looks like your fiancé might be the hero today after all, Fräulein!" he says brightly to Nicolette like some garish court jester.

"Maybe Colonel, but it's not over yet."

August storms into the Auto Union garage and makes a beeline for the Streamliner and the team swarming over the car.

"I smelled it again at about 120, it's the Benzo leaking," Timo says to Rene.

"How bad?"

"Bad! I couldn't breathe. Had to back off and let the cockpit air out," he says, pushing his hair back from his forehead as August arrives.

"What?" August bellows. "You backed off because of some fumes?!"

"Sir!" Timo says with a start. "I had the throttle wide open but then the smell hit me. It wouldn't go any faster, it just made the fumes worse."

"Goddamn swine, I knew I should have made Bernd drive today!"

"Sir, just give us some time, we'll get it sorted and I'll take it back out!" Timo says, Rene nodding behind him.

August scowls at the driver.

"You've thirty minutes, Timo — and you'd better be right!" August screams.

Bernd walks over to the scene just as August leaves.

"What was that all about?" Bernd asks.

"Nothing, Herr Horch was just making suggestions," Timo says flatly.

"So what happened? Engine?"

"No," Timo says, shaking his head. "I think it was a fuel leak."

Bernd winces. "Really? How bad?"

"Bad. It's got to be a leak in or by the injectors. I'm pretty sure it's not in it. If it was, the fumes wouldn't be so bad," Timo explains.

Rene jumps in. "Okay, I'll check the hose clamps and the pressure. If the pressure is too high, those clamps would leak and spray the Benzo everywhere which is probably what you were smelling."

"*Ja,* okay," Timo nods. "Do me a favor and put three clamps on the input hose where it mates to the injectors. And make sure they're tight. We'll get this!" Timo says excitedly.

Rene gives a thumbs up as he dashes off and Bernd pulls Timo aside. "Timo, look. Be careful. If you smell something again or it just doesn't feel right, back off. There's plenty of time to test. Okay?" he says, holding Timo by the shoulders.

"No, no it's fine, Herr Rosemeyer, we'll make it work!"

"Just be careful. Promise me?"

"Don't worry Bernd, I'll get it right," Timo says. He gives Bernd a wink and a smile; Bernd can see how determined he is to win this, even though there's technically nothing to win.

Back in the pits, Rudi's sitting in the W125. The massive V12 is growling like a lion, waiting to be released. The mechanics do their final dance before giving Rudi the thumbs up.

The timekeepers check with each other and give a signal—it's a go.

Rudi guns the engine and shifts into first, slightly spinning the rear wheels in the process. *Shit! I just lost a 1/10 of a second with that wheel spin*, he thinks.

The engine roars and Rudi flies down the autobahn shifting into 2nd and 3rd. He's already at 140 and is three and a half miles down the track. He looks to the left and sees street cars and trucks casually driving down the other side of the open autobahn.

Rudi is now doing 200 in fifth gear. He's got the throttle pegged and the car is absolutely gulping its fuel. There's so much air pressure in the front of the car that the engine can't move it any faster; now it's up to the aerodynamics and the streamlined shape of the big W125.

At 230 something hits Rudi. It feels like someone took a sledgehammer to his chest. Fractions of a second later, he hears a loud bam! He expects the car to flip any second. Did he blow a tire? He looks around and everything looks normal. All the gauges look okay. What was that?

With one mile to go, the big W125 is screaming down the autobahn. Rudi feels the front of the car lifting as if it wants to actually fly. Hitting 242, Rudi backs off the throttle and flies through the timing booth. He gingerly applies the reduced brakes to slow the car.

The mechanics rush to him and places his car on a dolly so they can turn it around and get him ready for the next run. After a brief stop and more fuel, Rudi is ready for the return journey. He guns it again.

He's tearing down the autobahn at 244 miles an hour. Rudi passes under the bridge and *bam!*

241

He's hit in the chest again, this time more violently. The car shimmies to the left and Rudi gently tries to counter steer. He's speeding dangerously close to the edge of the track. Another fifty centimeters and he'd be dead.

He passes under another bridge and bam! The car jumps back to the center of the road.

He passes the timing booth and slows the car. His whole body is shaking. He can't believe he just survived that run. What was happening out there? He gently touches his chest; it feels bruised.

The mechanics surround the car, patting him on the back, whooping and offering congratulations to Rudi as he gets out.

Rudi says not a word and strides to where Fischer is talking to a mechanic. Before Hans can say anything to the driver, Rudi throws a punch, but Hans is too quick and easily dodges Rudi's fist.

"What the fuck are you trying to do, kill me?!" Rudi roars.

Hans holds Rudi's arms by his sides, not sure if he's got another punch in him. "You hit 244 Rudi!" he yells with excitement.

Rudi jerks out of Hans' grasp, screams, "I almost died! That car almost killed me, you idiot!"

"What?" Hans asks, confused. "How—what?"

"Every time I went under a bridge I thought the car was going to come apart!"

Hans is perplexed. "I, uh, I don't know Rudi!"

"Well that's *it*!" Rudi shouts. "Until you figure this out, I'm not driving!"

Hans scratches his head. It doesn't matter if Rudi doesn't drive anymore today, they already got a record in the books! He shakes his head and smiles, conceding to Rudi. "Okay, okay, we'll look into it, Rudi."

Rudi stares at Hans and says nothing.

"Come on, let's go talk to Pietro, he might know what happened," Hans says.

"You talk to him. I need to sit down."

Rudi, with great effort, slowly walks to the garage and sits with his head between his knees. He's still shaking.

38. A Night of Knives

It's just two days until the record attempt and spirits are high. Most of Hitler's commanding officers, the teams from Mercedes and Auto Union, and their VIPs are gathered for a glorious evening, an anticipatory celebration of the impending event.

Not far from the Ministry of Propaganda and Hitler's Chancellery, the Hotel Aldon sits proudly in the Mitte district of Berlin. The Aldon is dressed handsomely for the evening; massive swastika banners hang from the elaborate ballroom ceiling and crystal chandeliers glow brightly, casting golden shadows on the attendees.

A banquet table lines the far wall providing local fare—schnitzels, spaetzle, roasted pork hocks, duck, sauerbraten, and Alsatian apple cakes. A large orchestra is playing Strauss. Beer and wine are flowing and the guests mingle and talk among themselves.

Bernd has arrived alone and is making his rounds, talking to team members, businessmen and various socialites who are enjoying the festivities.

Bernd is in a reflective and solemn mood, still processing the events of the past week. He chit chats, but does not engage with the entourage who wants to swim in his wake of popularity.

Thirty minutes later, Nicolette arrives, entering the hotel alone. She bites her lip to distract her from the pain her new shoes are causing. She runs gingerly up the enormous, carpet-lined staircase and enters the ballroom. She is immediately greeted by Frau Hilga Risk, an older socialite with even older money.

"Good evening, Fräulein von Dries!"

"Good evening, Frau Risk!" Nicolette says. She subtly twists her foot in her shoe, hoping to relocate the heel strap that is creating a blister, as they greet each other with cheek kisses.

"So wonderful to have you here tonight! Where is your handsome fiancé, Herr Caracciola?"

"Wonderful to see you too, Frau Risk," she says with a warm smile. "I hope your family is well?"

"They are fine my dear, but where is Rudi?" the woman asks.

Nicolette has had no success in the shoe area nor in dodging Frau Risk's question; she reaches down and twists the strap into place with manicured fingers.

"Unfortunately, he's tied up. I received word this evening that he was delayed at the factory. Something to do with a supercharger. But everyone is working hard to set the record, so sacrifices must be made," she says.

She now stands tall, her shoe dilemma resolved. She accepts a glass of champagne from a passing waiter and takes a sip, waiting for the next round of questions from her host.

"And you happen to be one of them. What a pity, my dear. But it shall be a wonderful evening!" Frau Risk says, turning cheerful once more. "I expect a fabulous turn out. So many interesting people are here.

"Please get some food and say hello to your friends. It's just wonderful to see you again!" she says, squeezing Nicolette's free hand. "And say hello to your father for me."

"Ah, I just left Father at the Chancellery. He too is busy tonight, but I promise to give him your regards."

Nicolette gives Frau Risk a peck on the cheek and the two separate.

***

Across town, a different scene is unfolding. In Mariendorf, a tiny Berlin district, tall ash trees line the promenade. A group of starlings somberly sing in the cold, dark air as the streetlights dimly illuminate the Martin Luther Memorial Church.

The church is a beautiful Gothic creation, built only recently in 1935. Soaring, barreled ceilings and terracotta arches span the altar. Adorned with typical Christian symbols, it also features depictions of Christ flanked by a member of the

246

Hitler Youth and a uniformed Wehrmacht soldier. It is here the ceremony will take place.

Göring, Himmler and Mengele are secluded inside a darkened nave illuminated by hundreds of candles. Twenty black-robed men stand in two lines of ten facing the pulpit where the triumvirate of Germans waits

Each man holds a candle, their faces hidden by the darkness and the hoods on their robes. They are silent, still; their breath rises in small clouds as they exhale.

The triumvirate addresses the men; "Tonight is the Induction. You will remember this night for eternity."

"Tonight is the last night you will be men, for after, you will be soldiers in the most noble pursuit known to man."

"We are Aryans, we are pure, we are good. We are the light that shines brightly in the darkest corners of the world. We are here to fulfill our destiny. We are the Reich and we are powerful.

"Proceed."

The two lines of men slowly march toward the altar. The soft click of their booted heels reverberates off the church's stone walls, their robes slowly swinging in rhythm with their movement.

The two lines form a semicircle around the altar and the three commanders. The twenty men kneel in unison and place their candles in front of them.

***

In the ballroom, Bernd, in a white tuxedo jacket and well-tailored black pants, is talking to August about race preparations when Colonel Schwartz approaches. Schwartz spent most of the day in meetings with Göring, Himmler, and others discussing a secret operation. He hopes to relax a bit before returning for more meetings that will extend well into the night.

"Gentlemen! Guten nacht!" says Schwartz, who beams at Bernd.

"Guten nacht, Colonel," the pair replies.

"You two look like you're enjoying yourselves, sequestered all alone. No doubt plotting something nefarious?" Schwartz asks, chuckling while looking around the room for a waiter.

"Schwartz, you dolt," August begins with a scowl. "We were discussing how to run the session on the autobahn that you won't close!"

Schwartz quickly grabs a glass of champagne from a waiter, saying, "Ah yes, well, as you know the autobahn is for the people, gentlemen. They use it to go to work, make deliveries, et cetera. I think it's only fair that you pay for its disruption." He offers to clink glasses but no one returns the favor.

August narrows his eyes. "That may be so, Colonel, but it's a pain in the ass to try to drive at 250 with cars in your way," he says, jamming a finger at Schwartz's chest, well-decorated with medals.

Schwartz, feigning hurt feelings, whines like a child. "Bernd, my friend, is this true? Are you not the greatest driver and Nazi officer known to Germany—is a little traffic going to bother you?"

"I'm not the greatest, Marcus, I'm just good," Bernd says. "And yes, the traffic is dangerous. Perhaps you'd like me to take you for a drive so I can show you firsthand? Maybe tomorrow?" His words hover somewhere between offer and threat.

Bernd knows Marcus won't accept the offer. He has sensed a change in Schwartz as of late, and suspects he has something to do with Margi's disappearance. Every time he calls Schwartz's office to request a meeting, he's been denied. He ponders Schwartz's involvement quietly.

Marcus waves away the offer with his free hand. "The invitation is tempting, but I'm afraid I'll be very busy tomorrow."

"Busy doing what? Traipsing around the world looking for secrets?" grunts August.

"I'm afraid my activities are classified, Herr Horch, but I will tell you this: change is coming to Germany. Big change. You'll read about it in the papers soon enough." His words trail off, an air of doom leaking out of them.

"Well, if change means you'll close the goddamn autobahn for the run, I'm all for it," August growls and drains his glass. He swiftly removes another glass from a passing waiter.

"Tsk, tsk. Such tiny thoughts from a little man. No August, this has nothing to do with your little race."

Bernd interjects before Horch can make a rebuttal. "I'm intrigued, Colonel. A man of your standing holds only the most tantalizing gossip. Can't you give us a little hint?"

"Oh Bernd, always such a charmer," Schwartz coos, sneering slightly to make the comment seem like a joke. "I'll tell you this. There are some in our country that incorrectly believe we are on the wrong path. These people are enemies of the state and they are everywhere. Some are deeply embedded in our government and military. Tonight, those enemies will be dealt with so that Germany can move forward unencumbered."

"Jesus, Marcus, should I be worried?" Bernd asks, eliciting a slight guffaw from August.

"Why would you have anything to worry about Bernd?" Schwartz asks, feigning surprise and dismissiveness. *Oh, my little Bernd, if you only knew how much I know about you*, he thinks.

"I don't, but the way you're talking makes it sound mighty threatening," Bernd replies. He pauses, searching Marcus' face for a tell, trying to sense what Marcus is really saying.

Schwartz is silent for a moment—then a chuckle escapes him and he blurts, "I frighten the great Rosemeyer? You've got nothing to worry about except going faster than anyone else in the world, my dear friend!" Bernd cracks a smile, but sees a mischievous glow in Schwartz's eyes, a harsh flame that contradicts his jolly response.

August senses there's something going on between these two, but doesn't care enough to get involved. "I'll drink to that," he says gruffly and gulps down his last bit of champagne. "Gentlemen, I'm dry, shall we move to the bar?"

***

The strong scent of incense hangs thickly in the cold air. At the altar, the triumvirate now stands backlit by candles, the hoods of their dark red robes draped over their heads. They produce a long scroll; written in large gothic letters are twenty names.

A chill runs through the church as Göring says in his slow and prophetic voice, "For our father, for there can be only one father."

"There can be only one father," the crowd responds in unison.

Göring holds a large golden eagle above his head, SS symbols emblazoned on its chest.

"Tonight is the night we purge those that would defeat us, defeat the Reich and defeat the Führer. Tonight we pledge ourselves to cleanse the world—but first we must be clean. And to be

251

clean we must first be pure."

The twenty men bring their hands in front of their faces, their palms facing together in the prayer position of monks.

One by one, they join together the fingers on each hand, forming an arch. "Hitler is the only father," they chant.

Twenty men kneeling. Twenty men with arches covering their faces. Twenty men ready to kill in the name of the Fürher.

"Tonight, our enemies shall know our wrath. We shall strike them down as they would strike us down. The names on this list are to be executed tonight, for tonight is the Night of Long Knives. You shall each be given one name. This person shall be dealt with, shown no mercy no matter who they are nor what they may say. You will do this deed with haste and ruthlessness.

"Your assigned teams await outside."

The trio descend from the altar, each with their own aspergillum filled with water from the Rhine, Elbe and Danube. As they approach each man, he removes his hood. The aspergillum deposits a few drops of water on his forehead which slowly tumble down his face.

Göring whispers a name on the scroll into each man's ear. The man re-hoods, bows, and departs the semicircle, making his way quietly to the back of the church.

The last man in the group is approached by the holy trio. He's alone. The last disciple. A small bead of sweat drips from the man's nose.

Rudi Caracciola removes his hood and is ordained with the cold, odorless water. The water leaks down the side of his face and is absorbed by the rough tunic engulfing his neck.

"General Mathias von Dries," Göring whispers.

***

Bernd is speaking casually with Maurice Becker, a wealthy industrialist who supplies parts to Ford AG.

In between small talk, Bernd notices a beautiful woman, her neck and back sparkling under the soft glow of the chandelier. The woman is talking to Michael Jäger, another socialite from Austria involved in agriculture. It appears he's trying to get her to dance to Ich Tanz Mit Fräulein— "Dolly Swing".

The woman laughs at a joke and turns slightly to her left, exposing a radiant smile that Bernd recognizes immediately.

Outside the church, Rudi stands amid the large group of men. The twenty disciples and their teams of ten SS officers are making plans to carry out their orders.

Rudi is stunned, a fog descending over this mind. General von Dries? Who in the hell would assign him this task! How can he kill his fiancé's father, for Christ's sake!

He would be fine spilling someone else's blood, someone who deserves it, some low life officer who is a spy, someone who is working against the Reich.

But von Dries? *He's a general! A war hero! Is he really the traitor they are making him out to be? A traitor to be knifed and gutted, an example made of?* His thoughts swirl as feelings of despair, confusion and bitterness well inside of him. He resolves to fix this disaster, and fix it quickly.

Rudi sees Captain Hans Baumgarten standing with his team and approaches him. He's not close to Baumgarten, but they've met each other several times at events and parties. Baumgarten is a large, well-proportioned muscular man and is known for his good nature—a perfect target for Rudi's plan.

"Rudi, good to see you," Baumgarten says, nodding.

"Yes, good to see you too. Could I have a word?" Rudi asks, motioning to a shadowy area not far from the church.

Rudi and Boris make their way over, stopping beneath a tree. It provides a bit of cover from the rest of the men.

"What's on your mind," Baumgarten asks as he lights a cigarette.

"I need a favor," Rudi replies, betrayed by a sliver of nervousness in his voice.

"Of course, if I can." Baumgarten blows smoke out through his nostrils and spits at the ground.

"You know I'm as committed as any German to these orders, yes?" Rudi says quickly.

Baumgarten pauses. He looks at his cigarette and contemplates the SS officer standing before him. "I don't know that, Herr Caracciola. After all, you're an *Honorary* SS officer, without a commission." He spits again. "As I said, what can I do for you?" he asks flatly.

"Look, I've been given a name that is an issue for me. It's not that I don't believe this person is an enemy, it's ... it's just that ... "

"It's what, Rudi?"

"It's just that ... it's my fiancée's father," Rudi says. He glances toward the group of men.

"General von Dries? Yes, I heard he was on the list," Baumgarten replies casually.

"Yes, so I was hoping to trade names with you," Rudi says softly.

"Ah, I see. You can't bring yourself to execute your fiancée's father?"

"Well, no, I can, it's just that well. It's a problem," he stammers.

"And you think I can help you?"

"Yes, yes. A simple exchange allows me to do my duties without this becoming an issue for me," Rudi says hopefully.

"For your fiancée or for you?"

"Look, I can do it. I *will* do it if I have to," Rudi says sternly but pleadingly. "It's just cleaner if we trade."

Baumgarten pauses, then asks politely, "Rudi, might I make a suggestion?"

A suggestion! Yes, Rudi has done it, he's going to trade names! His head clears. "Yes, by all means!"

Baumgarten spits again at Rudi's feet. "Go to hell Rudi," he hisses. "Forget we had this conversation. Get your team together and do your duty. Auf Wiedersehen."

Baumgarten walks away. Rudi stands alone beneath the tree, dumbfounded, then slowly follows his team to where Captain Schlager waits.

"Ready, Herr Caracciola?"

"Yes, Captain," Rudi says robotically.

"Sir, our orders are to make our way to the general's office at the Chancellery. We should arrive just after midnight."

"Very well Captain, bring the vehicles around," Rudi says distractedly.

"*Jawhol!*"

***

Bernd approaches Nicolette. She's standing alone, watching couples glide across the dance floor. Her ballgown is an off the shoulder number adorned with red and black jewels along the neck and waistline. Her hair is in a tight bun, highlighting her cheekbones. She wears little makeup but looks radiant nonetheless.

"Nicolette! I thought I recognized you from across the room. How are you?" Bernd asks warmly.

"Bernd, so great to see a friendly face tonight! I'm fine," she says. Suddenly, her heart is beating faster and she must work to regulate her breath.

"Where's your handsome Rudi?" Bernd asks, looking around. "Fetching the most beautiful woman at the ball a drink?"

"Oh Bernd, stop, you're going to make me blush. No, Rudi didn't make it tonight. Something about the car and the supercharger ..."

"Well, that's too bad for him and absolutely wonderful for me," he says softly, giving her a wink and a smile.

She laughs. "Well, you might be right. I'm

bored to tears and need a friend to talk to. If I have to ward off another blitzkrieg from Michael Jäger I might break down and cry."

"Ah, Jäger. Does he smell funny to you?"

"Like potatoes left in the sun too long!" she says, surprised anyone else had picked up on the scent.

The two laugh quietly and clink glasses at their joke. Bernd leans in close to her left ear. "We're horrible aren't we?" he whispers with a smile.

"Incorrigible," Nicolette says, reveling in the ease of their conversation and the closeness of their bodies.

"So, I have a question for you" she says, looking up at him.

"I promise not to lie." Bernd draws a cross over his heart.

"Hmmm. In that case, let me ask a different question—since the stakes are so high."

Bernd narrows his eyes, but can't keep from smiling. "Oh dear, what have I gotten myself into?"

She hesitates for a moment, looks at the dance floor. "Do you think what we're doing is right?"

He pretends to misunderstand. "Dear, we're just talking!"

Nicolette swats his arm playfully. "I'm talking

about Germany, you dolt!"

"Ah, I see," Bernd says, putting his hands in his pockets and looking out at the dancing couples. "Well, we have to be careful dear. There are ears everywhere. How about we make a deal. You dance with me and you can ask anything you want. Deal?"

"Deal."

Bernd guides Nicolette to the dance floor as the orchestra begins to play a slow waltz. He gently places his arm around her waist and pulls her toward him carefully. He doesn't want people to get the wrong impression—everyone knows of her engagement to Rudi. He also respects this woman and wants to show her that his intentions are noble and true.

"So, about Germany?" Bernd asks quietly.

"Yes, about Germany. Every time I turn around I hear about some horrible new thing we're doing in the name of the Reich. I'm sick of the aggression, I'm sick of death."

Bernd nods in agreement. "Yes, I know what you mean."

They're both good dancers. As they glide across the floor their bodies move closer together unconsciously; it feels comfortable, it feels right.

"I look around and I don't recognize Germany anymore," she says with genuine concern. "We've disappeared. Our people are gone, replaced with zealots. There's just so much evil ..."

"I feel the same," he says as they turn a corner of the floor. "I'm tired of the death, the secrets, the deceit ..." His words trail off.

"Thank God!" she whispers. "It makes me hopeful that someone else sees things my way."

"I may not show it often enough, but I'm concerned as you are. If only ..."

"If only you could help? Could do something?" she asks, looking up into his eyes.

"Yes," he says, his sentence not seeming quite finished.

"But you are, aren't you?" she asks.

"Helping? I suppose ... not really anything significant."

Nicolette hesitates for half a second. "Is that what Margi would say?"

"What?" Bernd inhales. "Margi? Who are you talking about?"

"Margi Wardenberg."

"How do you know Margi?" he asks, looking down into her eyes.

"I came to her and her children's aid a few weeks ago in the park. Some brown shirts were threatening her and I paid her fine. She invited me to her apartment for tea. Her children are wonderful," she says with a smile as tears begin to spring up.

"I see," he says. "That ... that was very kind of you. And yes, her kids are special. Very special." He stares at her, amazed. What are the chances she and Margi would meet! His smiles at the thought of these two taking tea together.

They continue to dance in silence, each contemplating the exchange.

"I saw a photo of you in the apartment," she states softly. "You were with her husband."

Bernd's throat clenches for a moment. "Michael? Yes, he was my childhood friend, we went to university together, we were close." The pair stare at each other's shoulders as they continue in circles around the dance floor.

"Is he the same man you mentioned the night of Rudi's medal ceremony? The one who got tired?"

"I told you about him?"

"Not in so many words, but yes. You mentioned that you had a friend who got tired and took his own life. He left behind a wife and two children," she says gently. "I assume these two are the same?"

Bernd is unsure where this is heading; he remains cautious. He doesn't want to drag Nicolette into what is becoming an increasingly dangerous situation, given Margi's disappearance.

"Your deductive skills are as impressive as your beauty and intelligence, Nicolette," he says, trying to avoid the subject.

"Thank you Bernd. But are they the same man?" she asks firmly.

He looks at her inquisitive face, half-smiles at her ability to get him to talk. He sighs "Yes. The family needed help after Michael's passing. It was a huge shock to them, and to me. I simply did what I'd want someone to do for me if the situation was reversed."

They dance slowly, the heat from their bodies mixing, comforting them both.

"I see. I'm truly sorry about your friend," she says quietly. "But I'm also happy that you helped them. That was very kind of you. Your compassion is amazing, really. We need more of it, don't you think?" she asks softly.

"The whole world needs more compassion."

Nicolette rests her head on his shoulder. "I agree. I'm glad we had this chat. Thank you for sharing your secret with me," she whispers. "Rest assured, it will stay private."

Bernd looks at her head resting on his shoulder. "I'm the one who should be thanking you," he replies. "I must confess, whenever I'm with you, things look brighter. The world seems better," he says quietly.

"And my dancing?" she asks, looking up at him with a playful grin.

"You move like a swan on a lake." He smiles and holds her tighter.

***

The clouds have moved in and blocked out the moonlight. Shallow, weak streetlights struggle to illuminate the road crossing the Spree River that leads to the Chancellery.

On the short drive, Rudi's mind races, struggling with his orders. How in the hell is this possible? The general is a good man, albeit naive. Maybe the rumors of von Dries' involvement with an anti-Reich setup are true? But why Rudi, why has he been assigned to kill von Dries? Is Schwartz behind this? Maybe it's because of his letter. Maybe this is payback for exposing Bernd. Or maybe it's a test, a test to see if he's committed. *Well, Colonel Schwartz, I will show you how committed I am,* he thinks as the truck slows.

The truck drops the ten stormtroopers and Rudi at the Chancellery's main entrance. The guards see the vehicle and immediately approach.

"Heil Hitler! Captain Caracciola, what brings you here tonight?" the smaller guard asks.

"We have a meeting with General von Dries, Captain," Rudi says.

"Very well, do you require assistance?"

"No, we have everything under control," Rudi says sternly. "See that no one enters the Chancellery until we depart."

"*Jawhol* Captain!" the guard replies, saluting.

The entourage walks quickly up the steps and into the main foyer. They make for the staircase that leads to the main offices.

Rudi's heart is beating rapidly. He knows he's been sent on this mission to test his commitment to the Reich, knows they sent him to take out von Dries to make sure. Any less and they will deem him unfit to remain a part of the SS, deem him unfit to drive for the Reich. His worst nightmare, and that's one of the better options—if he doesn't do this, if he doesn't murder von Dries, the chance that he will be alive for any foreseeable amount of time is slim. He must prove he is loyal. He must do it for the Reich. It's all he has—*Belgium's gone, Rudi. This is your life now. Your perfect life. You're a god, Rudi. You saw the eagle. You know your destiny. Fly the silver bird.*

"Let's keep it quiet Captain," Rudi says in a low voice.

"*Jawhol.* The offices should be empty this time of night, but I expect there will be some still working."

Rudi blinks. "The general's office is 420 in the South wing. If we encounter any resistance, your men are to use whatever means necessary against those that would stop us," Rudi says stonily.

"*Ja*, our men have silenced Lugers and of course, knives."

"Good. I'll provide final instructions when we reach the target."

"*Jawhol.*"

Walking softly down the dimly lit hallway, they pass priceless art stolen from the Musée d'Orsay and the Louvre softly illuminated by sconces. If the Chancellery wasn't the epicenter of war, it would make a beautiful museum.

***

Bernd and Nicolette sip champagne after their dance and mingle with the crowd separately. Seeing Nicolette alone, Frau Risk approaches.

"Fräulein von Dries! I see you are enjoying the evening!"

"Very much so," she says with a nod of gratitude. "It's a wonderful event, Frau Risk."

"And I see you're conspiring with the enemy?"

Nicolette is taken aback but manages to maintain her composure. "Sorry, what do you mean?" she asks.

"Herr Rosemeyer of course. He's your fiancé's competitor, is he not?"

Nicolette laughs. "Ah! Yes, they do race against each other, but they're actually good friends."

"Yes, I heard Bernd actually saved Rudi's life at Monza," Frau Risk says, her eyes wide.

"Yes, he did," Nicolette says, stealing a glance in the driver's direction. "He was very brave."

Frau Risk nods, then pauses. "I've always held Bernd in high regard."

"Yes, I'm beginning to as well, Frau Risk."

"A word to the wise," the old woman says softly, her eyes gleaming in the chandelier light. "There are some who think poorly of Herr Rosemeyer. He has a reputation of being a womanizer. Some even speculate he's less than pure—not of direct German descent. Be careful Nicolette, there are many eyes watching tonight."

Nicolette's heart drops with the insinuation. Coldly, she says, "Thank you, Frau Risk, for the advice. I'm *well* aware of Bernd's escapades, but I assure you he is an honest man. Maybe even a noble one."

"Yes, dear. I can see that."

"See what?" Nicolette asks.

"I can see that Bernd is a noble man with a good heart. I can also see you like him, maybe more than a friend should?"

Nicolette is growing angry with the woman.

"Frau Risk, I'm a bit offended!"

Frau Risk pats her arm. "Don't be," she says coolly. "I've known you since you were five years old and have watched you become a beautiful woman. A woman with compassion and honor. I've known Bernd for almost as long.

"Once, when Bernd was just a teen, I saw him give his coat to a gypsy who was freezing to death. His mother scolded him and when she asked why he had given his coat away, he simply said someone needed it more than him.

"A boy that young with a heart that large always matures into a loving man—despite what others may say."

Nicolette is silent for a moment. Softly, she says, "I had not heard that story. But that does sound like Bernd."

"If I may be so bold, you two have more in common than most. Sometimes, life and love are fickle, don't you agree?" she asks, a hint of a mischievous twinkle in her eye as she grins.

Across the ballroom, Bernd is watching the exchange between the two women. What is it about Nicolette that makes Bernd ache so badly? She's not like any other woman he's ever met. Every time he sees her, his heart fills with joy. Just watching her makes him want her, not because of her beauty, but because he sees her soul, her compassion, her love. He feels her integrity, her honesty, her depth. He's bewitched, hopelessly in love.

He feels conflicted, confused. He watches as Frau Risk takes her leave; he takes a deep breath and makes his way to Nicolette.

"Thank you again for the dance," he says gently as he approaches.

"My pleasure Bernd," she says. Her hazel eyes momentarily rob him of any comprehension. "And thank you for the chat. It's funny," she glances after Frau Risk, "every time I talk about you, the mystery grows."

"Mystery?" he asks, spellbound.

"Yes, Frau Risk just shared an interesting story about when you were young. It seems you've been helping people, been being kind from an early age. It's funny, your *reputation* doesn't mesh with the Bernd I know."

He gathers his courage. "Nicolette, might I have word with you over here?"

"Of course," she replies. Her heart tingles.

They walk toward a dark corner with a door leading to a small balcony. They step outside, alone on the balcony, the moon hidden behind a low, dark sky. Soft candlelight from the ballroom peeks through the heavy drapes, splashing softly on Nicolette's face. Her eyes sparkle.

Bernd takes Nicolette's hand, looking down at it in his own.

"I'm not sure how to begin," he says softly.

Nicolette looks deeply at him, her heart skipping, her face hot. She says nothing.

"Since I've met you, I seem to have become ... different. I seem kinder—no not kinder, better. You make me better, Nicolette," he confesses, looking at her.

"Oh, Bernd," she whispers. "I'm not sure what to say."

"Every time I'm with you," he continues, "I get a feeling ... it's hard to describe. And I love that, the effect you have on me."

Her eyes glisten, her lashes fluttering. "Bernd ... what a beautiful thing to say. I ... I feel the same way. I don't care what others say about you, what they think about you. I know you. I feel like I've known you all along."

Bernd takes her other hand and slowly draws her to him. She trembles as their bodies touch lightly.

"I think I'm falling in love with you," he says, lost in her eyes. "I know I shouldn't tell you this, but I can't help myself. You're everything to me. Right now, right this instant ... I could die in your arms and be happy."

Their faces have drawn closer. Bernd leans forward, making to bridge at last the gap between, but backs away at the last second.

"W—What's wrong?" she asks.

Dropping her hands gently, he steps back. "I can't do this. We can't do this! You're engaged to Rudi," he says, taking a step away. "I should know better, I'm sorry!"

She grabs his hands. He doesn't struggle, just looks at her.

"Bernd. You're a good man, an honest man. I know this!"

"I'm sorry Nicolette, I should have never told you how I feel," he says. He looks fearful.

"No, I feel the same! But I'm confused too, I'm not sure what I should do or feel! But I do know this." She holds his hands tighter. "I love you Bernd, with all my heart. I really do."

He gently pushes away, shaking his head. "Oh Nicolette, please forgive me. I should have never put you in this position. I'm so sorry."

He looks back at her, sees her eyes in the night, sees her soul. It shines brightly like the North Star. He feels her humanity, her love, her goodness. He takes another step, turns and walks away.

Tears in her eyes, Nicolette stares as he walks away. She trembles, her mind racing. Each step he takes away from her twists her stomach further. What is she doing? She just told Bernd she loves him! What about Rudi?

She leans against the balcony railing, looking at the dark sky. In that moment, as the moon peeks through the clouds, she knows what to do.

***

Arriving at office 420, Rudi and his men gather outside the door, knives and guns drawn, five men on each side of the door.

"Schlager, let me go in first," Rudi whispers.

"The general will have his aide close by, perhaps in the office foyer. Maybe we should come with you?"

"No, I'll take care of this. I'll call if I need you."

Rudi enters the large office foyer. Colonel Vogel sits behind his desk. He's engrossed in a report and looks up, startled at the intrusion. Behind him is a closed door that leads to the general's private office.

"Captain Caracciola, what brings you here this late?" Vogel asks suspiciously. The assassination plan isn't to take place for another four days, but he knows there are rumors. There are always rumors. He eyes Rudi carefully and wonders if word has leaked. Have they been discovered?

"Heil Hitler!" Rudi says rigidly. "Colonel Vogel, I was hoping to have a word with the general. About the wedding. Is he available?"

Rudi palms a small SS Degen dagger and conceals it in his sleeve cuff; he extends his hand to Vogel, as if to shake, as he approaches the desk.

As Vogel rises to shake Rudi's hand, Rudi slips behind him swiftly and slashes the dagger across Kaufman's neck, immediately slicing his jugular artery.

Before Vogel can yell, Rudi grabs him by the head and places his hand over his mouth. He then plunges the knife into his larynx, silencing Vogel once and for all. The man falls to the floor by the desk; blood slowly pools under his limp body.

Rudi wipes the blood off his dagger on Vogel's jacket, adjusts his uniform and looks at the closed door. You're next, von Dries.

***

It's well past midnight and the ball is growing raucous. The crowd is dancing, drinking and drugging. Bernd's got a big day tomorrow and he's exhausted. His confession to Nicolette has left him shattered. His thoughts swirl around him and he feels simultaneously elated, terrified, and ill. He's never known anything this intense, not even when racing. He floats down the hallway and arrives at the elevator door just as it opens.

Looking up, he sees Nicolette standing alone in the lift. Their eyes lock. Bernd enters the elevator. They stand facing each other; her face shows confusion, joy, desire. The door shuts softly and they are alone.

The elevator lurches and he stumbles. They touch. Bernd stares at her for a moment, slowly reaches for her hand. He is falling. He's light-headed now, his vision blurring.

He takes her head gently in his hands and kisses her softly. "Oh Bernd," she murmurs in response.

"I love you Nicolette," Bernd says softly. "Ever since I met you I've loved you."

***

Rudi opens the general's door and finds von Dries standing at the window, his back to Rudi.

"Guten nacht," von Dries says without looking.

"Heil Hitler!" Rudi replies loudly.

"What can I do for you, Rudi?"

"I think you know, General"

Dries turns to face Rudi. "Yes, I do. A pity it has come to this. Whatever happens tonight won't change anything, Rudi. Except for perhaps your wedding."

"My wedding has nothing to do with this, General," Rudi hisses.

"Yes, I suppose you're right. It doesn't matter. Germany will be defeated just as it was in the last war," he says nonchalantly.

Rudi shakes his head, takes a step closer. "I don't think so, General."

"So Hitler thinks that he can win by eating his own? He's an imbecile and a coward!" von Dries spits. "If he was a real man, *he* would be here, not some racecar driver pretending to be solider!" he proclaims loudly.

"The Fürher has better things to do than deal with traitors," Rudi says snidely.

Dries laughs. "A traitor? I think not, Rudi. You see there are many like me, more than you can imagine. Men who are willing to risk their lives to do the right thing. And the right thing is to get rid of this madman who is destroying Germany!"

"You're mistaken," Rudi growls, anger rising up in him. "It is *your* kind that are mad. How dare you insult the Fürher! He has changed Germany into a power that the world has never seen!"

Dries takes a slow step toward his assassin; as he does, he expertly slips a knife from a hidden pocket in the sleeve of his field jacket. He holds it in his right hand. He may die tonight, but he won't go down without a fight.

"Perhaps, but at what cost, Rudi? Hitler has done unspeakable things to our own. He and his henchmen are killing German citizens, not just Jews."

"To make a soufflé, you have to break some eggs," Rudi quips. "And as for the Jews, they're swine and don't deserve anything but what they get at the hands of the SS. The less of them, the purer we become."

Disgust spreads over von Dries' face. "Such a shallow perspective, Rudi. But then again, I would expect nothing more from someone like you."

"You mean someone like your future son-in-law?" Rudi sneers.

The general chuckles. "You must be joking! Nicolette knows who you really are. She'll have nothing to do with you, soon enough."

"Well, we shall see, General," Rudi says, burning with confidence.

Dries can sense the end is near. He needs to make a move soon. Rudi is younger, faster, and a bit taller but the general has experience. He senses Rudi is on edge, unsure what to do next. He needs a distraction to make his attack work. He may not make it past the guards waiting for him outside his office, but at least he can take Rudi with him.

"There's nothing to see, Rudi," von Dries says, cracking a smile. "Nicolette has already told me she won't marry you. Seems she's got a new interest, a new admirer. Someone with courage and morals, unlike you. Perhaps you know him? A certain ... Bernd Rosemeyer?"

"Shut up you old fool!" Rudi snaps. "There's nothing between Nicolette and Bernd! She loves me and we will marry soon enough!"

Dries eggs Rudi on. "Well, then I guess you haven't seen them together like I have? Quite the couple in my opinion. I saw them together at your medal ceremony. Alone. Kissing." He knows this last lie will set Rudi off.

Rudi's face turns bright red. His rage chokes him momentarily; just as Rudi begins to respond, von Dries grabs an ashtray from his desk and hurls it at Rudi's head. It hits its mark. A large gash in his forehead gushes blood as the ashtray clatters to the ground. Rudi is blinded by the pain and the blood which drips down over his eyes; he stumbles back, holding his forehead.

The general darts out from behind his desk, grabs Rudi's arm that holds the knife and twists it behind Rudi's back; the knife falls easily from Rudi's hand. Rudi may be fast on the track, but in close-quarters combat, he's a child.

Dries raises his knife overhead, ready to slice open Rudi's neck. Suddenly, a guard bursts into the office—he fires a silenced round and the bullet hits the general in the back. von Dries grunts loudly, the wind knocked out of him. He idles for a moment, then collapses slowly to the ground. Rudi, shocked from the counter attack, stands over von Dries' body, shaking.

***

Bernd's hotel room is dark and quiet. Soft lights from the street illuminate two bodies standing silently in the middle of the room. He holds Nicolette tightly.

They kiss passionately and deeply. He slowly removes the hairpins holding her bun in place;

her hair falls with a hush onto her shoulders. He pulls back and looks at her; shimmering lights from passing cars sneak into the room and dance like crystal across her hair and face.

He kisses her again. He gently turns her around, kissing her neck softly as he slowly pushes down the shoulders of her gown. Her breath is coming quickly, her heart is beating fast and deep. Bernd kisses her shoulders and spins her again to face him. She gasps softly as he begins to kiss her chest, then her breasts.

He gently pushes her dress again—it slides off gracefully, landing in a puddle at her feet. Standing in her panties in the darkness, she pulls Bernd toward her and kisses him.

They stay that way for what seems like hours. She takes his hand and leads him to the bed. They touch each other, exploring each other's bodies lovingly. She kneels on the bed and helps him get undressed.

Naked and exposed, they tentatively kiss. Then with hunger, they intertwine their bodies with force, with passion, the desire becoming too much to control. They are ravenous for each other.

Nicolette mounts Bernd. As he enters her, she gasps with desire. The heat from their bodies is intense and they sweat with passion. They climax together and collapse in the bed in a heap of contentment. Bernd holds her tightly; as they drift off to sleep, perfectly nestled in each other's arms, Bernd whispers, "I love you."

***

Rudi, standing over von Dries, clears the blood from his eyes with a handkerchief.

"Sir, are you alright?!" the officer shouts, still holding the smoking luger in his hand.

"I'm fine!" Rudi barks. He looks at the man's limp body on the ground—he's still breathing. "I was about to send this miserable swine to his death before you came in!"

General von Dries struggles to his knees and places his hand over the exit wound in his chest. Blood seeps out from between his fingers as he screams, "You bastard! Couldn't defend yourself so you had to rely on your goons! I could have taken you with me, you little shit! Me, an old man! Doesn't say much about your manhood does it Rudi?"

Rudi's eyes are cleared of blood and he has regained some composure. He smiles sinisterly. "Perhaps, old man, but who's lying on the floor dying?"

"You're a weak piece of shit. I hope you burn in hell, but not before you see Bernd and Nicolette together," von Dries says, panting and lightheaded.

Rudi swiftly kicks the limp man in his side. "If I do, I'll see you there you traitorous bastard!"

With one long, swift swipe, Rudi slits von Dries' throat. Rudi stands above him as the general lays dying. "To the victor go the spoils, old man."

Rudi feels something inside him harden like steel; he realizes, at that moment, he has crossed a line. There's no return from his destiny.

***

Bernd wakes in the morning to the sound of birds chirping sweetly outside his window. It's a beautiful day; the sun has chased the low-lying clouds away. Bright light streams in, warming the hotel room. He rolls over, expecting to find Nicolette nestled in the soft white sheets, but the bed is empty. She's gone.

He sits up with a jolt and looks around. There's not a trace of her. He can just barely smell her perfume lingering in the room. He lies back in bed and recounts the night. A profound warmth spreads through his body, confirming what he already knows. He loves her. He loves her as he's never loved anyone in his life.

A knock on the door startles him. He jumps up and grabs one of the two terry cloth robes that the hotel has generously provided. He wishes she was still here, wearing the second robe, having coffee and pastries, wasting the day away in bed.

He opens the door and finds a hotel porter with a small box in his hand.

"Herr Rosemeyer, this was just dropped off for

you."

"Thank you. Who is this from?"

"My apologies, sir, but I don't know. I was only told to bring it to you."

"Thank you," he says. The porter takes his leave.

Returning to bed, Bernd opens the small gift box. It is elaborately wrapped; he removes the gift paper, wondering who it could be from. There's no note. He opens the box and finds a necklace inside.

He picks it up gently by the chain and dangles it in front of his face, inspecting it. A Star of David pendant hangs from it.

He looks inside the box and finds a small hand written note:

"For those who have the courage of kindness.

Love, Nicolette"

39. A HARD RAIN FALLS

It's sleeting heavily. Bernd pulls at his rain-soaked hat; it bends at the brim, leaves him looking like a sad, lost dog.

He's making his way to Margi's apartment to check in on her and the kids. Hard to believe it's been almost a month since he's seen them—*this last month has been as much of a tempest as this storm*, he thinks. On cue, the rain whips up and pounds against his face as he shivers beneath his topcoat.

As he lumbers down the dark street, his thoughts turn to the time he spent with Margi and Michael at university. It was 1932 when the three had started at Humboldt University in Berlin. The three of them were inseparable for nearly four turbulent years.

Bernd and Michael had grown up together in Berlin's Schöneberg neighborhood. It was a place where wealthy actors, industrialists and politicians lived, their mansions tucked away in a tree-lined hamlet just twenty blocks south of Nollendorfplatz, the heart of Berlin's gay scene. The two loved the slow walk to town that shifted more from affluence to seediness with every step.

Both their families were wealthy, Bernd's family from real estate and Michael's from steel. They spent their youth together doing what young boys do—playing army, hunting for bugs, shattering a neighbor's window while playing stick ball.

They were thirteen when they built a secret hideout behind Michael's house. The fort became a place of sanctity, of firsts. Cigarettes were smoked, sex explored, dreams were made and shared. They made a pact that they'd attend university together—Michael was going to be a doctor, Bernd a history professor. But the truth of men always takes a different trajectory than the chrysalis of youth.

By the time they got to university, all they could think of was girls, beer and how to break curfew without getting caught. And then they met Margi.

She was stunning, stubborn, and a proud Jew.

On May 10th, 1933, Students of the National Socialist Student Union, along with many of their professors, burned over 20,000 books on a warm night. The university allowed, condoned, even encouraged this book burning, which pissed off an already angry Margi even more.

The books, which made up the bonfire, were mainly by Jewish, communist, liberal, and socio-critical authors. The SNSSU ignited the lot in front of the Old Library as a small band from the SS's paramilitary detachment played Horst-Wessel-Lied, the anthem of the Nazi party, over and over. The books burned as the students sang along.

Margi was already a strong and enraged fighter for women's rights, and this event took her anger to a new level. Yes, women got the right to vote in Germany in 1918, but it had taken too long—women had been critical to WWI and had stood shoulder-to-shoulder with men in every way. And now the Nazi Party was threatening to eradicate the ideology and history of her people, the people who had stood up to tyranny and given her the right to vote. She was a radical feminist before they had invented the category.

"You can all burn in hell!" Margi yells as the students toss more books into the fire, her face illuminated by the dancing flames.

Bernd and Michael, looking on warily from the grass in front of their dorm, overhear the stream of insults the young woman hurdles at the SS.

"Who the hell is that?" Bernd says.

"I don't know, but she's divine!" Michael responds in awe.

"Go ask her out." Bernd glances at Michael, who stands dumbstruck next to him. "Michael, go!" Bernd barks.

"Me? She'll just want to go out with you Bernd," he says, his eyes never parting from Margi's fiery silhouette. "Remember Tina? I carried her books home all year and all she did was talk about you! No, look at you Bernd, look at me. I don't stand a chance."

"Bullshit," Bernd says flatly. He knows Michael's right about Tina, but Michael won't get much of anywhere in this life if he can't stop comparing himself to others. "Get over there and talk to her. She's perfect! I've never heard such colorful insults, even when Herr Kakov tried to give you detention 10th year!"

"I don't know Bernd, she looks scary."

"Michael, get your ass over there. She'd be fool to not talk to you! Ask her if she needs some help."

Michael swallows, then walks slowly toward the flames. Margi is screaming for the SS to leave. "Excuse me, Fräulein," Michael shouts over the singing and music.

"Fuck off, unless you want to help me stop these bastards!" she screams at him, her eyes wide.

And with that, Michael reaches down and grabs a pile of smoldering books from the edge of the fire. He stands, a devilish smile spreading across his face.

She is momentarily stunned by Michael's actions. Something changes in her eyes. She tosses her head back and laughs. "Let's get you out here, you marvelous bastard!" she whispers.

The pair sprint off, clutching armfuls of hot smoldering history as shouts of protest recede behind them.

That night in Michael's dorm, they had talked until 5 AM, delving into politics, literature, love, and their families. They nearly missed their classes the next day after falling asleep reading passages from the outlawed books. The fact that they were both Jewish made their chance encounter even richer. They were infatuated with each other. Their romance blossomed over the next year, and they spent all their spare time together either making love or bitching about the low-lifes taking over their country. Bernd, unaccustomed to being the third wheel, fell into a comfortable role as Michael and Margi's relationship grew. He supported Michael's love of Margi and could see that Michael was growing and thriving in her company. He was so proud of Michael, though Margi's presence had displaced his own position as Michael's best friend. But Bernd was equally enthralled with Margi's feistiness. Her stubbornness and tenacity impressed him and her passion for life inspired him. She was a truly remarkable woman, and he loved them both separately and as a couple.

One night, as Bernd and Margi walked back to their dorms, she asked, "Bernd, I've been meaning to ask you. Why don't you have a real girlfriend?"

Bernd laughed. "I do! I have many!" he said with a boastful smile.

"That's my point! I know there's more to you than this playboy you want people to see." Margi always spoke bluntly.

"Ah, but there are so many fish in the sea. And besides, I'm not ready to be with just one person," he had said defensively. He wasn't used to being questioned about his relationships.

"Yes, I can see that. But you don't mean to keep this up forever, do you? Don't you want to have someone special in your life?"

"I do!" he replied, looking ahead to the dorm. "I have you and Michael—the rest is just filler."

Margi was silent for a moment.

"Bernd, I've known you for a long time now," she began slowly. "I see how you treat women. I'm not saying you treat them poorly, but it's almost like they're not enough for you. It's like you're searching for something else, for something more," she said gently.

Bernd glanced at her, then back at the dorm. He sighed. "Well, to be honest, it's just that I find everyone so damn interesting. When I meet someone new, it's like I want to crawl inside their body—get to truly know them, to really understand them. And every time I do, it ends up leading to some kind of romance. I can't seem to keep my emotions in check. I meet someone new and I just dive in and forget about who I was just with."

Margi had chuckled. She'd seen it happen many times. Nearly every weekend, if she recalled correctly. "Does this apply to all people, or just pretty girls?" she had asked.

"I don't know, Margi," he replied, deep in thought. He trusted her fully; he could say anything around her. "Really, I don't know. Men, women—everyone's so interesting. I want to meet everyone." Margi smiled at the ground. "Is that wrong?" Bernd asks, a breathless excitement in his voice.

She had grabbed him by the arm and pulled him closer as they walked. "No Bernd, there's nothing wrong with that!" she'd said reassuringly. "But I do worry that you'll never find enough, be it man or woman, to satisfy your curiosity."

His chin dropped to his chest, his breathing growing a little shallow. "Shit. I don't know what I'm doing, Margi," he said. "I see what you and Michael have and I want that too, but I'm torn. I want more than just one person. True love to me means I shouldn't have to limit myself; it should be everywhere and with everyone. Man or woman. Isn't that what freedom is? And isn't freedom when you find love?"

Margi had thought about it for a moment. "Yes, freedom to love is important. Maybe the most important thing in life. It's okay, Bernd. Michael and I will always be here for you. You'll sort it out. We'll sort it out. Together. You know we love you unconditionally, right?"

It was in that moment with Margi that Bernd knew his sexuality would be a work in progress for many years to come.

It's 5 PM, a drenching dusk settling in as Bernd approaches the alleyway to Margi's apartment. The kids should be home from school and Margi would be helping with homework and getting dinner ready. Maybe he'll stay a bit, play with the kids, talk to Margi about her exit papers, maybe reminisce.

Sadness swirls about him and mixes with his longing to be with Margi and the kids. He misses them dearly.

As he climbs the stairs and enters the long hallway leading to the apartment, a vivid image of the necklace Nicolette sent him after their night together flashes through his mind. God he misses her. The five-pointed star looked familiar, but there are thousands of them in Germany. He clears his head and his thoughts return to Margi and the kids. He's practically running down the hallway with anticipation.

Arriving at the door, he uses their coded knock. He stands tall with a smile, hoping to give her a hug. He waits.

Silence. No footsteps, no odor of freshly baking bread creeping out from below the door.

He knocks again. Nothing.

They should be home. Maybe they're at the park? In this rain, not a chance. A strange wave of foreboding washes over him; it settles in his gut. Something isn't right. The feeling rumbles through his soul.

Bernd walks down the hallway, descends the stairs and exits into the alley. He locates the fire escape for the building just to his left and pulls it down. Remnants of snow and ice part from the ladder and lightly dust his overcoat. He grabs the first rung, the cold steel stinging his hands through his gloves, and begins to quietly climb the three flights to Margi's apartment.

He ducks as he passes open windows on the way up, smells cooking sausage and hears children playing from the other apartments. He grows more concerned as he gets closer. The lights aren't on.

Arriving at Margi's window, he peers inside through the wet, streaked glass. It's dark inside, but he can make out more details as his eyes adjust. He rapidly compares it to his memory of the apartment—and everything is wrong. The furniture is new, the bric-a-brac is prodigious and garish, and the photos he can make out through the smudged window show a different family. He sits down heavily on the fire escape and realizes something horrible has happened to the Margi and the kids.

Before he descends, he pulls his water-soaked hat down tighter and conceals his face just a bit more.

He reaches the ground and knows in his soul Schwartz is behind this. His shoulders slump as he shuffles in the dark.

As he walks, the thought of the necklace returns. It was Margi's necklace, the same one she wore at university. The one that Michael gave her.

40. A Stab in the Dark

Schwartz saunters into Cafe Rix, taking off his overcoat as he approaches a table. He hangs it on a nearby rack and takes a seat.

"So, what can I do for you, Herr Caracciola?"

"Your little prank wasn't funny, Colonel," Rudi says gruffly.

"Prank?" Schwartz asks, cocking his head as he feigns surprise.

Rudi continues in a low voice. "I know the purge was needed. There are conspirators, I *know* this, we all know this. But why the games? Why did you assign me von Dries?" he asks, sounding almost frantic as he holds Schwartz's eyes in his own burning gaze. "To prove my loyalty?"

"Ah, I see," Schwartz says with a knowing smirk. "Games? No, it wasn't a game Rudi—it was a test. You need to understand that as an honorary SS officer, there are some who think you're not as committed as you should be." He lights his cigarette, his beady eyes still trained on Rudi's.

"Committed!" Rudi spits, incredulous. "Colonel, *I'm* the one who told you about Bernd's activities, his sympathizing! *I* told you about the Wardenbergs and you didn't even believe me!"

"Yes, all true," Schwartz replies his eyebrows raised as he exhales smoke.

Rudi lunges his upper body over the cafe table, hissing. "Look, I'm willing to do what the Reich needs, even kill if need be, but now you've placed me in an awkward position! How am I supposed to marry the daughter of a traitor? I killed her father, for Christ's sake!"

"Indeed, these are good questions, but you must realize that it was necessary. We uncovered von Dries' assassination plot just in time. While we know what he was planning, we still don't know who, besides himself and Vogel, is involved. We had to make sure you, his daughter's fiancé, weren't involved. And as for your marriage, well I suspect you're reconsidering?"

"You're goddamn right I am! I doubt she had anything to do with it, but I sure can't marry her now!" Rudi says, running a hand violently through his hair.

"We have no evidence that she was involved, but we haven't questioned her yet," Schwartz says.

"Why not?" Rudi asks; he sounds like an angry child. He wishes Schwartz would just make her disappear. If he did, he could walk away, albeit tainted from his relationship with her, but most would sympathize with him —duped by a traitorous bitch.

"There are bigger fish to fry, Rudi. I'm looking for the Polish connection, and I'm close. In a few days we'll have exposed all of the conspirators. Then we can take care of your little Nicolette."

"Fine," Rudi says, slumping back into his chair. "Just make sure she disappears. Quickly."

He is feeling better. His concerns with von Dries' murder are slowly evaporating, like gasoline spilt on a hot summer day. The general was a traitor and died like the pig he was.

While he still may have feelings for Nicolette, they too are quickly evaporating as his resentment for her grows. A slight smile spreads across his face at the thought of Nicolette's imminent arrest. Things are falling into place.

41. SABOTAGE

It's the day before the final speed record. Back in Berlin, Schwartz is meeting with Hitler and Göring at the Chancellery.

Göring addresses the group. "Gentlemen, there is the Bernd Rosemeyer matter to discuss; shall we get started? I've read your report, Schwartz. It seems we have some egg on our face. I suggest you get rid of him as soon as possible," he says dryly. "We can't have a Jew break the world speed record. We would look like idiots."

"The attempt is scheduled for tomorrow, correct?" Hitler asks.

"Correct, mein Fürher. The people of Germany are very excited to see our new cars on our new autobahn!" Schwartz braces himself for outrage. "And to that end, I'd like to keep Bernd around for a bit longer."

"Why?" Göring shouts. "He's a Jew! The sooner he's gone, the better!"

"General, if you'll allow me to explain," Schwartz says firmly, yet delicately. "Bernd's untimely death before the race would make our efforts look weak. As you know, Rosemeyer is the best-known driver Germany has. Plus, if Caracciola doesn't set the record and Bernd is dead, we have no way of securing the record." His weak argument falls on deaf ears.

"Bullshit, Colonel! *Mercedes* can set the

record, I've seen their car! Get rid of him," Göring barks. "And I hold you personally responsible for letting a Mischling into the SS ranks!" he adds, pointing at Schwartz.

The euphoric effects of the Eukodol now washing over Hitler, he bids, "General, hold on. The colonel may have a point." He realizes that it might be useful to have two horses in the race instead of one.

"Thank you, mein Fürher," Schwartz says with another bow. He addresses Göring carefully, "Think of Bernd as insurance. If Rudi is slower than Bernd—and that's a big if—Germany can claim the record. However, before the race, I would simply persuade Bernd to denounce his past and people, so should he be the winner, Germany will still have a clean victory. If he is unwilling to do so, I will make sure Bernd never sets the record."

"Tell us how—and it better be good," Göring growls.

"Well, if need be, we can make sure Bernd's car malfunctions ... to ensure Rudi wins."

"Hmm," Göring grunts. "That might work," he says gruffly.

"General, the record is far more important for Germany than Bernd ever could be. Imagine the world reading of our achievement! I can handle Bernd, trust me," he says, looking firmly into Göring's eyes.

"Yes, you do have a point Colonel, the record is incredibly important," Hitler, now feeling the electricity of the Eukodol, says.

"Immensely so, sir," Schwartz says flatteringly. "I've spoken to August and there is a plan for all contingencies. Rest assured that we *will* set a record tomorrow and it *will* be by a pure German driver."

"So you've spoken to August about this?" Hitler inquires. "How does he feel about having a Jew driver?"

Schwartz shakes his head slightly in acknowledgment, saying, "Herr Horch is understandably disappointed. He has assured me that we can work together to solve this small issue. Keep in mind that only a small group of people know of Bernd's ancestry."

"Colonel, need I remind you that this is the worst-kept secret in the Reich." Göring senses something queer in Schwartz's hesitation to nip this problem in the bud. Little Schwartz must be in love, he thinks. This pansy must have a plan to save that dirty Jew. Probably his only hope to get Rosemeyer to give him the time of day.

"It's only a matter of time before this is known by all," he continues. "I suspect, given your ... sexual proclivities, you might have a soft spot for Bernd? Maybe that's how he got into the SS in the first place? With your help?" he challenges, waving a hand accusingly at Schwartz.

"I assure you that is not that case, General!"

Schwartz snaps.

Göring stares at Schwartz. It's unlike him to address a commanding officer in this manner. He's sure Schwartz is up to something. If Schwartz hadn't delivered Red Hat, he'd seriously consider shooting him on the spot. Instead, he steels himself as he sits back in his chair.

"Perhaps, perhaps not," he says, crossing his arms. "In any case, this is on you, Colonel. We expect to set the world record tomorrow with a pure German driver. Understood?" he commands.

"Of course, General," Schwartz says through gritted teeth.

"And Colonel, one more thing."

"Ja?"

"Make sure Caracciola wins!" Göring spits.

"Jawhol, General, and thank you both for your flexibility. Tomorrow will be a great day for the Reich."

"See to it," Göring mutters. "And keep your dick in your pants, Colonel."

42. Backup Plan

That afternoon, Schwartz arrives at the Auto Union offices; men are streaming by as he walks up the stairs to August's office. He knocks, hears August grumble, "Komm herein."

Schwartz takes a seat. "So August, I'm sure you're aware of our little problem?" he asks, his beady eyes flat in the dim office lights.

August pushes back in his chair. "You mean that fucking Rosemeyer?"

"Our leaders would like *us* to take care of it."

August shakes his head, a faraway look in his eyes. "I've worked hard on this car, but I'll be damned if I'll let a Jew win! I can't believe we've come so far and now a Jew is going to screw it up! This is *your* fault Schwartz!" he bellows, shaking a finger at the colonel.

"Easy, August. Bernd's ancestry is as much as a surprise to me as it is to you. But that's water under the bridge now."

"It's still your. Fucking. Fault, Schwartz! You should have never allowed him into the SS and into my team! *You* need to fix this!"

"I will," Schwartz says flatly as he lights a cigarette. "Look," he exhales smoke, "here's the situation. If Bernd is faster than Rudi, we'll need to make sure we have options."

"Yeah, like what?" August grunts.

"Well, first I can speak to Bernd personally and let him know that winning isn't in his interest."

August guffaws immediately at the suggestion. "You're kidding, right? Bernd is a driver and drivers live to win. You think you can just ask him nicely to throw the race?"

"In fact, I do. We maintain a certain relationship. Once I tell him that there will be consequences, he'll listen."

"Bullshit!" August yells. "Just because you two homos—just because—that doesn't mean he'll listen to you!" he stammers.

Schwartz stares August in the eyes and blows smoke into his face. "First," he says, bitingly, "my activities are of no concern to you, you little shit. Second, if Bernd won't cooperate, we'll need to make sure we have a backup plan."

"Yeah, so what's your backup plan, Romeo?"

"Well, that's why I'm here," Schwartz says calmly. "It's not my first option, but if he's faster we'll need to break his car somehow." August winces at the suggestion. "Tell me how to create a mechanical issue on the car that will prevent him from winning. Something easy, something I can do that isn't too complicated."

"You want me to sabotage my own car?!" August bellows. "I'd rather just put a bullet in him and be done with it, the stinking Jew! And while I'm at it, maybe put a bullet in you!"

Schwartz bangs his open palm on the desk. "Need I remind you who you're talking to!" he yells with startling force. "*Despite* how you feel, Bernd is a hero to the German people, you idiot! If we simply shoot him, there will be questions! He will become a martyr! If he loses, he will be discredited. Can your pea-size brain comprehend that? If you make a threat like that to me again, it will be your last!"

"Fine! And after he loses, we put a bullet in him! He's cost me the race and my reputation, the fucking traitor!" August shouts.

"Let's take it one step at a time August," Schwartz says, kneading his forehead as he thinks of a way to diffuse August's temper. If he didn't need Horch right now, he'd take his ass to prison. "If Bernd is winning and I can't get him to back off, I'll take care of the car. If Rudi is winning, there's no problem."

"Bullshit! Mercedes will *not* be faster, you idiot! My car is *much* better!"

"Oh Jesus, August, perhaps, but let's see how it plays out. Can you tell me how to sabotage the car or not?"

"I say kill him now and be done with it," August mutters under his breath.

Schwartz does not give up, decides to play to the only thing motiving Horch—a win. "August!

Don't you want the world to see the Streamliner? It's fast and beautiful, a tribute to Auto Union! Wouldn't you rather see it compete than sit idle with no driver?"

August sits silently, his eyes fixed on the desk. Schwartz has a point. He settles a bit. Horch struggles to think of a solution to their common problem. Then it comes to him. "Okay, Okay. I can't believe I'm going to tell you this, but I think I know what to do."

"Tell me."

"Look, we can't have the car develop a mechanical. It would look bad for us—Auto Union unable to make a reliable car, not good for us. What if the car crashed? It would look like driver error. Much better. Stupid Jew couldn't drive. Not our fault," he says gruffly.

Schwartz sits back in his chair and waits for August to explain. "Ah, I see. So how do you propose we make the car crash?"

A crash! The thought of Bernd mangled makes his stomach flip. He prays August's plan won't be fatal—he just needs Bernd sidelined, not dead. He still has hope that he'll be able to persuade Bernd to renounce and avoid this mess.

"Easy. At the turnaround, the mechanics will be busy refueling. We simply remove one of the two steering pins. That'll be enough to cause the car to crash once he's at speed."

"Interesting," Schwartz says. "If the

Streamliner bests Rudi on the first run, you can still claim—prove," he corrects himself as August opens his mouth to object, "that the Streamliner is the better car. We can then pull the pin for the return run. Auto Union looks good, Bernd looks incompetent, and *someone* sets a fucking record!"

"Maybe it's a solution for you, but I'm still pissed! We've worked our asses off! We should win this!" August says, his voice rising once again.

"Look, August, I know you've worked hard, but we need to be smart about this. The record is what's important and we can't have a Jew winning."

"*Ja, ja* I know," he says reluctantly. "I understand it but it doesn't mean I have to like it," he huffs.

"No you don't, my friend. I completely understand your predicament. Let's hope I can talk some sense into Bernd. There's still a chance I can get him to renounce the Jews. It wouldn't be the first time we've converted a Jew into a Nazi, albeit an impure one," he says.

August waves his arms in the air dismissively. "Honestly, I don't give a fuck anymore. The chances Bernd will back off are slim. As much as I'd love to see our car win, we need to make sure a *true* German wins."

"Understood. Let's meet before the race so you can show me the steering pins and explain how to remove them."

"*Ja*, okay," August says conceding. "But this whole thing is shit! You owe me, Schwartz. I'm sacrificing a lot to take care of your problem." He points at Schwartz.

"It's not for me, my friend—it's for the Reich."

43. Convert or else

Colonel Marcus Schwartz sits alone at table in the dimly lit bar of the Hotel Grand. He sips B&B from a crystal snifter that smells of coriander and cloves. Its sweetness dances on his tongue before it slides down his throat and warms his belly.

The hotel is busy. From his vantage, he can see the lobby, the main entrance and the large windows; Berliners pass in and out of the frame as they bustle along the streets.

A well-dressed Bernd enters the lobby and shakes the cold from his expensive grey wool overcoat. He looks around, spots the bar, and takes off his coat. He spots Marcus; Bernd gives him a nod as he confidently approaches.

"Thanks for meeting me tonight, my old friend," Schwartz says, standing and shaking Bernd's hand.

Bernd tosses his coat on the spare chair and replies with a faint smile. "How could I refuse a drink with my friend?"

"It's been a long time, eh?"

"Too long."

"Excited for tomorrow? Everything ready?" Schwartz asks, sipping his B&B. "My apologies," he says with a start. "Would you care for something?"

"I'll have whatever you're drinking," Bernd responds.

"Waiter, bring us two please. I might as well order another for myself." Schwartz turns again to Bernd. "Can't have you drinking alone, can we? So about tomorrow, everything is good?"

"As good as it *can* be. The car is ready and so am I." He pulls out a pack of Junos and lights one; the smoke rises slowly, partially obscuring Bernd's face.

"The people love you, you know," Schwartz says.

"I suppose some do."

"Some more than others?" Schwartz posits. "I'm familiar with that—you know when you love someone and they don't share that feeling?" Schwartz says, a shade of melancholy appearing in his eyes. "Sad, don't you think?"

"I suppose."

"Yes, I'm sure you understand this..."

"How's Dominique?"

"Haven't seen her. Been too busy," Schwartz replies in monotone.

"You do seem busy. I called your office several times last week but I was told you weren't available." Schwartz shrugs and stays silent. "But now we're here and you're not too busy for me. I appreciate that."

"I always have time for my good friends. You should know that," Schwartz says. The two men sit facing forward at the bar, but Schwartz casts a gaze toward his visitor. "How long have we known each other? Three years? We've had some good times, haven't we?

"Many."

"So many memories! We've always trusted each other, haven't we?"

"Of course Marcus..."

Bernd falls silent as the waiter brings two crystal snifters to the table before turning on his heel and hustling away. The men toast each other. "To memories!" Schwartz says.

Bernd replies, "To memories!" as they lift their glasses.

"Trust," Schwartz says as he sucks at the flavor in his mouth. "Funny thing. It takes two, don't you think?" he asks inquisitively.

"Of course. Trust is mutual. If it isn't mutual, it isn't trust."

"Yes, you're right, so right. So then—why didn't you trust me?"

"Excuse me?"

"Your secret." A glass shatters in the hotel kitchen. "You could have told me. I maybe could have helped."

Bernd sets his glass down slowly and stares at the colonel. "I'm afraid I don't know what you're talking about, Marcus."

Deep inside, he already knows why Marcus has agreed to meet with him. He suspects Marcus will want *something* in exchange for information on Margi and the kids. He sits back in his chair and waits silently.

"I know about the Wardenbergs," Schwartz says.

Bernd stiffens at the mention and remains silent.

"I know you don't trust me, but did you underestimate me too? You know I always find out, don't you?

Bernd extinguishes his cigarette aggressively, contemplating what Marcus has said. Visions of punching him in the face flitter through his mind—he quickly dismisses them.

"No. I just thought that you wouldn't care. They mean nothing to you. Nothing to Germany," he says bluntly.

"Mmm, I see. But I do care. Just for different reasons than you might think."

"What do you mean?" Bernd asks, defense coloring his voice.

Schwartz sighs. "We know about your blood

certificate. Your ancestry. We know it all, Bernd."

Bernd is momentarily stunned—but he quickly relaxes in the truth. It feels ... good.

Now exposed, he feels refreshed. As if a large weight has been lifted from his soul. He suddenly feels this surfacing of his true identity could be a good thing, something he can use to help Margi and the kids.

"A Jew *can*not hold the world speed record, my friend," Schwartz says as he swirls the B&B in the snifter. "You, more than anyone, should know this."

Confused by the shift toward the record, Bernd asks, "What? What are you talking about, Marcus?"

Schwartz sets his glass down and leans closer to Bernd, catching a whiff of his scent. He breathes it in heavily through his nostrils—movie memories of him and Bernd in Frankfurt flash in his head.

Forgetting for a brief moment the task at hand, Marcus shakes his head clear and says quietly, "Let me lay it out for you, my dear friend. You are a Jew and a sympathizer, and we have proof. You cannot win tomorrow unless you renounce the Jews."

"You want me to renounce my own people? So that I can win a race? I'm surprised, Marcus, but I guess I shouldn't be."

"Bernd, look at me," Marcus commands. "You have set certain things in motion, things that are out of my control. I'm trying to help you. I'm trying to save Margi and the children.

Bernd's fists clench at the mention of Margi and the children's safety falling from Schwartz's mouth. *The son of a bitch* does *know what happened to them.* He glowers at Schwartz, every muscle in his face straining.

"What about Margi and her kids? What have you done?" he hisses in Schwartz's face.

"They are safe for now, but their fate lies in your hands. Renounce the Jews and I'll make sure they stay safe."

"You fucking bastard," Bernd spits in a whisper.

Marcus, giving a slight wave of his hand, says, "Not my proudest moment. But surely you understand that we can't allow you, a Jew, to win the race."

Bernd's stare darts between Marcus' beady, conniving eyes. Can he trust him?

"So if I renounce, you'll let them go?" he asks stonily.

"Yes."

"And what guarantee do I have? How can I trust you?"

"You have my word."

A strong wind blows outside. A woman's umbrella turns inside-out as she passes the hotel.

"And if I don't?"

Schwartz winces. He has all the cards; he's left nothing for Bernd to play with. Nothing except a bluff, which Bernd seems to be pursuing. He's seen it before. Men in desperate situations, backs to the wall, searching for a way out—they either cave or bluff. Bernd is bluffing, there is no doubt. He cares too much for the Wardenbergs. Marcus decides to make it clear.

"I can guarantee you this, my friend. You will not win tomorrow, no matter what," he says. He has assumed no threatening tone, but something about the statement rings eerily, like some unshakeable declaration by the fates. "If you try, you will be sending the Wardenbergs to their death. And yourself as well."

Marcus' words hang in the air. Bernd sits in silence, his shoulders drooping imperceptibly.

"Bernd, I know this may shock you—or maybe you don't care. But I do have feelings for you. You must know that by now," Marcus says. Bernd knows he's telling the truth. "Please, I'm begging you. Make the right choice. The right choice for you and for the Wardenbergs."

Bernd bites his tongue and looks away.

"You have until tomorrow to think it over."

44. FOR THE RECORD

The blueberry jam stains as she slowly spreads it onto a stale piece of bread. She takes a small bite. She runs to the bathroom and gags, her stomach doing flips. Back at the kitchen table, she sits with her head in her hands and thinks.

Her mind is a mess, reels of her thoughts playing at extreme speeds. She recalls the night with Bernd and her heart swells with emotion. God, it felt right! She feels her love for him deep in her soul. Her jumbled thoughts surge again and Rudi's face appears, her bliss replaced with guilt.

Her love for Rudi has gone, that much is clear—it's drained away as water does in a sink. Her engagement nags at her. Is this who she is? A woman who sleeps with her fiancé's competitor? *Schiesse*! She needs to call it off, but when? Today? Before the race?

She shakes her head, tries to think clearly. If only her father were here, she could ask him, but he's been missing for over twenty-four hours and it's the day of the race. She wrings her hands in silent desperation; he should be here!

Thoughts of him being caught, captured, tortured flash through her vision. Her mind throbs with concern, guilt, thousands of horrible thoughts. She needs desperately to talk to her father.

As she slowly rubs her temples, she hears a

knock on the door.

Her heart beats fast in her throat, her shoulders, behind her ears. She prays it's someone from her father's office, someone who knows what's happened! She runs to the door, and throws it open. She's greeted by a familiar face, Herr Hugo Boss, the head of the Metzingen based clothing company. Her hopes crash down.

Boss, who is a member of the German Labor front, the SS, and is a prominent supporter of the Reich, has been invited to today's race.

"Guten morgen! Ready to go?" asks Boss jovially.

"Herr Boss, good to see you," she says, attempting a smile for her visitor. "Have you heard from my father?" she asks quickly.

"Why no, not since a few nights ago when he invited me to the race," he says, puzzled as he shuffles in and stomps his cold feet. "Where is he?" Boss asks. His black overcoat absorbs all the morning light in the foyer, creating a new darkness from what was sunny only moments ago.

As she closes the heavy wooden door after him, frowning deeply, she says, "I wish I knew. It's unlike him. It's a big day and I know he was planning to be there."

Boss shrugs. "Knowing your father, he probably got tied up with something and went to the race directly."

"Perhaps," she says. He would have called. *Boss doesn't know shit.*

"Come, let's go and see if he's there," he suggests as he checks his watch. "It starts in two hours and it's going to take a while—damn German traffic."

"*Ja*, let me grab my coat," she says.

Herr Boss looks around. "Where's Rudi?"

"Probably at the track," she replies as she picks up her coat.

"I thought you two would go together?"

"No, he's too busy and so am I," she says flatly.

"Are you okay?" Nicolette feels a pang at his genuine concern.

"Fine. Or I will be, once I find my father."

A small two-engine Siebel Si 204 plane circles the Frankfurt-Darmstadt autobahn, the starting point for today's race.

A low-lying mist lines one side of the autobahn. The highway is made up of long straights sliced with bridges, imposing beasts made of steel and concrete, that cut the highway into sections every two miles. From the plane, the highway looks like a gigantic tic-tac-toe board.

The plane touches gently down in the brisk morning air and taxis to a waiting car. Bernd unbuckles himself and climbs down from the plane. He enters the car and finds the keys in the ignition. Starting it, he turns on the heater and drives fifteen minutes to the Auto Union garage where the team is preparing the Streamliner.

It's a cold but clear day in Frankfurt. Hitler's new autobahn is state-of-the-art, another masterpiece of German engineering. A new type of concrete has been specially formulated for the project, adeptly applied by Germany's ever-busy construction crews—it's as smooth as glass. The highway, now closed to traffic for today's event, is regaled with Nazi flags and iconography.

Close to the highway is a large building constructed for the upcoming speed event. Divided into two sections, one for Mercedes and the other for Auto Union, the garages are humming with efficiency and cleanliness.

August and Schwartz stand by the gleaming Streamliner Type-C, now containing a massive 6.3 Liter V-16 engine that produces more than 545 HP. A mechanic is silently working on the car.

"You there, get us some coffee," August grunts to the nearby worker. The mechanic gently puts his tool down on a soft piece of cloth carefully draped over the Streamliner's skin and scurries away to find coffee.

They are alone with the vehicle. "Step to the

front and kneel down," August commands Schwartz.

"Okay. Now what?" he asks from the nose.

"Here's the plan. When the car is being refueled, the mechanics will be busy," August says quietly.

He points to an air intake on the side of the car. Looking in, Schwartz can only see a mess of steel and aluminum suspension, hoses and part of a tire.

"It's dark, I don't know what I'm looking for," Schwartz gripes.

"You see the two large cross-sections? That is the semi-trailing arm. There's one on each side of the car. The steering rods are connected to them with cotter pins. You see the pins?"

"*Ja*, I think so. Do they look like a woman's hair pin, but bigger?"

"*Ja*, those are the R clips. They hold the pin in place and prevent it from coming loose." August explains. He lowers his voice further; "All you have to do is remove the R clip and the pin will come loose. Not immediately, but with enough vibration, it will fall out. Once it's gone, the steering shaft won't work."

"Ah, got it. Okay," Schwartz says from the ground. "You said there are two? One on each side?"

"*Ja*, but don't worry about the other one, one will be enough. Trust me," August says, shaking his head.

Nicolette and Boss arrive at the Mercedes garage and walk to meet Rudi who is busy overseeing his car's preparation. She scans the entire venue, looking for her father as they approach.

Rudi is fidgeting as he watches the mechanics do their work. He's nervous, more than usual. This speed trial is the most important race in his life—as a driver, a Nazi, and a German.

Rudi spots Nicolette and grows annoyed, somewhat surprised that Schwartz hasn't arrested her yet. He gathers himself and greets the pair; "Morning. You ready to see me set the record?"

"Have you seen my father, Rudi?" Nicolette asks.

"No," Rudi says. "I've been here since seven and he hasn't come by to wish me well."

"Rudi, not everything is about you." Her brain flashes a possibility in front of her—telling him about Bernd right here, right now—but she bites her tongue. She's got more important things to do. She's got to find her father.

"It is today!" he quips back. "Mercedes and I will set the speed record and prove to the world that German engineering and my bravery are a powerful combination!"

She dismisses his egotistical sermon. "Great. So if you see him, let him know that Hugo and I will be in the stands. Can you do that?"

"Sure," he says, nodding tightly. "Wish me luck even though I don't need it."

"Good luck Rudi," she says blandly. She turns and walks away, Boss in tow. Rudi's jaw clenches.

Nicolette and Boss sit in the stands among various Nazi officers and dignitaries. It's a full house and everywhere you turn the air is charged with excitement. A large scoreboard has been erected. There are three columns labeled First run, Second run, and Average speed. Below are two rows: Mercedes and Auto Union. This is where the speeds of each run will be tallied for the attendees.

In the Auto Union garage, Bernd sips hot tea as he thinks about today's event.

The stakes are high, incalculably high. A win today will mean that he will be the fastest driver in the world. A Jewish champion. But it also means that the Wardenbergs will be sent away to an internment camp, or worse.

The driver in him knows he can win. He's as sure of this as he is of his love for Nicolette. He can win this, not for himself, but for his people, for the Jews. He can prove to the world that his people are just as capable and deserving as any other race.

If it were his life he was sacrificing, the decision would already be made. But it's not. It's Margi and the kids. His head aches with the thought.

If he renounces the Jews as Schwartz has demanded, he can save Margi and the kids and still win. But what becomes of the millions of Jews he will sacrifice in the process? His denouncement will only help accelerate the dehumanization they've already experienced, will deal them yet another blow, something the Nazis couldn't even produce on their own. He would be as guilty for their deaths as the SS. He can't help send these people to their graves!

His mind races. Can he really trust Schwartz? Would Schwartz really let them go? His stomach flips with every possibility.

He touches the pendant under his suit. He wishes Margi was here, wishes Michael was here. But more than anything he wishes he could talk to Nicolette. She would know what to do.

Next door in the Mercedes garage, Rudi is nervously giving orders to the team when Hans Fischer approaches.

"Where's Wilhelm? He should be looking after the final preparations. Doesn't he care?" Rudi complains to him.

"Wilhelm is in the stands, Rudi. And he does care."

"He hasn't even come by to check on me, wish

me luck," he says moodily.

"I'm here, Rudi. Good luck," Hans says flatly.

"Yeah, well, thanks." The start time creeps closer, Rudi hyping himself further each minute. "So, will today be the first of many victories for Mercedes or the last of many failures for Auto Union?"

Hans finds his comment sleazy. "Rudi, both cars and drivers are the best Germany can provide. Regardless of the outcome, it will be a great day for Germany."

"Bullshit, Hans! I'd appreciate a little more support from you. I will win this race today!"

"I hope so."

Rudi stands alone in the garage, his mind struggling as he contemplates what he's just been told by August and Schwartz.

Their plan assures him of a win today, regardless of how fast he goes. He will be the fastest man in the world! He brims with pride as he thinks about the accolades, the fame, the celebrations.

An amazing development, but it sits oddly with Rudi.

Maybe it's because, deep down, Rudi wanted to prove to Bernd that he is a better driver. He shrugs off the thought. A tainted victory is better than none.

Nicolette is fidgeting endlessly in her seat; she decides to go to the garage and see if Rudi has heard from her father.

"Have you seen him?" she asks.

"No—can't you see I'm busy!" he snaps. "Have you asked Fischer?"

"Yes, he hasn't seen him either," she says, fiddling with a loose thread on her dress sleeve.

"Well, we're all a bit busy right now. I'm sure he'll show up eventually," he says, his back to her.

"There's something we need to discuss."

His heart lurches into his stomach.

"What? Can't it wait?" he asks, a feverish sweat cropping up on his forehead.

"Yes. We can talk tonight at the reception."

"I'll be quite busy tonight celebrating the victory, but okay," he says, turning to face her with a proud smirk. "Good luck finding your father."

Bernd is reviewing the latest reports on the injectors when Schwartz approaches.

"Guten morgen, Herr Rosemeyer! Ready?"

Schwartz says. To the average passerby he would sound cheerful, enthusiastic.

Bernd replies without looking up. "Allo, Marcus."

"So, did you have restful night? I need you as sharp as a tack today, old boy," Schwartz says as he sidles up next to Bernd.

"Hardly, Marcus," he says, gravely serious. He looks at Schwartz with an acidic stare.

"Pity—but given the circumstances, I would have expected as much. Have you thought about our conversation?"

Bernd has to unlock his jaw before answering.

"Yes."

"And?" Schwartz asks with a jolt in his chest.

"And what?"

"Bernd, I need to know what you intend. There are many who are waiting," he whispers.

"Too bad," Bernd says, putting down the report.

"Look." Schwartz's toes tingle from the refreshed conflict. "I gave you my word. Just renounce and let's all get on with our lives," he urges quietly.

"Lives?" Bernd asks with disbelief. "You want me to publicly admit that the Jews are a plague and should be exterminated? What about *their* lives?" he asks.

"Bernd, let's not be overly dramatic."

"Dramatic?" he snaps, taking a threatening step closer to the colonel. "We are killing thousands of Jews every day and for what, Marcus!" he says. His voice rises too loudly; both pause and look around to see who might have overheard.

Schwartz gives a short sigh. "I see you're conflicted. I understand. I guess you're not the man I thought you were."

"Oh, I am," Bernd says stonily. "But not in the way you think."

"So, you're not going to renounce?" Schwartz asks plainly.

"Here? Right now? No!" Bernd hisses.

"I see." Schwartz replies. There is a tinge of remorse in his voice.

"We'll talk after the race," Bernd says, his hands on his hips. He turns to leave, done with the conversation.

"I'm afraid that's not an option," Schwartz says to Bernd's profile. "As I mentioned, things are in motion and you will not win today."

Bernd turns back to look at Marcus.

"Watch me."

45. Run!

The time recording crew is on the course making final adjustments to their equipment when the head timekeeper gives the five-minute signal. Seeing the event is about to start, the crowd makes their way to their seats.

The first car to run will be Rudi in the Mercedes. The team has towed the car about one mile behind the start line. Rudi will make a flying start and will trip the timing trigger going well over a hundred miles an hour.

At over 250 miles an hour he'll cover the seven-kilometer course in just less than a minute. He'll stop, be given his time while the car is refueled, and then begin his second run. He'll trip the timing trigger back at the finish line and the timekeepers will perform the necessary calculations and post the average speed. Rudi already knows it will be one for the record books.

The current world speed record stands at 255, set by Bernd the previous day. Rudi knows he'll win today, but the competitor in him has kicked in. He'll beat it, he'll beat Bernd, or he'll die trying.

Rudi sits alone in his car. He envisions the run in his head, replaying each shifting point, each bridge crossing, each throttle movement.

His focus is clear. He feels a stiff gust of wind blow across the car, gently rocking it on its suspension. He feels the dimpled aluminum steering wheel under his gloves. He's part of the car.

"Push me and let's get started!" he yells to the crew.

The team gathers behind the Rekordwagen and push-starts the car. Rudi drops the clutch; the car's rear wheels bite into the tarmac and it stutters for a few feet. The massive engine turns over, fuel is injected, and the engine catches. It roars to life. Rudi depresses the clutch and lets the engine idle while the car coasts to a stop.

It's so loud that the crew doesn't even bother to speak; they hold up one finger telling Rudi he has one minute before the start of his run. Rudi acknowledges, shaking his head.

The team checks to see if the timing crew is ready, then give Rudi the thumbs up. Rudi guns the engine, places the car in first gear and slowly applies the throttle while he lets the clutch out. The car leaps forward, a plume of blue exhaust left in its wake.

The crowd cheers as Rudi starts his run.

Rudi accelerates. He hits 103 as he trips the first timing trigger. The crowd hoots as he flies by, Nazi and Mercedes flags waving in the stands.

Now in second, Rudi hits 163 and shifts immediately into third. He doesn't want to create wheel spin when he mashes the accelerator, and a higher gear will help turn the torque into speed.

Rudi is at 189 and sets a blistering pace. The first of two bridges is rapidly approaching. He braces himself for the familiar concussive blow.

He times his shift into fourth to coincide with the arrival of the first bridge. *Bam*! The force smacks Rudi in the chest but the car continues to accelerate.

Shifting into fifth at 244, Rudi has already covered 3.5 kilometers. He presses the gas pedal all the way to the floor. The engine howls. He hits the second bridge and he's through.

He notices that the steering is light. The nose of the car is creating lift. He wills the car to stay on the ground as he spots the end of the course in the distance.

He blasts through the finish line in a blur and lifts his foot from the gas pedal. The car responds immediately. Without torque being delivered to the rear wheels, the nose lowers slightly as the weight shifts to the front of the car.

He gently applies the brakes and the car begins to slow. As he approaches the turnaround crew, he can see he's done well. They're clapping their hands and waving excitedly; he must have broken the record!

As he finally comes to a stop, the crew swarms the car. One of the mechanics approaches and tells Rudi his speed. "It's 261, Herr Caracciola!"

Rudi sits elated, buzzing with excitement as they refuel the car. Two hundred sixty-one, six miles an hour more than Bernd's record! He's done it! He just needs to make this last run and the record will be legitimately his. The wind is now behind him and is gusting to over twenty knots—he knows he can go even faster on the return leg.

The car refueled and the engine at idle, Rudi is given the thumbs up signal. He's ready.

He repeats the run with the same shift patterns, same acceleration. Anticipating the bridges, he braces for them and coasts through. It's a quick and clean run and he knows it went well. With the extra push from the wind, he's confident that he went even faster on this run.

He comes to a stop and the Mercedes team runs out to greet him waving Mercedes and Nazi flags. Fischer jogs up, pats him on the head and yells, "You did it Rudi, you did it!"

"How fast?" Rudi shouts, his eyes adjusting as he removes his helmet.

"Two hundred sixty-six on the way back! Combined, you set a 263.5! You are the new record holder Rudi! Congratulations!"

As Rudi exits the car, he hears the crowd cheering as the timekeepers post the numbers on the board. He hears the announcer confirm to the crowd what he already knows. He's the fastest man in Germany! He's the fastest man in the world!

Rudi is suddenly surrounded by a large group of people, all trying to shake his hand or talk to him. The crowd is cheering madly, everyone standing to applaud his run. Despite all the commotion, he notices that the one person who should be there congratulating him isn't. Nicolette is nowhere to be seen. *Maybe Schwartz finally did his job*, he thinks. Bernd walks to the car where Timo is making final preparations.

"Herr Rosemeyer, everything is set," he says, seeing Bernd approach. "We adjusted the clutch. Shouldn't slip in fourth gear. We tested it at six kilometers and it's solid. Exhaust has been fixed too.

"We also triple-checked the injector hoses and slightly reduced the air pressure. It should be good."

"Thanks, Timo."

"Set the record, Herr Rosemeyer," the mechanic says, looking firmly and faithfully into Bernd's eyes as they shake hands. "Set it for all of us."

"Hello!" Rudi calls to Nicolette. He is surprised to have found her in the VIP stands. "Did you see that? I'm the fastest man in the world, Nicolette!" His excited declaration bears a drop of anger.

"I did. Congratulations, Rudi."

He drops his hands to his sides as his smile drops from his face. "That's it?" he asks in a huff. "Nothing more than a 'well done'?"

"Rudi, I'm really worried! My father still isn't here. He wouldn't miss this. I'm afraid something bad has happened!"

"Jesus Nicolette, he's probably just tied up with work. Or maybe he's meeting with some of the VIPs in the garage," he says dismissively, wishing she'd just shut up. "I expected you to be more supportive!"

"Rudi, can't you see I'm worried!?" she cries, tears in her eyes.

"I can see that you care more about your father than me!"

"Go to hell Rudi, you ass!"

"I may be an ass, but I'm the fastest ass in the fucking world!"

The Auto Union garage is a beehive of activity. In just a few minutes it will be Auto Union's turn at the attempt. The team is anxious. They've worked hard to get to this point and they've paid a high price.

Bernd is getting ready, pulling on his race gear as Schwartz walks in.

"It's time, my friend."

Bernd sighs with contempt when he sees his visitor. "I'm busy, Marcus."

"You need to decide."

"I already have."

"It's your last chance, Bernd. Make the right choice," Schwartz says, a piece of his soul burning bright with fear—fear of loss.

Bernd glares at Schwartz. "All my life I've thought that if a man applied himself, he could achieve greatness. If he worked hard, his work would speak for itself. That's why I race so hard, in pursuit of the grace that surrounds true, honest work. I believed in objectivism.

"But thanks to you," he says, throwing his gloves onto the bench, "I've realized that a man's achievements, if pursued for individual purposes, are shallow. A lie.

"A man's greatness isn't determined by ego or work, it's determined by kindness and compassion. A willingness to sacrifice himself for the greater good."

"Oh, don't give me this bullshit altruism!" Schwartz snaps. "I need an answer!"

Bernd plunges his hand into his driving suit and pulls out the necklace. He gently places the Star of David pendant so that it hangs over his heart, plainly visible.

"This is your answer."

Bernd leaves Schwartz standing alone in the garage. He climbs into the car, says a silent prayer for Margi, and puts on his helmet.

Mechanics are getting ready to tow the car to the start line as Bernd makes a few final adjustments inside the vehicle. Timo notices the star and looks at Bernd with wide eyes.

Bernd sees his stare. "For us," he says.

Timo smiles and tears well in his eyes, but he quickly blinks them away. "Ready?"

"Yes."

August Horch is just arriving. Schwartz approaches him immediately.

"Well?" August barks.

"He's a fool."

"I told you. I knew he wouldn't do it," he hisses in a low voice.

"Let's get down to the turn around. We've only got about twenty minutes before he arrives."

"You're going to pull it?"

"Let's see how he does on the first run," Schwartz says, staring out at the track.

"He's going to smash the record. I guarantee it," August grunts.

"We'll see."

"A shame ... it's a great car. Give me a moment."

August walks up to the vehicle and pats Bernd on the head.

"This is what we've worked for, Bernd," Horch says wisely. "I only ask that you do one thing for me."

"What's that, August?"

"Go fast." Horch gives a final pat to the car's sleek exterior.

The crowd is eagerly awaiting Bernd's attempt as the Auto Union team tows the car to its start location. Just as Rudi did, Bernd will make a flying start. The breeze has kicked up and winds are gusting to thirty knots.

With only minutes to spare, Nicolette runs up to Bernd's car.

"Nicolette!" he says.

"Bernd, I just wanted to wish you luck!"

"Thanks," he says with a laugh. "I'm so glad you came!"

"What's that?" she asks, pointing to the necklace.

"Someone gave it to me," he says calmly, looking up at her through his goggles. "Any idea who might have sent it?"

"A good friend, I'd say. Someone who loves you." The two lock eyes knowingly for a long second.

"Well, if you see them, tell them I love it. And I love you!" he shouts over the noise of the track, not caring who might overhear.

"I will, my darling! I'll see you after the race!" she says, backing away off the tarmac.

"Count on it!"

The mechanics give Bernd the one-minute signal and bolt his new windscreen to the car. He's alone now, in his own world, but his mind is on fire. He's 100 percent focused.

His sweet, brief encounter with Nicolette has made the perfect end to his preparations. He's completely focused now. He prays Margi will forgive him. His senses tingling, he tests the pedals and steering. Everything he touches with his hands and feet feels alive. He relishes the feeling.

The mechanics give him a thumbs up and push-start the car. He pops the clutch and the car roars to life, belching blue exhaust smoke. The smell of benzidine and acetone fill the air.

Bernd checks the gauges, waiting for the massive engine to reach temperature. He can see vapor leaking from the front of the car where the dry ice is swiftly cooling the water being pumped into the engine. It quickly swirls away like a dust devil in the wind.

The car is growling, straining; it wants to be released. It's impatiently waiting for the command to go. Bernd gradually adds throttle and disengages the clutch. The car jumps forward and small vortices of blue smoke swirl in the wake of the departing car as he begins his run.

The crowd is on their feet as Bernd charges through the recording trigger. Even with a stiff headwind, he crosses the start line at over 110 miles an hour.

At 162, Bernd shifts into second and adds more throttle. The rear tires subtly spin; he feels the car being pushed to the right, so he gently counter-steers, bringing the big Streamliner smoothly back to the center.

At 191 and fourth gear, Bernd sees the first bridge approaching. He feels the car under him; it's got more to give if he can just keep it straight. He's also beginning to smell that wretched scent. The one that almost killed him the last time. He braces for the concussive impact of the first bridge. *Bam*! The force of the air hits him like a sledgehammer.

Shifting into fifth at 260, Bernd shakes his head clear. The fumes are coming at him, not as bad as last time, but they're there. He sees the next bridge coming at him rapidly. Air is being jammed into the front intake with such force that the seam where the new nose meets the side skirts is buckling.

Three rivets start to yield, then pop off and fly through the air. The edge of the aluminum side skirt catches the air and bends slightly. No longer aerodynamic, it creates drag which nudges the car to the left.

Bernd hits the next bridge at 267. The new nose is creating too much lift and the car wants to take off like a plane! With the nose acting like a wing, the front tires aren't being pushed into the ground, making steering almost impossible.

With the little steering that can be achieved at this speed coupled with the drag created by the loose side skirt, the car is moving, moving rapidly to left. Bernd fights to control the massive beast as it hits 270.

He's drifting dangerously close to the left side of the road, the front tires now barely touching the ground. With millimeters to spare, he dabs the brakes ever so slightly to plant the front wheels on the ground so they bite, then gently steers the car away from the edge.

As he blasts through the finish line and trips the recording system, he gently applies pressure to the tiny brake system and begins the torturous job of slowing the massive Streamliner.

He sees his crew waving at him, giving him the thumbs up. He knows he was fast, but was he fast enough? At that moment he realizes he doesn't care about being the fastest *man* in the world. What he wants more than anything is for the fastest man in the world to be a Jew.

He quickly thinks of Nicolette and Margi and wonders if he's made the right decision.

He did; he had to do this. He did this for hope, for humanity.

He pulls up to his waiting crew. They pat him on the head and scream "Two hundred and seventy miles an hour! You did it, you did it!" Hearing the good news, Bernd relaxes and lets the crew turn the car around so they can begin to refuel.

At the rear of the car, the crew pours the witch's brew of Benzo into the fuel tank.

August and Schwartz walk up. August yells over the tremendous noise of the idling Streamliner, "That was fast Bernd!"

"*Ja*, the nose is creating too much lift, hard to steer!" Bernd shouts back.

"*Ja*, it looked like you were struggling after you hit 200!"

"I think the side skirts saved me. They created just enough downforce to keep me on the road, but we have to fix the nose!"

"Okay, let me check it," August yells.

August kneels down by the front tire, pretending to inspect the nose. Schwartz follows him. Kneeling by the front left tire, he reaches his hands inside the air intake, groping for the R clip.

August rises again, fiddling with his jacket pocket.

"*Ja*, I see the problem!" he calls to Bernd. "The front splitter isn't large enough, but I can't do anything about it! Let me push down on the nose and reset it!"

Schwartz stands up. He looks at August and gives a subtle nod, indicating that the deed is done. August moves to the middle of the nose and gives it several aggressive downward pushes to reset it.

"Okay, I think that should do it!"

The crew finishes refueling and signals to Bernd that the car is ready to go.

Back in the stands, the crowd cheers as the timer puts up the first speed on the large board.

Bernd guns the engine and drops the car into first gear. He touches the Star of David as he starts his second attempt. With a twenty-knot wind at this back, Bernd knows he can take the world record.

"You did it?" asks August.

"*Ja*," Schwartz says.

"Let me see it."

"See what?"

"The clip, you idiot!"

Schwartz stares ahead at the Streamliner in silence.

"You fucking coward!" August hisses.

"I—couldn't find it!" Schwartz says.

"Schwartz, I always suspected you and Bernd, but I didn't think it would come to this!"

"I tried!" Schwartz shouts in August's face.

"Well, you're lucky."

"I am?" he asks, perplexed. "How?"

August holds out his hand. In his palm is an R clip.

Bernd shifts into second gear at 164. He feels the wind pushing at his back—he can do this! He's blasting down the autobahn, already ahead of his previous pace.

He clears 190 as he shifts into third and sees the first bridge in the distance. The car feels strange to him, looser than before.

At 240 he hits the first bridge, the air pressure disrupting his vision for a split second. *Bam!* The force of the air slightly lifts the nose of the car. Bernd feels it immediately and struggles to keep the car in the center.

In fifth at 270 he sees the second bridge rapidly approaching. He knows if he clears it the run will be all but over; after this bridge, he'll cross the line in less than five seconds. Then he'll know if he's set the record. He can hardly believe it. He's going to do it. He's doing it for his people!

As the car crosses under the second bridge, the concussive force of the air pressure lifts the front of the car another ten millimeters. Lifts it just enough. As the nose lifts, the eight-millimeter pin holding the steering linkage disconnects from the steering shaft. The front right wheel immediately turns sideways and the tire bursts into flames.

The car becomes a missile, no longer under Bernd's command. It veers across the autobahn and hits the median. It launches forty meters into the air, flames trailing off the back.

The crowd rises and gasps in unison as they watch the Streamliner pirouette in the air—it slams to the ground, where it erupts in flames and smoke. The heat is so intense that they can feel it from the stands.

The crowd is frozen by the spectacle. Cries and screams slowly break out as realization sets in, hitting a crescendo just as the sirens on the emergency vehicles begin to blare, their frequencies merging and mixing with each other, creating a nightmare soundtrack to the hellish scene before them. They've just watched the death of the most famous driver in Germany— maybe the world.

Emergency crews race to the scene but everyone already knows the fate of this driver. No one could have survived this.

Boss, Nicolette, and Rudi are standing side by side in the stands.

"Oh my God! No, no!" she screams, clutching the guard rail.

"Let's go," Rudi says in a low, urgent voice.

Smoke obscures their vision as they run to the wreck; the intense smell of burning Benzo and rubber assaults their nostrils. Workers swarm the flaming car as they try to put out the fire. The three spot another crew fifty meters away, close to the median. They run over to see what's happening.

Bernd's body lies on the ground. He's been thrown from the car, his helmet smashed, his arms and legs at unnatural angles.

"Oh my God! Bernd!" Nicolette wails.

Despite everything, Rudi is torn at the sight of Bernd's mangled body. He holds Nicolette back. "I'm afraid he didn't make it," he says softly.

A car pulls up, brakes screeching. Schwartz and August jump out and rush over to Bernd's body. Nicolette and Rudi walk slowly over to what remains of Bernd.

"Shit!" August says.

"I can't believe this!" Schwartz gasps, stunned at the gruesome sight.

"He's—he's dead!" Nicolette sobs. "No!" she shrieks, doubling over and sinking to her knees.

Schwartz approaches Bernd's body, reaches out to touch his sleeve. The body has no reaction; he hangs his head and looks at August, hate burning in his eyes.

"Come on Nicolette, we can't do anything more here," Rudi says quietly. "You shouldn't see this." He takes her arm and gently guides her away.

"Okay, come on everyone," August says. "Let's let the crews do their work. Get in the car and I'll drive us back to the garage."

They pull Nicolette away from the scene, nearly carrying her limp body. She's sobbing uncontrollably. Just as they reach the car she screams. "Wait!"

She sprints back to Bernd's body, leaving Schwartz, Rudi and August standing by the car. Just as the medics place a sheet over his body, she reaches Bernd's mangled body. Her breathing ragged, she pulls the sheet down, snatches the Star of David from around his neck and cradles it against her chest.

As they drive slowly back to the garage, the four are silent. Nicolette's sobs have been replaced by a profound numbness. They reach the garage; they disembark from the car and take a few steps in no particular direction. What are they supposed to do? Celebrate the record, Rudi's win? Confusion descends over them and the teams that surround them.

Schwartz gently pulls Nicolette aside.

"I know what you went back for," Schwartz says softly.

"What?" she says. Her stare is blank, seeing nothing though directed at Schwartz's face.

"I know. Did you get it?"

Nicolette wordlessly opens her palm. The star sits in her palm, covered in Bernd's blood. Her hand trembles and closes.

"He was a good man, better than you know," Schwartz says, a single tear falling down his cheek. "I loved him as much as you did," he confesses.

Rudi and August stand together alone in the back of the garage, away from the team. In the front, the Auto Union crew stands quiet and solemn; they can't believe they've lost another friend.

"Well, August, I didn't want it to end like this, but it did. I won," Rudi says softly, firmly.

"Yeah. I didn't want it to go like this either. We had the better car, and you know it."

"Maybe, but I was the better driver. I set the record for Germany."

"Oh fuck you, Rudi," August growls tiredly. "He was on pace. He would have beaten you if we—if he hadn't crashed, goddamn it!"

"Perhaps," Rudi replies, staring out at the bright sky. "But I'll tell you one thing, August."

"Yeah?"

"A Jew like him could never win. His kind will never win. Never."

16. Confrontation

The next day, Nicolette is at her airfield. She sits alone at a small picnic table. Hendrick walks in and joins her. It's a cold, dark February day and Nicolette's body is being frozen by the cold.

"Hello, Nicolette."

"Hello, Hendrick. Thank you for coming."

"My pleasure," he says somberly. "How are you doing?"

"Horrible." She takes a moment to regain her composure. "I still haven't heard from Father. And Bernd's death—it's too much!" she cries, her voice breaking and tears falling anew. "Have you heard anything about my father?" she asks Hendrick with pleading eyes.

He stares back at her in silence.

Her stomach lurches. "Hendrick! What have you learned!? Please, tell me!"

"I'm reluctant, Nicolette. A person can only take so much. I know you're grieving Bernd."

"Hendrick, please, I need to know!" she cries. She gulps air, but can hardly breathe.

"Very well. But please understand that what I'm about to say is unfortunate beyond words."

"Oh God!" she utters quietly. A numbness casts over her body. She waits, her breath

343

shallow, nearly nonexistent.

Hendrick holds her eyes in his steady gaze. "Your father was murdered in the Night of Long Knives, along with nineteen others. The Warsaw assassination plot was uncovered by the SS. They found out everything. They knew what your father was planning. They know about me. Frankly, I'm baffled that I haven't already been arrested. As for you, I believe they think you knew nothing of the plot, but we can't be sure."

Her head hangs. "I can't believe this," she manages to whisper to the table. "I knew he would be caught!" Tears fall on the wood.

"He did what he thought was right, Nicolette," Hendrick says softly. "You must always remember that. He was a great man trying to do the right thing."

"I know, but they murdered him!" she yells. "I can't believe it's come to this!"

"I'm afraid it gets worse."

She cradles her face in one hand, her elbow propping her up. "How could it possibly get worse?" she sobs.

"We know who killed him."

Nicolette looks up at Hendrick, her face wet with tears.

"It was Rudi," he says.

She is momentarily stunned, confused. "No!" she whispers. "You must be mistaken! Rudi is horrible, but he's not a killer!" Her eyes frantically dart between Hendrick's.

"I wish it weren't true," he begins, "but our sources have confirmed it. He was given the order by Göring himself. Apparently, Rudi tried to trade victims with another officer but was refused."

"Oh my god, Hendrick!" she screams, her body beginning to buzz. "You're sure it was Rudi?"

"One-hundred percent."

She jumps up, picking up a wrench lying on the table and hurls it at the hangar wall. "I'm going to kill that fucking *bastard*!" she screams. "Take me to him, take me to him right now!"

"Easy Nicolette!" Hendrick urges.

"I'll kill him with my own bare hands!" she shouts, shaking and flailing about.

"Let me take care of it," Hendrick says, rising from his chair. "Right now we need to think about how we're going to get you out of Germany."

"I won't leave until that bastard is dead!" she yells.

Hendrick takes her firmly by the shoulders and looks her in the eyes as she tries ferociously to free herself from his grip. "I promised your father that I would see to your escape and that is a promise I intend to keep. Tonight, you and I will fly to Poland—to some friends who will refuel us. We'll fly to Sweden from there. There, you will be safe."

"I won't!" she cries. "I'm not leaving until I kill Rudi!" she screams.

"I'm afraid that's impossible, Nicolette. He's well-guarded, as you can imagine, and they already suspect you. You won't get near him."

"Shit!" she yells, thrashing away from Hendrick. She kicks the leg of the small table, sending its contents scuttling over the hanger floor. The noise of the tools clattering silences her for some reason.

Hendrick takes a step toward her. "I know this is hard, the hardest thing you've ever done. But we've got to leave. Get your things together. We'll depart in thirty minutes," he says, comfortingly but unyielding.

He turns and leaves Nicolette alone. He cries quietly as he prepares the plane and gathers the supplies they'll need for their twelve-hour flight to freedom.

Nicolette sobs, feels like she'll never stop. She realizes that Hendrick's plan is the only way to survive.

And survive she must. She will live and she will fight, and she will eventually take her revenge.

Then it hits her, she knows what to do.

Sitting with pen in hand, she scribbles a brief note. She addresses it and slips it into the airfield mailbox.

She stands alone in the hangar watching dusk approach. Her head is filled with rage and sadness. Her thoughts flash, turn to her father, her dear father who sacrificed his life to try to stop the madness, the death, the war. Her father who Rudi murdered.

She pulls out the necklace from her pocket and holds it in her hand. The plane's engine starts and exhaust fumes fill the hangar. She takes the necklace and fastens it around her neck, hanging it over her heart.

A tear falls and lands, for the last time, on German soil.

47. THE FUNERAL

Five days later, a National Day of Mourning for Bernd Rosemeyer is declared. Tens of thousands of people gather at the Potsdamer Platz, just south of the Brandenburg Gate, to pay their respects.

Bernd was loved by many—Germans, French, Italians, Jews, Gypsies, the rich and the poor. His flamboyant life, good looks, and racing successes made him one of the most popular celebrities in modern German history. The news of his death brought sorrow to many in an already tense and tired Germany.

But one small group, unknown to many, knew a different Bernd. To them, he was not a racing hero—he was their savior. They knew him as a kind, loving, gracious, and moral man, a man willing to put his own life at risk to help them. These fifty people, Jews, just like Margi, owed their lives to Bernd and his charity.

Today, the small group assembles on the periphery of the ceremony. They stand quietly. They wear the Blue Star with pride today, unashamed that they are Jews. They show their respect in the open for their fallen comrade, knowing full well of the harassment and internment that will surely come. A man like Bernd, who gave his life in the pursuit of their freedom and equality, is to be honored regardless of the outcome.

Together, their Blue Stars moving slowly in rhythm, they light candles and chant a prayer in Hebrew.

"Birth is a beginning and death a destination,

But life is a journey.

A going, a growing from stage to stage;

From childhood to maturity and youth to old age.

From innocence to awareness and ignorance to knowing;

From foolishness to discretion and then perhaps, to wisdom."

Within moments of finishing the prayer, a group of brownshirts approach and haul the group away to waiting trucks. Spectators stare at the arrest, wondering why these Jews have shown themselves so publicly.

They shrug at the encounter and turn their attention back to the speaker, Colonel Marcus Schwartz, who is in the middle of a tribute to Bernd Rosemeyer.

48. Mail Time

Rudi, the fastest man in the world, sits at the dining table in his new luxurious Berlin apartment, mulling over the last few weeks. The smell of fresh paint and strong coffee float through the air on this sunny, cold morning.

His successes have brought him adoration from all corners—from the masses, from the elite, even from Hitler himself. The parties, interviews, awards and appearances have inflated his already immense ego to new heights.

He has been promoted to a full colonel of the SS and enjoys all the accompanying perks. He walks to the mailbox located in the hallway by his front door and gathers the mail that has finally caught up to him since his move to the new apartment.

He sits at the table and takes a sip of coffee while he flips through the mail, most envelopes being addressed not to him, but to the previous occupant. He notices a small envelope, his old address written on it in familiar handwriting. He sets his coffee down quickly, grabs the letter, and opens it with his small Degen dagger—the same which slit von Dries' throat mere weeks ago. He begins to read.

"I know what you did. You're a coward and I pray you rot in hell for killing my father.

But you have no idea what I did, do you? I

loved Bernd with all my heart. He was my lover the night you murdered my father.

While Bernd may be dead, he won't be forgotten. We made love the night of the gala and with any luck I will be the mother of his son. My son will be named Bernd and he will make sure your kind will never win, in race nor in war.

N"

49. Orange You Glad to See Me

It's 1956 and the world is at peace, at least for now. London has been rebuilt and its citizens no longer duck their heads when they hear a loud noise or a buzz, they no longer worry about Blitzkriegs or V2 rockets.

Bernd's son lives in London with Nicolette. He's taken to racing like a duck to water. Nicolette takes him to go-kart practice every day and loves what she sees.

Young Bernd is a natural. He's faster than anyone his age, and a skinny young man with mangy brown hair has taken notice. One cold winter day, the man approaches Nicolette.

"Your son is fast! Quite the speedster!" the man says in a thick Kiwi accent.

"*Ja*, he gets it from his father," she replies as they watch Bernd Jr. whip around the track.

"That so? Who's his dad?"

"No one you would know," she says offhandedly. "But he did like cars and driving."

"Yeah? Me too! Hey look, miss, I've got a garage in the west end and I'm trying to put together a team. Your boy is still too young to drive, but if he wants, he can come over some time and watch. You know, learn the ropes."

"I'm sure he'd love that," she says, smiling.

"I'm sorry, I didn't catch your name."

"McLaren, Bruce McLaren."

"Nice to meet you, Herr McLaren."

"Just call me Bruce."

Acknowledgements

Writing a book was easier than I thought but editing it was a nightmare!

None of this would have been possible without my family. Laura was my cornerstone, Chloe my collaborator and Dominque my cheerleader. They stood by me during every struggle and all my successes. That is what families do. I love them to the moon and back!

My friends Christopher Knight and Dario D'Angelo offered suggestions and encouragement. My racing friends Kenton King, John Mai, Baily Woods, David Rahemi and Rick Sutherland all lent a supporting hand (and car) when needed. And lastly, my friend Vesta Lall provided the final bit of inspiration I need to get this over the finish line!

So much research went into this book to ensure its accuracy. The Mercedes and Audi web sites and their archives were incredibly helpful for engineering facts and information related to car designs. Aldo Zana's web site was insightful for details on race events and historical information. Peter Stevenson's "Driving Forces: The Grand Prix racing world caught in the maelstrom of the Third Reich" was also illuminative.

Thank you to everyone who helped me on this journey!